BIMBO HEAVEN

Marvin Albert

FAWCETT GOLD MEDAL • NEW YORK

A Fawcett Gold Medal Book
Published by Ballantine Books
Copyright © 1990 by Marvin Albert

Library of Congress Catalog Card Number: 89-91543

ISBN 0-449-14623-5

Manufactured in the United States of America

First Edition: April 1990

this one's for the gendarmes of Eze and Cap d'Ail

1

A SUNNY PLACE FOR SHADY PEOPLE—THAT CRACK ABOUT the French Riviera has gotten so old that not many give serious thought to it any more. But it's still on the money, often enough. So I tend to reserve judgment with strangers. Until I get to know them better, or worse.

The September sun was shining with all its might the day this charming stranger showed up at my place with her healthy tan, clever eyes, and worried smile. She came to me like Venus, out of the sea. Breathing hard from her swim and a steep climb up the wooded slope. Wet chestnut-brown hair plastered flat around her head and neck. Her nicely filled bathing suit dripping a trail across the sun-warmed bricks of my patio.

The patio is on the long side of the house that looks out and down over the Mediterranean. I was outside between the patio and a curve of lemon and orange trees that defines the eastern limits of the property, using a handsaw to cut tree branches into short logs that would fuel the fireplaces on cool nights.

There were two fireplaces in the house. The one in the living room got used most. I only used the bedroom one when Arlette Alfani was staying over with me. Which was whenever she wasn't totally immersed in preparing cases for the law courts and I wasn't off doing a sleuthing job some-

1

where else. Not often enough; but that added to the excitement, of course.

I had been available for the past few days. But Arlette was off in Ireland, acting as legal liaison between a well-off French family and the Irish attorney representing their son, who'd been jailed in Dublin on a hit-and-run charge. Which left me to work off excess energy with hard physical labor. Stripped to an old pair of shorts; the rest of me gleaming with sweat under the Mediterranean sun as I added four fresh-sawed logs to the stack beside the toolshed.

I was lifting another heavy tree branch off the pile next to the sawhorse when my dripping wet visitor brightened the day by coming off the slope and onto my patio.

I set the branch down as I registered the anxious look she cast behind her toward the sea. I looked in the same direction, but couldn't spot what it was that worried her. Some people were sunning themselves on the narrow beach below. A few more were swimming in the little cove. Three pleasure boats were anchored just outside the cove. The big white car-ferry from Corsica was coming over the bright blue horizon on its way to Nice.

Everything peaceful. Nothing unusual. But my visitor moved swiftly across the patio and into the shade of the olive tree, putting it between her and the sea.

That tree has been around for close to half a millennium. Though battered and torn by the storms of those centuries it remained more than broad enough to hide her—from whoever she was hiding from.

She forced a smile. It was a nice smile in spite of being forced. A small attempt at humor tried to force its way through her anxiety.

"If you are not Pierre-Ange Sawyer," she said, "I am in big trouble."

2

HER FRENCH HAD AN EAST EUROPEAN FLAVOR. I GUESSED her age as late twenties. It was difficult to be sure. She was the type who had probably looked much the same five years before and still would five years hence. Durable.

Her face and figure had the full, vibrant curves that the models for Rodin's voluptuous nudes would have had if regular workouts had been fashionable back in those days. Her hands were unusually muscular. There was a ring on her right middle finger: one large diamond, and a number of tiny diamonds circling the gold band. Her lips looked like they would be soft and warm.

I admitted I was Pierre-Ange Sawyer.

Her smile became less strained. "Sonia Galeazzo told me you prefer to be called Peter or Pete," she said. Establishing what she wanted to: though strangers to one another we shared a mutual friend.

"I don't mind Pierre-Ange," I told her. Not in France I didn't. Back in the States though, Pete was less likely to cause trouble. I would have had to back up the name my French mother pinned on me with too many back-alley brawls.

"My name is Ilona," she told me. She didn't give me a last name to go with it. Instead she added to her credentials as a friend of a friend: "Sonia told me you are only half French. You father was American. And his father was a police captain in Chicago when you were going to school there. Sonia thinks that's what led you to become a detective.''

"How did I come to be the subject of conversation?''

''Sonia admires you. We were on a yacht cruising past here a couple years ago and she pointed out this house of yours. That is how I knew where to come this time.'' Ilona No-Last-Name looked me over without any hint of coquetry; more like she was mentally weighing me. ''Sonia did say you are big and very strong.''

''I wanted to be another Fred Astaire, but we've all got to work with what we have.''

What she had was an attractiveness of the quiet, comfortable-to-be-with variety. Nothing spectacular, just pleasant. She wouldn't draw many stares away from the beauties who parade around Monte Carlo, Cannes, and Saint-Tropez at the height of the season. But the more a man looked at her the more he would like what he saw.

Not that he would necessarily get what he liked. There was more to this Ilona than something soft and sweet to bite into. Her eyes were the stiffener, balancing that vulnerable mouth. They were too wise for her to be anyone's marsh-mallow.

Those eyes were searching mine now. ''Sonia also said you are tough and honorable. Someone that people who need help can depend on. She said you are one man she would trust with her life.''

''Sonia sometimes has that tendency to exaggerate.''

''Not on the good side. Especially not about men.''

I nodded. I take my friends the way they come. And expect them to accept me the same way. Sonia Galeazzo, in addition to certain small flaws from a male viewpoint, was one of the roughest of the international band of paparazzi. Known to the illustrious unfortunates victimized by her fast and fancy camera work as the Milanese Monster.

''I need a favor,'' Ilona told me. ''I have to get a message to someone who lives up in the hills near Lucéram.''

''Use the phone in the house.''

She shook her head. "The problem is, there's no phone at *his* place. I'll have to write the message, and I need someone to deliver it for me. It has to reach him quickly. And I have to get back to the boat."

"One of those three anchored off the cove down there?"

She nodded, studying my face, measuring whatever Sonia had told her about me against what she saw. Finally she nodded again, to herself this time. "Will you do it? Take my letter for me—right away? I'll pay whatever you ask."

She hugged herself, gripping her wet shoulders with those strong hands. A breeze had started, and she was getting goosefleshy in the cool shade of the olive tree.

I said, "Come inside."

"I'm afraid to cross your patio. He might see me. . . ." She peeked around the olive trunk at the cove below. "He was asleep when I left the boat. But if he wakes up and starts looking for me with binoculars . . ."

It could have been confusing, if the change in her tone hadn't made it clear that "he" down on the boat and the one up near Lucéram were two very different men.

"There's nothing wrong with my swimming ashore. And taking a rest under the trees behind the beach, where he wouldn't be able to see me. And with all those bushes and trees covering the slope he won't be able to see me climb down. But if he spots me up here with you he'll want to know why. *That* could be—unpleasant."

I took one of her wrists and led her away from the patio, around through the cover of the citrus trees and flowering bushes and in through a side door of the house. Hidden from the cove all the way.

I studied her while she put on the terry-cloth robe I got from the bathroom. When she tied its belt I handed her a towel. She began kneading her wet hair with it.

I said, "If you're worried about the man on the boat, why go back?"

"I have to."

"You could tell me what's going on. Sonia may exaggerate, but I have been known to be of help on occasion."

"I can't talk about it. Will you just do what I've asked and no questions? Please?"

What the hell, it wouldn't be the first time I'd taken on a job without knowing what it was about. Usually the reason I didn't know was that the client had lied to me. At least this one wasn't spinning a phony story for me to untangle. And what she was asking seemed simple enough. In addition to providing a guilt-free excuse for not doing any more chores around the house that day.

I led the way into the kitchen. When she was seated in one of the basket-weave chairs she let the towel hang around her face while she removed the gold ring with the diamonds from her finger. "This is worth more than you are likely to charge me. Even if he's not home when you get there and you have to devote some time to finding him."

She placed the ring on the breakfast table in front of her and resumed toweling her hair. "If he isn't there," she added emphatically, "*don't* leave my letter with his wife. That's important. I don't want her to know about this. Or about me. Just find out where he is and get it to him. Nobody else."

She nodded at the ring on the table. "I'll come back with enough cash to pay for your trouble and redeem this."

"When?"

"I don't know. Soon. A few days, probably. I'll phone and let you know."

"All right." I took a brandy bottle from the liquor shelf, poured a judicious amount into a cut-glass tumbler, and set it down before her. "You look like you can use this." I went off to my study for writing materials.

When I returned Ilona had finished off her brandy and was neatly folding the damp towel on a corner of the table. Her hair stood out in half-dried spikes going every which way. On her it didn't look bad at all. Just gave her what the French call a piquant accent.

I gave her pen, paper, and envelope, and left her to

compose her message in private. On my way through the living room I picked up my binoculars. Stepping out through the sliding glass doors onto the patio, I crossed to the shade of the olive tree and focused on the boats anchored outside the cove.

There were only two down there now. The smaller one was a sport-fishing job with twin outboards and a tiny forward cabin. Two women were indulging in a spot of nude sunbathing in its cockpit. Very nice, but I managed to switch my binoculars away to the larger boat. A luxury cruiser with a long main cabin and a covered flying bridge. Nobody was in sight on that one. I spent some time studying its cabin windows. But if there was someone inside, scanning the shore through his own binoculars, I didn't spot him.

Ilona came out of the house via the route I had used taking her in. The side door and the cover of the citrus trees. She'd left my bathrobe behind and she had the envelope in hand.

I lowered the binoculars and told her I didn't think her man on the boat was awake yet.

"I hope you're right." She gave me the envelope. She had sealed it firmly after folding the letter inside. There was nothing written on the outside. "His place doesn't have a normal address that I know of," Ilona explained. "It is on some little mountain road outside Lucéram, and it's called *La Vieille Ferme*. His name is Desiré Brissac. Anyone in or around the village can tell you where to . . ."

"I know Brissac," I interrupted. "And I've been to his place. He used to live near here. The other side of the Lower Corniche, in Saint Laurent d'Eze."

It wasn't much of a coincidence. The Riviera and its back country cover a lot of territory, but for its year-round citizens it's just a stretched out small town. People know each other. They move around without entirely losing contact. A kid you went to school with in Menton turns up as your dentist in Valbonne, your baker in Saint Raphael quits and reappears as a florist in Nice.

Ilona had tensed. "Do you know Brissac's wife, too?"

"Sure," I said offhandedly. Not adding that I knew her longer and better than I knew her husband.

"But you won't tell her about this—or about me?"

"Did Sonia neglect to list trustworthy among my other sterling qualities?"

Ilona's laugh was short. "I am trusting you, God knows. You will get this letter to him as quickly as possible?"

"Don't worry," I reassured her.

A little prematurely, as it turned out.

She looked anxiously toward the slope below my patio. "Now I must get back."

I showed her the best way to reach the path without being spotted. She started past me, then unexpectedly turned back. "Thank you. . . ." She raised up on her toes, pulling my face down to hers and kissing me gently.

I'd been right about her lips: they were soft and warm on mine. Her nicely filled bathing suit was cool and damp against my bare skin.

It was not a lingering kiss, but I was not left unaffected. She drew back, regarding me thoughtfully.

"Well," she said, "one thing Sonia is definitely wrong about. You *don't* have your emotions under iron control at all times."

"Sonia has never shown any interest in learning different."

"No, she wouldn't, of course. . . ." For a moment there had been a flash of pure deviltry in those clever eyes. Then that was gone and so was she.

I watched her fetching derrière vanish between the trees and around a hedge. Maybe it was time to take myself a short holiday in Ireland. If Arlette had to stay over there much longer. My libido was getting unruly.

Ilona reappeared on the beach at the bottom of the slope. She ran gracefully across its stony incline and dove into the surf as soon as it was up to her knees. She swam with athletic power, covering distance swiftly. After a while I had to use the binoculars to keep track of her.

She climbed aboard the big cruiser. It was not so big compared with many of the yachts along the Côte d'Azur. Not something that it would take more than one person to run. But bigger and sleeker than anything I could afford.

The name painted across its wide transom was *La Dolce Vita*. Which might or might not mean it was owned by an Italian. It could have been named by an Italian and gone through six different owners since then. It could have been named by a Swede in love with the Fellini movie.

Painted under the boat's name was PANAMA. Which told me nothing at all. Every harbor along this coast had vessels registered in Panama for tax avoidance reasons. It didn't mean any of them had ever been within two thousand miles of Central America.

I kept watching through the binoculars after Ilona disappeared inside the boat's long cabin. Five minutes dragged by with nothing further developing there. I went into the house.

Getting a knife from a drawer in my study I sliced Ilona's envelope open. I removed and unfolded the single sheet of paper inside.

I couldn't read her letter.

It was in Hungarian.

The only two words I understood were names, at the beginning and the end. The bottom one was "Ilonka." With a *k*. In Hungary, Ilonka is a common affectionate diminutive for Ilona. Like using Judy for Judith in the States.

The name the letter was addressed to was "Dezsö." Brissac's given name in Hungary, before he'd mangled it into the French name Desiré after defecting to the West some twenty years ago. I didn't know his original family name.

Two exiles meeting in France and discovering they shared a common homeland would be a natural beginning for some sort of developing relationship. Exactly what sort was the question. One of several. I liked Brissac, but this wasn't the first time I'd had cause to wonder about him.

Desiré Brissac was fifty. As far as I was aware he was a solid husband and a devoted father to his ten-year-old daughter. Unlikely to be messing around with a woman the age of Ilona-Ilonka.

Unlikely didn't mean not possible.

It *could* be a May-December romance.

It could also be quite a number of other things.

It was none of my business.

But whatever was going on, it more than worried Ilona. It frightened her.

And you don't stay a private investigator unless you're afflicted with more than your share of curiosity about people's tangled lives. It's an onerous profession without that kink.

I took an identical envelope from my desk, folded Ilona's letter inside and sealed it. Then I had a fast shower and got dressed. Freshly laundered jeans, denim shirt, low-top sneakers. I took along a corduroy jacket, socks and a crew-neck sweater, in case finding Brissac took me into the night. If it kept me out longer than that there was the full overnight bag I always kept in my car. I switched on my telephone answering machine and the house security alarm system before leaving. Outside I crossed the patio for another look at the cove.

The boat she had swum back to was gone.

3

LUCÉRAM IS FAIRLY TYPICAL OF THE MEDIEVAL VILLAGES YOU find tucked away among the folds of the Maritime Alps behind the Riviera. Huddled stone houses clinging together ever more tightly as they mount a rugged mountainside. A patchwork of slanting orange-and-brown tiled roofs. A tall slender church tower pointing to the preferred destination for its six hundred souls.

It's only sixteen miles inland from the Côte d'Azur beaches as the crow flies. Crows don't have to drive the twisting gorges that slice their way up into those mountains. And from my place I had to swing around behind Nice before entering the gorge road I needed. Nevertheless, I made it in under an hour.

The village was in sight ahead when I crossed the bridge over the deep Paillon Gorge. I turned away from it on the other side, taking a sharp left into a road that did some intricate curling around a high hump of adjacent mountain. The road was a rudimentary one-lane affair. If you met another car, one had to back up and find a spot where it could ease over onto the verge and let the other slip past.

There were some small farms on terraced slopes on both sides. And an occasional old house that city folks had renovated as a weekend or summer retreat. The road climbed higher and the land suddenly became bleak. Living trees

11

were few, scattered and very small. There were plenty of big, old trees, but they'd all turned into black skeletons.

One of the fires that hit the Riviera backcountry most summers had scourged a path across the region three years before. It had swept up one side of this mountain hump and killed everything on the crest—including a couple trapped in their farmhouse—before the wind reversed and drove it back on itself. In the wasteland left behind property values had dropped to a price Desiré and Mireille Brissac could raise.

The crest was a jumble of wide knolls and hollows. I drove down a long dip past a farm where workmen were building a new barn near the incinerated remains of the old one. When I came up out of the dip the Brissac place appeared atop the next crest.

The winding dirt track from the road onto their land was steep and bumpy. Second gear most of the way; a couple places where I had to shift down into first. There were long views in every direction. High mountain peaks to the north. Lucéram on its lower summit to the east, far enough below to be a toy village. The widest view was south toward the sea: a series of long ridges with mist rising from the depths between them.

The grim view was to the west, where entire forests had burned. But their dark gloom was softened now by the fresh young green of new undergrowth. The land, enriched by the ashes of the killed trees, was reasserting its will to live.

I hadn't been up here in over a year. Since I'd spent a free week helping the Brissacs put a new roof on the fire-gutted house. I hadn't been the only helper. Other friends of Mireille and her husband showed up when they could to lend a hand. The thick stone walls had survived the fire, but not much else had. A couple of Desiré Brissac's friends had been new to me. What I'd read in them had started some interesting thoughts about his background.

Brissac's past, before he'd met Mireille, was a subject he

never cared to discuss much. There were gaps, as well, in any conversation about the decade he'd spent as her husband.

When a friend is so obviously reluctant to talk about something you don't press. But that doesn't stop you wondering what he's concealing.

There were still some interior building materials stacked close to one side wall. Tiles for the kitchen and bath, weathered planks for partition paneling. And the pipe that carried water to the house from a deep well two hundred feet away hadn't been put underground yet. But the integrated flower beds and flagstone paths, hedges and young trees that Brissac had planted were already converting the place into an artful oasis in the surrounding desolation. Landscape gardening was Brissac's trade.

The dirt track ended at a wide graveled area separated from the side garden by a low curve of brick wall topped with potted plants. Mireille's aging Volvo station wagon was parked there, next to a black Mercedes sedan that had Paris license plates. The Renault Traffic van that Desiré Brissac had still been using when I'd seen him in Monte Carlo a couple months ago wasn't there.

I parked behind Mireille's wagon. She hadn't come out to greet me, though she must have heard my Peugot grinding up the slope. And she would have seen it was me from any window on three sides of the house. But the Mercedes might belong to a buyer from one of the big stores, come down to place an order for woodwork decorated by Mireille's folklore paintings. If so they were probably in her workshop, at a crucial point in their bargaining. Mireille would expect me to just knock and walk in. Say hello and go off to fix myself a drink in the living room until they finished talking business.

I went through an opening in the low brick wall and followed a flagstone path leading between flowering bushes toward the side entrance. The door opened when I was three steps away. But it wasn't Mireille who opened it.

It was a man. He was wearing an expensively tailored,

Italian-style summer-weight suit. Dark gray. And a florid silk necktie. Maroon and gold. He looked at me with a tight smile. The gun he was aiming at a point somewhere between my solar plexus and my belly button was a long-barreled target Luger.

4

HE WAS A TALL MAN. AS TALL AS ME BUT WHIPCORD THIN. With a high-bridged nose and a deep groove down each side of his gaunt face. Both grooves started below his high cheekbones. The left one was shorter, ending just past the corner of his mouth. The other continued around his prominent jaw to the hollow of his throat. I didn't know what a physiognomist would make of that imbalance. At the moment I was more concerned with the way he studied me while the gun in his hand concentrated on my midsection.

I said, "*Bonjour*, Roland. Who are you working for these days?"

He said, "What are you doing here, Sawyer?"

We'd met several times over the years. None of our meetings had become a treasured memory for either of us. But we had acquired some practical knowledge about each other.

Roland Mari. A workmanlike gun for hire. Good enough at his trade to discourage me from trying a broken-field run back to my car. Where it would take another eight seconds to dig my emergency pistol out of its hiding place inside the rear seat.

Nor did I give serious consideration to any of the tried and proven methods of diverting a man's attention long enough to disarm him. Roland Mari was not someone it was wise to make sudden moves around. His tight smile didn't mean he was in a friendly mood.

I watched him consider what he knew about me while I considered what I knew about him. "I'm here to see Madame Brissac," I told him politely. "Have I come at an awkward time?"

"Maybe not. Come in and join us." His own polite tone was given a note of insincerity by his failure to lower the Luger.

But he wasn't your crazy-type killer. Roland had discovered his ability with guns in the army, where they'd upped him to sergeant during his tour in Algeria. He'd retained that rank until he was mustered out. Which meant he was even better at strictly following orders than he was with guns. The French are no exception when it comes to the almost universal military distaste for independent thinking.

Roland hadn't changed basically since then. And since he hadn't been expecting me it was obvious he hadn't been given orders by anyone to come up here and kill me.

So he wouldn't. Unless I made it absolutely necessary. Something I intended to avoid. The day didn't *have to* end badly.

I accepted his invitation to come in. He backed up as I moved forward. When we were both inside we were still exactly the same distance apart as we'd been outside.

The side door led directly into Mireille's workshop, with its tangy odor of paint and turpentine and freshly sanded wood. A local firm that made unpainted furniture supplied the items she decorated. Some newly arrived stock—a cupboard, two doors, and a chest of drawers—were on one side of the shop, waiting for Mireille to paint them with designs culled from her library of books on folk art. Near the opposite wall there were three coffee tables, two with their designs completed, the third not quite finished, its paint still wet. The designs on the three were entirely different. One of Mireille's sales points: each piece was unique.

She stood next to the unfinished table, a smallish woman

of thirty-six with clean-cut, pretty features and a short mop of blond curls. Her white cotton overalls had some paint stains. Not many; Mireille worked neatly.

Her back was pressed against the stone-block wall that was part of the original house. Her fists were clenched at her sides. She looked scared, angry, confused. But mostly scared.

A young thug, about nineteen, held a switchblade knife to her throat. Its sharp point touched the skin, not drawing blood but forcing Mireille to tip her head back and stand very still.

The boy with the knife was a full head shorter than Roland Mari but weighed more, with much of that weight in muscle that strained the material of his T-shirt and jeans. He had tiny blue eyes and a nose like a chunk of putty someone had stepped on. His rusty-colored hair was clipped close to the skull except for a fringe that fell across his forehead halfway to his rusty eyebrows. It didn't have far to fall.

He had the look of a pit bull. Strong, fast, and mean.

"Madame Brissac," I demanded before Mireille could give voice to her surprise at seeing me, "what the hell is going on here?"

She caught the ball instantly. "I don't *know*, Monsieur Sawyer," she told me swiftly, hurrying the words. "They're looking for my husband. I *told* them the truth—that I don't know where he is and haven't heard from him in two days . . ."

That was enough information. I interrupted its flow, telling Roland, "That *is* the truth." I looked back to Mireille. "I'm sorry to report, Madame Brissac, I've spoken to all the people down along the coast that you suggested, and none of them have any idea where he's gone. So . . ."

"Wait a minute," Roland snapped. "She hired you to look for Brissac?"

"You heard. Why are *you* looking for him?"

"That's not your business, Sawyer. When did she hire you?"

I shook my head. "I've already said more than I should. My dealings with a client are private."

The boy with the knife had a suggestion for Roland: "Easy to make *her* tell it. All I got to do is start drawing an *X* in her cheek with this . . ."

"Hurt my client," I told him, "and I'll come looking for you. You won't have a face left after I find you. Or elbows, either. Your arms wouldn't be much use to you, ever again."

His sneer went from me to Roland. "He don't seem too worried by that gun you're holding on him."

Roland got the look of a man trying to exercise patience and finding it difficult. "Thing is, Max-Emile," he told his pit bull, with one of those tight smiles, "that Sawyer knows he's got nothing to worry about—unless he does something foolish."

"We've got no argument there," I said. "It's just a job. And one that's hit a dead end, anyway. So unless I turn up some new lead to her husband . . ."

"Don't," Roland told me. "*Don't* look for him any more."

"Why not, Roland?"

"Because at this point, Sawyer, nobody's told me to kill you. If you stay involved with this Brissac thing, they might tell me to. Clear?"

I nodded. "I get the message."

"Good." And to Max-Emile, Roland said, "And you, you don't cut her. Because nobody told you to do that. *Did* they?"

"No," Max-Emile admitted. But he didn't like it. He was apparently *not* someone who took naturally to strictly following orders. People like him were what tough sergeants were made for.

"Go face the wall over there," Roland told me, and pointed with his free hand at a spot some five feet from Mireille. "Hands behind your neck, elbows against the wall."

I took the position. Roland ordered me to move my feet backward. I did that, too. When half my weight pinned my elbows against the wall, he told Mireille to stay where she was and ordered Max-Emile to find out if I had a gun on me. "But first put away that knife," he said. "I don't want Sawyer grabbing it from you and using you as a shield."

I knew Roland, but he knew me, too.

Max-Emile didn't know any of the things Roland did. He laughed. "I'd like to see him try."

"No," Roland said dryly, "you wouldn't like it."

I said, "Sounds like you're down to teaching kindergarten, Roland."

"The new ones have to learn from somebody. Only some of them don't know they have to."

Max-Emile closed his knife with a sullen look and stuffed it into the back pocket of his jeans. He was starting toward me when Roland snapped at him: "And *don't* get between me and Sawyer while you search him."

Max-Emile stopped and glared at Roland. "Damn it, I'm not some stupid fucking kid you got to . . ."

Roland cut him short with a voice suddenly gone very quiet—a whisper of ice and steel: "You don't use that tone with me. I get respect from people like you."

It was like a shock of cold water. Max-Emile sobered and dropped the glare. "I-I'm sorry, Roland. I didn't mean . . ."

"Did I ever give you permission to address me by my first name?" Roland asked him in that same whispery voice.

"No—I'm sorry, Monsieur Mari." The young thug said it meekly, temper and street pride breaking as he abruptly recalled what Roland was.

"Fine," Roland said, "now do what I told you. The way I told you."

"Yes, sir." Max-Emile was careful not to move between Roland and me as he did the frisk. When he was finished he stepped away from me and said, "No gun."

"Then let's go," Roland told him.

"And just leave these two?" Max-Emile was surprised, but there was no iota of disrespect in his question.

"Why not?" Roland's voice had eased up. He was back to the tight smile and the hard patience. "We were sent to find Brissac. We looked and he's not here. I don't think either of them know where he is. So . . . go out and start the car.''

Max-Emile hurried outside. Roland backed to the open door and waited there holding the Luger on us. Mireille remained frozen in place, taking slow, deep breaths through her open mouth. I continued to lean with my elbows against the hard stone-blocks of the wall.

The Mercedes engine purred to life outside.

Roland Mari vanished from the doorway.

I listened to the Mercedes driving away as I unlocked my hands from the back of my damp neck and shoved myself off the wall.

5

"I WAS WORRIED ENOUGH ABOUT DÉSIRÉ BEFORE THOSE TWO came along," Mireille said raggedly. "Now I know I was right to worry. Worry isn't the right word for it—I'm scared."

"Did they say anything at all about why they're looking for him?"

"Nothing. I asked and they wouldn't answer. They just searched through the house for him and kept trying to make me say where he is. I wish I knew."

I was driving her down to Lucéram. The government hadn't yet gotten around to running a telephone line up to the Brissac place. But people wanting to contact either of them—usually about their work—could phone a bistro at the bottom of the village and leave a message. It was also at that bistro that Mireille was supposed to pick up her daughter, Hugette, who was spending the afternoon at a girlfriend's house. Hugette wasn't due there for another half hour, but Mireille was anxious to find out if her husband had phoned since she'd last checked that morning.

I didn't remind her that when a call was urgent one of the couple who ran the bistro would drive up with the message right away, knowing they'd be well tipped for the extra service. She needed to be doing something, anything, to help get her nerves back under control.

"All I do know," she said as I carefully descended a hairpin bend in the one-lane road, "is that I haven't heard from

21

him since he drove off early yesterday morning.'' Mireille frowned and qualified that: "I haven't heard *from* him—I did hear about him, though. Some man who wouldn't give his name phoned the bistro. He said he was calling for Desiré— and for them to tell me he was all right but wouldn't be able to contact me for the next few days. They said he sounded nervous. He hung up while they were asking his name.''

"When did this man make the call?''

"This morning. More than twenty-four hours after Desiré went away.''

"He say where he was going?''

Mireille nodded. "Just to drive along the coast, somewhere between Menton and Saint Raphael. The way he usually does when he doesn't have a new job already lined up. Dropping into bistros along the way. They're the best places to find out if anybody local needs work done.''

I asked what she'd told her daughter.

"It's not the first time her father has stayed away from home for a few days,'' she told me. "He'll do that when he's got a very big landscape job to do. I've let Hugette think this is one of those times.''

I asked the next question as casually as I could: "Do you happen to know a woman named Ilona?''

"I don't think so. Why—what has she got to do with Desiré disappearing?''

"Nothing at all. She's just part of the tail end of a case that brought me up here. I've got a client who wants to find her.'' I described Ilona.

Mireille shook her head. "What is her last name?''

"I don't know that. Neither does my client.''

"That's odd.''

"It is and it isn't,'' I said vaguely. Mireille was too preoccupied with her own problem to pay real attention to what I was saying. Which made it easier to lie to her. "I can't explain without violating this client's privacy. All I can tell you is I ran out of the few weak leads he gave me, and then somebody thought they saw her once in Lucéram. I asked around there but no luck. So I came over to ask you and Desiré.''

"Why us?"

"This Ilona is from Hungary, like your husband. So are a lot of other people, of course, but . . ." I shrugged. "It was just a last thin possibility."

Mireille gave it a little thought. "No, I don't know any Ilona. If Desiré does, he never mentioned her to me."

"Then he probably doesn't. And that finishes that job. I'll have to tell the client I couldn't get anywhere with it."

We entered the main road through Lućeram. I parked near the bistro and watched Mireille hurry off into it. Almost running. She still had that same butt-rolling stride I remembered from when we'd first met, back in our teens.

That had been during one of my customary summers with my mother, at the house I now lived in on a semipermanent basis. Mireille and I had progressed from hello to flirting to rapture over one long night at a beach party in the cove below the house. Sharing bits of steak grilled in the bonfire. Dancing out of the firelight into the shadows. A long post-midnight swim. A little wine. Falling asleep wrapped in the same blanket. A hot romance that lasted to that summer's end, when I'd had to return to my dead father's parents and the next school term in Chicago. Parting with tears and vows of fidelity forever. When I came back next summer she had a new boyfriend. After some sulking I'd found another girl-friend—and we'd become two couples that went everywhere together.

We were the only two left of that inseparable foursome. The other boy went to Paris to study banking and died of an overdose when he was twenty-two. The other girl married a dentist, had two kids, and got killed in a hang-gliding accident when she was thirty. There'd been long periods since those teenage summers when Mireille and I didn't meet, and other periods when we ran into each other once or twice a year. No matter how long the times between, our friendship never entirely lost its special ingredient: a memory of that first passionate kiss under the stars near the smouldering embers of a dying beach fire.

Desiré Brissac had showed up twelve years ago. A stocky political refugee with a rugged, hard-boned face and hair already turning prematurely white. Wary eyes and a slow, quiet smile that hadn't had much practice. Big shoulders and hands that looked like they could crush stone. What little he was willing to tell about his Hungarian past confined to some rudimentary facts.

He had been a career soldier, part of a unit trained for antiriot and counterinsurgent actions. Some things he'd found himself involved in turned his stomach. Finally, while on a patrol assigned to stop border crossers the hard way, he became one of them—slipping through into Austria and then making his way to France.

No details. There were elements underneath that sketchy background that stayed too painful for him to talk about.

He came into our area looking for some new kind of work that a man trained in nothing but weapons and fighting could learn to do. Mireille's father, who had a small landscape gardening business, had hired him. Brissac had learned, quickly and eagerly.

"It's a nice profession," he told me once. "Everybody likes a gardener."

"At least," I'd said, "you don't have to worry about them shooting at you."

"And," Brissac had said, "you don't have to hurt *them*."

He was forty when Mireille married him. She was twenty-six, four months pregnant, and crazy about him. When her father retired, Desiré Brissac took over his business, paying for it in irregular installments over the years that followed. Handling small landscaping jobs alone; hiring helpers by the day for bigger jobs. It never brought a high income. But the Brissacs weren't out to get rich. The one thing that did bother them was that down near the sea rents were high. They couldn't afford the living space they wanted. Just a tiny apartment—too tight for comfort as their daughter grew—and a one-car garage Mireille used for her own business that her husband encouraged her to start.

Then they'd gotten their chance to shift to the burned-out hilltop near Lucéram. After that move life seemed to be giving them everything they felt they needed to be happy.

Until now.

Mireille came out of the bistro and shook her head as she got back into the car beside me. "He still hasn't called." She gripped her knees and stared grimly through the windshield. Her voice and nerves were under control. But the fear remained, sharp inside her.

"He's gone off other times," I said. "I'm not talking about a few days' gardening work. There've been much longer periods he's been away somewhere, doing I don't know what. Did he ever do that before and not phone while he was away?"

"Yes. Once for almost two months. But he always warned me, before he left. That he was going and I wouldn't hear from him until he came back."

"This time he didn't warn you."

"No—and this time we don't have any urgent financial problem. That's when he would go, before. When we needed money. More than we could earn normally, in a short time. Like when he wanted to back me in starting my own business. And the time we bought the property up here."

"Where did he go, those times?"

"I don't know. Desiré didn't want to talk about it. He said he didn't want me knowing that part of his life. All I do know is that whenever he came back he had the money we needed."

"Check or cash?"

"In cash . . ." Mireille looked at me fiercely. "Desiré is not a thief, if that's what you're thinking."

"But you haven't asked the police to help you find out what's happened to him."

"He wouldn't like having the police prying into his affairs.

He . . .'' Mireille hesitated. ''Look, what does he know how to do, other than gardening? He *was* a soldier, before that.''

''You think he hires out as a mercenary.''

''I did guess that was it, naturally. But when I told Desiré, he told me not to worry. That he wasn't going off to fight again, as a soldier of any kind.'' Mireille was looking at the windshield again, eyes narrowed as she thought back. ''When I pressed the subject, pretty hard, he told me the job he did when he was away was just teaching other men to do some specialized work. I couldn't get more than that out of him.''

With Desiré Brissac's background in Hungary, that almost certainly meant training third world troops in antiguerilla tactics.

''Who did he go to when he wanted a job like that?'' I asked Mireille.

''I have no idea. Who or where. None at all. . . .'' Mireille looked at me again. ''That job that brought you up here—you did say it's almost finished.''

''Completely finished,'' I told her. ''If you want to hire me to find your husband, I'm available.''

''We don't have much reserve in our bank account at this moment. I can't spare more than three hundred francs, as a retainer. But there's more due in soon. I'll pay you the rest in installments, as it comes.''

''Fine,'' I said. ''You can write me a check for the three hundred when we take Hugette back to the house.'' I didn't intend to cash any checks from Mireille until I was certain it wouldn't leave her strapped. But if this case brought the law down on me at some point, the check would serve as legitimate proof that I was doing lawful work for a respectable client. More legitimate than a ring left with me by a mystery woman with no last name and questionable motives.

Because Mireille had no likelier suggestions about people who might know where her husband went off to—this time and before—I asked her about the two thought-provoking friends of his who'd been helping rebuild the house the week I'd spent up there.

She told me their names were Klaus and Eric. "I don't know their last names," she said without remarking on the fact that I'd said the same about Ilona. "They used to come by to help quite often. Always together." She didn't know anything else about them—other than their being men Desiré knew from "somewhere," going back three or four years.

I probed her for any other possible lead to her husband. But she couldn't help there. She did say one thing that was interesting, though: "Young women have always found Desiré attractive. Look how young I was when I fell in love with him. He likes it, naturally. As far as I'm aware, though, he's never . . . taken advantage of it. But if that's what's happened—if he has gotten involved with someone younger than me—if those two horrible men were from some angry husband—I'd be relieved. Mad and hurt, but relieved to find out it's not something worse. But to be honest, I don't really think that's what this is about."

I refrained from telling Mireille that it was one distinct possibility.

I've never been a great believer in the unvarnished truth. Not when it's hurtful and serves no purpose. As in, "I hate to be the one to tell you, and if it wasn't my duty as a friend I wouldn't, but I saw your wife with another man and they look very much in love." Too often "being honest" is just a hook on which to hang a closet streak of spite.

Mireille's daughter appeared, coming down a stairway street from the interior of the older part of the village above us. We got out of the car to signal her. When Hugette saw me there with her mother she let out a whoop and came running. A slender ten-year-old with a pixie face and a pair of flaxen ponytails flying behind her small head.

She remembered the proprieties of her advancing age at the last moment and stopped running. She came the rest of the way at a dignified, graceful walk, said, "Bonjour, Monsieur Pierre-Ange," and reached up to shake my hand. I slapped her hand away and bent down and kissed her. Hugette kissed me back, a quick peck on each cheek. Then she drew back a half step and gave me an up-from-under-the-eyelashes look accompanied by a small coquettish smile.

A lot of American women work at being perky girls all their lives. Most French girls start practicing at being provocative women around age eight. It doesn't seem to make much difference in the end results, though. Either system, I keep noticing, somehow goes right on producing the most inspired creations in nature's storehouse of living treasures.

Hugette went back to being a little girl when we got into the car. She settled herself on my lap. I let her help me steer—the way we'd first done it when she was two—all the way back to the house.

And all the way I was sorting out priorities in the moves to be made in finding Desiré Brissac. One of the very first had to be another talk with Ilona. This time with no holds barred.

But that turned out to be easier to want than to achieve.

6

THE SMALLISH MAN WAS TELLING THE BIG ONE ABOUT THE time he had tried to assassinate him. It lay heavy on his conscience.

"I forgive you," the big man said. He took a noisy sip of strong tea, holding his glass with a paper napkin so the heat wouldn't burn his stubby fingertips and thumb. "At that time you considered it your duty to murder me."

"No, no . . ." the small one insisted, spreading his slim hands apart in a gesture of abject apology. "I was only frightened. Of what they would do to me if I did not carry out their orders. Coward. I chose to kill you so that I might live a little longer. Coward."

They were at the table to my left, middle-aged men in old men's suits, speaking French with heavy, melodic Russian accents.

The big one took a slurp from his glass of tea and winced as it boiled his tongue and throat. He set the glass delicately on the table. "Anyway, you failed. Probably because you did not *want* to kill me. One might even say that you put your own life in danger because the real you, inside, refused to obey orders. So, no coward—and no murderer, either."

But the small Russian wouldn't be consoled. "I failed because I was too nervous to take enough time to do it properly."

"The important thing is that you did fail." The big man's laugh was warm. "At least to me that is important."

"But it put you in the hospital for three weeks."

"Believe me, my friend, waking up in a hospital is better than not waking up in a morgue."

The *Père Tranquille* was a place for conversations like that. An old café near the ornate Russian Orthodox church in Nice. The church had been erected with money donated by Czar Nicholas II, back when Nice was the favorite place for Russian aristocrats to spend their winters. The café, bought in 1924 by a devout member of that aristocracy who'd escaped the Revolution, had in recent years become a haven for political refugees from Iron Curtain countries.

The present owner was a young anti-Soviet Marxist—a Bulgarian chess master who'd defected in the middle of a championship match in Paris, tearing up his party membership card in front of the TV cameras. Five months later he'd married a well-born *Parisienne* intellectual he met at the nudist colony on the Ile du Levant, and bought the café with her father's money.

The habitués of the big, brown-walled room represented every shade of political color between those two owners. A complicated tangle of mutually hostile ideologies. Back home they would have been mortal enemies. Here, they were all exiles together. In a zone of truce, but far from the tranquility of the café's name. The interwoven layers of anger and disillusion, regret and mockery, cynicism and nostalgia, were as dense as the cigarette smoke.

At the table next to me the failed assassin and his intended victim had fallen silent. They sat together gazing through the window, brooding on the night outside. I checked my watch. Pointlessly—there was nothing to do but to go on waiting. I'd already asked about Desiré Brissac. He wasn't known here. My description of Ilona hadn't rung a bell either. I finished off my drink—Polish vodka, red with pepper—and got out my current time-passer: a paperback of Ariosto's *Orlando Furioso*. Packed with more thrills, chills, and slapstick than *Star Wars*. Ariosto would have made a fortune if Hollywood had been around in the sixteenth century.

I was into the scenes of the beautiful Marfisa defeating nine male warriors in knightly combat, when Marie Hadjok came in.

Her saucy face and strong sinuous figure still made heads turn as she walked to my table. She wore a sleeveless, open shepherd's jacket over a white shirt and tight jeans. Her waist was cinched by a wide leather belt with a big buckle fashioned out of the word BOY. At sixty, Marie felt entitled to indulge little eccentricities. I stood and kissed her cheek. She patted mine and said, "If I weren't so passionately enamoured of you, I would never break in the middle of my own work like this to solve your little problems."

I assured her of my fervent gratitude and pulled out a chair for her. I had her favorite drink waiting on the table: the most expensive cognac in the place. Marie took a taste and made a purring sound of appreciation as I sat down beside her. I took out Ilona's letter to Desiré Brissac and handed it over.

Marie looked at it and said, "Let me read it slowly first and absorb the sense of it. Word for word translation is no good at all. Hungarian is a much older language, primitive and basic. While French is so deliciously ripe with nuance."

She took another sip of her cognac and began reading Ilona's letter. Squinting until she remembered to put on her reading glasses. Too many hours of straining over scrawled, typed, and printed pages had finally made the glasses essential. Translating Hungarian books and articles into French was her profession. Back in her native country she had worked the other way round, translating French into Hungarian. Until she translated and circulated an editorial from a French newspaper that infuriated the party politicians.

It had become relatively easy recently for people to get out of Hungary. It hadn't been when Marie had done it. She always enjoyed recounting the details of how she'd managed her escape. First persuading a lecherous party official that she needed a short vacation in Yugoslavia—with him—to rethink and correct her ideology. Then giving the official the slip and seducing an Italian tourist she selected from a Yugoslav beach. When the tourist drove back across the frontier into Italy, Marie was curled up "small as a snail" behind the rear seat of his little VW, with his dirty laundry piled on top of her.

She lived and worked just around the block from the *Père Tranquille*. In a single top-floor room, with a bathroom down the hall that she shared with a physics teacher whose apartment took up the rest of the floor. When I'd phoned, Marie had been working on a manuscript by a recently arrived Hungarian poet. She'd refused to interrupt until she finished the poem she was in the middle of translating. So I'd waited in the café. Her room was too small for me to wait there. Every horizontal surface was covered with her work. Including her bed. Which gave her the excuse, when she wished, to go down the hall and sleep with the physics teacher.

Hungarian women share certain traits with French women, but are more boldly direct about it.

Marie looked up from the letter. "I think your profession would be of equal interest for a mental voyeur or gossip columnist."

"Not so different, sometimes," I acknowledged.

Marie downed what was left of her cognac. I called for another, and paid close attention while she translated the letter aloud:

"My dear Dezsö,

"Are you crazy, intruding into my affairs like that? They have found out who you are! They don't know of my connection with you, but they will come after you. These people can be very dangerous, I warn you. If you are at your place when you receive this letter, go away immediately. To some place where they can't find you. If you are not at home, don't go back there. Stay away, for the next couple weeks. After that this should be over.

"And from now on please remember, my life is my own. You have your own life to lead. We are *not* part of each other's lives—that was *your* decision, don't forget.

"But, I still do love you. And I always will.

                                                "Your Ilonka."

⊠ **7** ⊠

ANTONIO ODASSO STOOD SIX-FEET-FOUR IN HIS SOCKS. AT sixty-five he still held his two hundred and forty pounds of solid bone and muscle ramrod straight. He had a broken-nosed face scarred by grenade fragments acquired fighting with the French Foreign Legion. His apartment in Cap d'Ail looked like it belonged to a young woman with an unrestrained taste for lacy frills and pink ribbons.

That had been his wife. He had married her after leaving the Legion and establishing himself as a local plumber. He'd adored her and didn't have the heart to change anything after she died in her late thirties. For a while after her death he came close to not having the heart to go on living. Local boys in their teens during that period—and I had been one of them—saved him from suicide. We had always liked hanging around Antonio, soaking up his battle stories. In that black year we never left him alone. Some would be tagging along wherever he went, telling him jokes and asking his advice on any personal problems we could think up; pushing him to retell his Legion experiences, eating the meals he liked to cook, sleeping over at his place or, when he couldn't sleep, playing cards with him until dawn.

And drinking with him. It hadn't been easy to keep up with him there; but we'd tried our best to. Finally Antonio got worried about turning us all into alcoholics, and he cut down on his own consumption. After that he'd begun climbing out of the worst of his grief.

We discussed Desiré Brissac in Antonio's kitchen while he cooked a dinner for the two of us. *Escalope de veau, sauce Perigueux*. He had added a good deal of culinary refinement to the basics he'd learned as an army cook, when his wounds had rendered him unfit for combat for almost six months.

"I don't really know Brissac," Antonio told me. "So I don't have any idea where he might have gone, myself. I only met him a few times, over drinks. There's a bar in Nice where old soldiers like to go and swap lies."

"I know the place," I said. "The Blue Devil. But I don't know any of the other men who go there, well enough. That's why I came to you first. They'd tell you things they wouldn't tell me if I walked in there alone."

Antonio made sure his sauce could simmer a bit longer. "We can drop in there together after we eat," he said, and began quickly whipping up a green salad for us.

I asked if he knew of Roland Mari. Antonio said, "Sure, in Algeria. He made sergeant. Rotten personality, but a good sergeant. Except he always stuck too tight to regulations."

"Ever seen him around here?"

"No." I hadn't expected an affirmative answer. Roland lived in and worked out of Paris.

Antonio set our meals on the table and opened a bottle of Fleurie. The wine was superb. The food was good—not three-star, but what reasonably priced restaurants call honest cooking. I made appreciative noises. Antonio grinned, as pleased as he'd always been when I'd been a kid.

I said, "I've got a reason to believe Brissac hired out as a merc, now and then when he needed extra dough."

"I wouldn't know about that," Antonio said. "I never had any connections with the mercenary business. Never wanted any part of it."

"I've gotten the impression around the Blue Devil that not all your old soldiers feel the way you do about that."

"Oh, sure—some of them still hire out. They always claim

it's for the pay, but mostly it's they miss the adrenaline rush you get around combat. Not me. I had my fill of it.''

Antonio Odasso's fighting career began when he was a teenager in Naples, waging secret street warfare against Mussolini, whom his father hated. Then his father was beaten to death by fascist thugs. Antonio killed two of them and fled to France. He joined the Foreign Legion to prevent French authorities from sending him back to Italy. He'd fought in North Africa during World War II, then in Indochina, then Algeria. He was entitled to feel he'd had enough.

''Me, myself,'' he added, ''I'm quite content to make my money with the other thing the Legion taught me.'' Legionnaires long ago acquired their reputation as fighters. Less widely known was that they spent much more of their time at construction wherever they were sent: building roads, railroad lines, forts, barracks. Each Legionnaire was routinely expected to be able to handle whatever was needed. But their officers liked it when some of them picked up special knowhow along the way. The specialty Antonio had learned was plumbing.

He stacked the empty dishes in the sink and began cutting up a fresh fruit salad for our desert. I said, ''Desiré Brissac has a couple tough friends. They look and talk like ex-soldiers that might still work at it, on occasion. Named Eric and Klaus; they seem to be a pair.'' I described them.

''They're in the Blue Devil most nights,'' Antonio told me. ''Used to be in the Legion. I got to know them in Indochina. They were already buddies. Klaus Troestler, he's German or maybe Austrian. Eric Savart, he's a *pied noir*.'' A ''black foot,'' a Frenchman born in North Africa when France still ruled there.

''I'd like to know if they're at the Blue Devil tonight,'' I said.

I followed Antonio out to the living room. The telephone was on a fragile-legged stand, sharing a lace doily with a lamp in the shape of a lavander cherub holding a beribboned shade. I listened over the extension receiver while Antonio made the call. He identified himself and asked if Eric Savart and Klaus Troestler were around.

"They usually come by a little later," the bar's owner said. "Have a couple drinks, go off if there's nobody else they want to talk with."

"I'll be there inside the hour," Antonio told him. "If they come in before me, tell them to wait until I get there. Tell them I said it's important."

We went back to the kitchen and ate our dessert.

◪ 8 ◪

THE BLUE DEVIL WASN'T A PLACE THAT TOURISTS OFTEN found. It was in a murky *cul-de-sac* inside one end of Nice's Old Town, not far from Place Garibaldi. It was a bar for regulars, private conversations, and slow but steady drinking. When a stranger wandered in conversations died. The stranger usually had one quick drink and wandered out.

It was a small, square box of a room, freshly painted with the national colors: red, white and blue. The bar stretched across the back, with six small tables between that and the front windows. There were three more little tables on the cobbles outside. I sat down at one of them and Antonio went inside. It was five minutes before he came back out.

"They're not here yet," he told me as he sat down. "Nobody in there's seen Brissac around for months. I told everybody to ask around and phone me right away if they hear anything. Made sure they know it's important."

The bartender came out with our drinks. A small local *marc* for me, a tall beer for Antonio. We sipped and waited. Half an hour later the pair we were waiting for appeared, strolling into the *cul-de-sac* toward the bar.

They were a Mutt-and-Jeff couple. Klaus Troestler was short, lean, and dark, with a liberal sprinkling of gray in his military-short black hair. Eric Savart was tall and wide with a blonde's complexion, and what little was left of his hair was shaved to the skull. What they shared was that they were both in their late fifties, had almost identical hard-case expressions, and walked with the same warrior's swagger. But they had done competent work on the Brissac house.

Antonio told them to join us. They remained standing by the table, their hard eyes on me.

"We've met," I reminded them.

Klaus nodded. "You were helping out at Desiré Brissac's place for a while. You're a friend of his wife."

"And of him, now. What are you drinking?"

They hesitated, looking from me to each other. Antonio told them, "I've known Pierre-Ange since he was a kid. I vouch for him—all the way."

Eric and Klaus sat down and said beer would be fine. Beer seems to be taking over from pastis as the slow-but-steady drinker's preference in France. Antonio shouted through the open door for three large beers and another *marc* for me.

"Desiré left home yesterday morning and hasn't come back," I said. "His wife doesn't know where he is, hasn't heard from him. She's scared he's in deep trouble. I think so, too."

"We haven't seen Desiré in a couple months," Klaus said. "What kind of trouble?"

"Two guys went up to his place today, trying to find him. They asked the questions with a gun and a knife. And wouldn't say why they're hunting for him. That kind of trouble."

It bothered them. Eric said, "This is the first we know about it. We can check with some people he might get in touch with if he's in real trouble."

"Do that," I said. "If you find out anything contact me fast." I pushed a card with my phone number across the table. "If I'm not in, leave a message on my machine. Or call Antonio—I'll check with him regularly."

The bartender came out with our drinks. He went back inside as Eric pocketed my card. I asked if Eric and Klaus knew Roland Mari. They didn't. I said, "I know Desiré has done some jobs as a mercenary. You two ever work with him?''

They tasted their beers and looked at each other. Antonio growled, ''I *said* I vouch for him.''

Klaus nodded slightly. Eric told me: ''Once. In Morocco. That's where we first got to know him. We were there teaching some Moroccan troops how to handle new weaponry. The kind they were going to use against guerrillas coming from Algeria into what used to be called the Spanish Sahara.''

''A chunk of worthless sand,'' Klaus put in, ''with a lot of valuable minerals underneath. Desiré was giving the same government troops lessons in guerrilla and antiguerrilla fighting. Same kind of assignment he had in Oman and the Congo, but we weren't with him those times.''

I asked, ''Which merc middleman did you get the Moroccan job through?''

Eric and Klaus looked at each other again.

I kept a tight rein on my voice: ''The same go-between probably got Desiré his other assignments. He'd be a natural for Desiré to go to if he needs help. He might even be the reason Desiré is in trouble.''

''We'll check with him and find out,'' Klaus said.

''I'd like to contact him with you,'' I said.

But Klaus shook his head. ''He wouldn't like us spreading his name and location all over. And we might need to do business with him again. *We'll* check, and let you know.''

I drank some of my second *marc*. It was more dignified than stamping my feet. I tried a different subject: ''Desiré wouldn't let his wife wonder and worry for two days, if he could contact her. Easy enough to come up with some reasons why he can't call her. One, somebody's holding him prisoner. Two, he's dead. Three, he's hurt, too badly to phone. I've already called all the local hospitals. He's not in any of them. Would you know a private doctor he might be with? The kind of doctor that wouldn't feel obliged to notify the law about a severely wounded patient?''

Eric and Klaus gave each other that damned look again.

"We'll check around and see what we can find out," Eric said. Same response I'd gotten on the subject of the merc go-between.

And that was the best I could get out of them.

There were two messages waiting on my answering machine when I got home. Neither was from Sonia Galeazzo, though I'd left messages with her answering services in both Milan and Cannes, as well as with her agent in Paris. None of whom had known where she was, or so they'd claimed. I guessed she was off on one of her secret missions.

The first message was from Mireille, less than an hour ago, telling me she still hadn't heard from her husband.

The other message was from my partner in Paris, Fritz Donhoff, asking me to phone him. Fritz was the senior partner. More important, he was our expert in gathering information by phone from a wide variety of sources. In his seventies, after fifty years in the business, he would have had to be very dim not to have acquired an immense network of informants all over Europe. Fritz was not dim. I called him, hoping for answers to some of the questions I'd left on his answering machine several hours earlier.

"My boy, how are you?" he said in that deep voice like a warm bear-hug. Fritz often treated me like an adopted son. Since my real father had died before I arrived in this world, I didn't usually mind that much. But it could be irritating when I wasn't in the mood for all that middle-European affection.

"What have you got for me, Fritz?"

"I didn't return to the apartment and get your message until less than two hours ago, Peter. So you'll have to exercise more patience than I hear in your voice at the moment. I was able to check the basics on Desiré Brissac rather easily. His name was originally Dezsö Kormany. Or Kormany Dezsö, since the Hungarians put the family name first. Hungary *is* where he is from. He obtained French citizenship by serving in the army for a number of years. There is nothing else of use to you in his records. And other than that all I've gotten so far are some negatives.''

"Such as?''

Fritz told me that the license number I'd automatically noted, on the Mercedes parked outside the Brissac home, belonged to Roland Mari. "So, no lead there. It is Mari I've concentrated on since getting home. People who know him say he left Paris about a week ago. None of those I phoned know who he is currently working for. They didn't even know he's now down in your area.''

"What about the yacht named *La Dolce Vita*?''

"I'll get on that tomorrow, with my contacts at the marine insurance firms here and in London. Now suppose you fill me in on the details of this case.''

I filled him in, starting with Ilona and ending with Eric and Klaus.

"Interesting,'' Fritz mused. "Tomorrow I will try to contact a man I know in Munich who sometimes acts as a broker in mercenary dealings, and ask if he knows Brissac.''

"Sure,'' I said, "but it's a long shot. I already phoned two I know, in Rome and in Brussels. They never heard of Brissac. Problem is, there's too many characters he could have gotten merc jobs through. Including a lot who do it as a sideline, along with arms dealing and other quasi-legal businesses.''

"Maybe we'll get lucky,'' Fritz said.

"Knock wood.''

"My boy,'' Fritz told me firmly, "it is time you outgrew these little superstitions. Luck derives from persistence and mathematics—not from magic.''

I didn't remind him of a couple cases where vital leads had come from something very close to the occult. Fritz has his minor prejudices.

The other person who hadn't left a message on my machine was Arlette Alfani. I'd phoned her yesterday. Today it was her turn to call. I held to that point of view for a full five seconds. Then I called long distance and the number of her hotel in Dublin.

She wasn't in her room. The switchboard paged her. When she came on the line I heard the noises of a convivial bar in the background.

"You've already lost the case," I suggested, "and you're getting drunk before booking the morning plane home."

She laughed, but very little. Arlette didn't have enough confidence yet to accept cracks about losing cases with good humor, like long-established attorneys. "I'm just having a last drink with John—he's the Irish lawyer handling our client's defense. He wanted to go over a few of the points we will present to the court."

"He wants to get into your bed, is what he wants."

"That is possible," Arlette said. "And he is charming. But I will remember you and keep my panties determinedly aloft. Promise."

"When are you coming back?" I said. "I miss you."

"Not for at least a week. They won't let our client out of jail. He did hit and run. They're afraid he'll skip the country. I'm trying to get across all the counterpoints I can. The boy is young and he's sorry. He's from a respectable family and back in France he doesn't have a single violation on his driving record. He wasn't used to driving on the other side of the road, the way they do here. It made him nervous. He was in a strange country where he can hardly speak the language. So he got scared and ran. I have his family getting me letters extolling their son's virtues from all the influential people they know."

"How's the man he hit?"

"He'll live, thank God. But he won't be out of the hospital for ten days more. Peter . . . ?"

"Yes?"

"I miss you too. How about your coming over here for a bit, so I'll have something to look forward to, nights. And won't be tempted by handsome Irishmen."

"I wish you'd asked me this morning," I told her. "I'd

already be there. Now I'm on a job. One I can't walk away from.''

"Too bad."

"Yeah."

I went to sleep that night without Arlette and without a single solid lead to follow the next day.

"YOU CAN COUNT ON ONE HAND THE ARTISTS THAT SELL before they're dead or too old to give a fuck anymore. Scandal sells *now*." Sonia Galeazzo had told me that some years ago, in the American brand of English she spoke as easily as French and her native Italian. It was one of her several explanations for having given up painting for what she'd been doing ever since.

I followed the directions she'd left for me, shortly past noon, with her answering service in Cannes. Parked my car at the seaside resort of Agay, east of Saint Raphael. Rented a small boat with an outboard motor and headed off between the dark red rocks jutting out of the emerald water. There were plenty of yachts anchored between the red rocks, but all too large. Further out, beyond the rocks, the anchored boats were fewer. I swung over toward the smallest one, not much bigger than mine but with a little cabin and forward deck.

It was the one I was looking for: the *Ocean Breeze*, in English, registered in Toulon. I tied up alongside and climbed aboard. Sonia was on the forward deck, looking like she was asleep on her tummy, her head and arms hidden under a gigantic straw sombrero. Her short, wiry figure was bare except for a black bikini bottom. What the sun was doing to her skin would turn painful by that night. Sonia wasn't accustomed to being outside without all her clothes on.

I stretched out beside her. In the shade of the sombrero, Sonia held a Nikon with a telescopic lens aimed at a yacht that was too far away for me to see anything interesting there with the naked eye.

She turned her pinched gamin's face from the viewfinder and looked at me with those huge dark eyes. "Get your clothes off, damn it. Nobody here but us dozing sunbathers."

I shucked off my sneakers, jeans, and T-shirt. Kept on my sunglasses and undershorts. The shorts were dark blue: at a distance they would pass for swim trunks.

"On your back," Sonia snapped. "I don't want them to start worrying somebody's looking their way."

I rolled over on my back. "Who are you crucifying with your camera today?"

Sonia had gone back to keeping watch on the distant yacht through her camera. She had the total, confident patience of an experienced alley cat waiting outside a mouse hole. "Rico the Rake and his new wife, that Swedish beauty he met at the Monte Carlo Beach Club."

That Rico was an Italian count who'd gotten the nickname for his addiction to gambling, fast cars, night clubs, and other men's women. He was also famous among the racier members of the international set for the lavish parties he could still host at his ancestral Tuscan palazzo, thanks to the enormous settlement his former wife, an American heiress, had paid to get rid of him.

"I've been shadowing them for over a week," Sonia said. "Ever since their wedding down in Florence. Right now they're inside the main stateroom, taking a nap I guess. But they'll be back out. I've already gotten some great shots of them. Sunbathing and scuba diving. In the nude," she added with relish. "Plus some snuggling, also nude. The Italian tabloids will eat it up. The Krauts and Brits, too."

"I was under the impression," I said, "that married people were allowed a little fun, in our western world, without other people getting excited about it."

"Licit or illicit, sexy fun is sin, and sin is scandal. My meat and drink."

Sonia wasn't called the Milanese Monster as a joke.

"And we've got a bonus over there this afternoon," she went on without taking her attention from the yacht. "Another couple's joined them. They like traipsing around bare-assed, too." Sonia named a top British actor. "The girl he brought along's a luscious hunk. Gorgeous tits and ass."

I'd seen some of the paintings Sonia had done before she quit. They were the work of someone who had spent a lot of time in museums studying the techniques of the old masters with eyes that understood what they saw. And she could, when she wanted to, carry her side of an intelligent discussion in a cultivated manner. But when Sonia went vulgar, she went all the way.

She tensed, suddenly, and began snapping off fast shots. About fifteen seconds' worth, then she stopped. "Damn it, she went back inside. . . ."

Sonia relaxed a notch but remained vigilant. "That was the limey's luscious girlfriend. They probably picked each other up in the bar at the Carlton. That's where he's staying, naturally. Nothing but the best. Maybe she'll get lucky, like Rico's bride. If not she'll at least party in luxury and center stage while he's here. And then go on the make for some other guy who can afford expensive young toys. No shortage of men with the loot along this coast. That's why the Riviera's so loaded with lovelies."

"Nothing new," I said. "The Côte d'Azur's always been a plush hunting ground."

"Uh-huh," Sonia said. "Bimbo heaven."

I said, "I'm trying to find an attractive young woman who knows you. Her first name's Ilona. She didn't give me a last name. She's from Hungary but speaks French without much of an accent. Yesterday she came to my place saying you told her nice things about me. She's supposed to phone me in a couple days but I can't wait. I have to talk to her."

"Ilona Szabo," Sonia said, and shot me a quick glance. "You're too young for her. Ilona likes older men."

"It's business," I growled. "Nasty business. Some people I care about are going to get hurt unless I can do something about it."

"Ilona in trouble?"

"I think so."

"She's a nice person. I liked her."

"I'll try to help, if I can find her in time." And if I could, I'd shake out of her what it was that Desiré Brissac had gotten himself into.

"I don't know where she is these days," Sonia said. Her attention was once more focused through the camera on the yacht. "I only knew her for about a week, and that was long ago."

"She told me you were both cruising past my place on a yacht when you got to talking about me."

"That's right. Almost two years ago—the first and last I saw of her. The yacht belonged to Marius Lejon."

"Of the Lejon supermarket chain?"

"Yeah."

"What was the boat's name?"

Sonia thought for a moment. *"The Big Fish."*

Not *La Dolce Vita*. Nice try, no cigar.

"And it *was* big," Sonia said. "He kept it in the Beaulieu marina, for when he came down here from Paris. I was sneaking shots of a party on it, from the dock, when he caught me at it. And invited me aboard. Lejon knew my work—thought most of it was more amusing than humiliating. His yacht was ready for a cruise down to Capri. He said I could come along and take any pictures I wanted."

"He must've left his brains in his office out tray."

"No, he was smart. Thought it would be funny to have a collection of my kind of pictures of him and his guests, for his private collection. Our deal was, he got first look. Any shots he liked—or that he or his guests wouldn't like other people seeing—he bought all rights to. For a good price. The rest I was free to sell elsewhere. Not bad for me, financially. And hell, I'd never been on a real luxury cruise before.''

A corner of Sonia's mouth quirked in a reminiscent grin. ''Also, it turned out to be a fun shoot. Lots of hanky-panky. Most of the guests were from the latest crop of Riviera bimbos—two for every male guest.''

''And Ilona Szabo was one of them.''

''I wouldn't call her that. Some might, but I wouldn't. She was the only female aboard I felt like talking with for more than ten seconds, all the way to Capri and back. But we lost touch after that week. Almost two years.''

''How did she come to be on Lejon's cruise?''

''That goes back to when she came out of Hungary,'' Sonia told me. ''She'd been trained in some kind of physical therapy there. Straightening out crooked spines and stuff like that. So that's how she earned a living after she came to France. She couldn't get a license to practice here on her own, but a doctor in Paris hired her as his assistant therapist. . . .''

''Do you know the doctor's name?'' I interrupted. She didn't. But Fritz could find that out, now that I had Ilona's last name. ''Tell me the rest.''

''Well, one of this doctor's patients was Marius Lejon. He had a tricky back. Used to go out of whack pretty regularly. Ilona was able to help with that.''

''And massaging his back led to further developments.''

''Ilona does like elderly men. And likes being able to make them feel good. Lejon made her his private, personal therapist. And mistress.''

''Cinderella meets her prince—only he's over the hill and in lousy health so no happy ending. Marius Lejon died a year ago.''

''I heard,'' Sonia said. ''Ilona must have taken it hard. She did like him. But I guess she came out all right. Lejon said he was gonna add something to his will for her.''

''You must have gotten some pictures of her while you were shooting the yacht trip.''

"Sure."

"I could use the most recognizable face shot you can find."

"All that stuff's in my Milan files. When I get a chance I can phone there and ask my lab girl to . . ."

Sonia severed connection with me abruptly. The motor attached to her Nikon whirred, snapping a sequence of fast frames while she moved the camera in a slow arc. Recording some new and saleable occurence aboard her victims' yacht.

I sat up and put on my jeans and T-shirt. I don't think she noticed when I climbed off her boat and headed back to shore in my rental outboard.

⊠ **10** ⊠

IT WAS LATE AFTERNOON MERGING INTO EVENING. THE EN-trance to the paved, one-lane road on Cap Ferrat had signs reading PRIVATE and NO EXIT. It cut through a wooded section of the cape toward two invisible estates. One belonged to a former prime minister. The other to the Duchatel family—the one with the construction firm responsible for so many of the insect-nest "New Towns" of France. I drove with due care. There was a nasty six-inch ridge across the road at several points. *Un flic qui dort*—a sleeping policeman—to cripple the cars of speeders.

I stopped at the Duchatel gate. It was as high as the walls, and the trees behind were higher. The estate remained invisible. An armed guard wearing the uniform of a Riviera security company got off a stool by the gate and came over, looking in my opened car window at me and frowning at what he saw. I had changed into a respectable-appointment outfit culled from the overnight bag in the car. Plain sports shirt, denim slacks, and jacket. A silk scarf around my neck, shoes and socks on my feet. That apparently wasn't enough.

"I'm not here for the party," I said, and gave him my name. "There's a man inside who's expecting me. Dixon Chess."

He went back to the gate and spoke into its intercom. Then he waited, keeping his frown on me. After a couple minutes he communicated with the intercom again. Whatever it told

51

him altered his attitude. He smiled at me as he waited some more. The gate began to open, remote-operated from somewhere inside. When it was open enough the guard waved my car through, still smiling.

The graveled driveway made a long curve close to an inner wall and was bordered by an impressive variety of roses. Twenty-three different kinds, according to an account I'd once read in *Nice-Matin*. Backing the rose bushes were palms and olive trees. Between them I got glimpses of a wide, perfectly manicured lawn sloping up to a white-pillared mansion that had nothing Mediterranean about it. The look was more Stately Homes of England.

The drive turned away from the house between lines of high hedges. It ended near a five-car garage. The parking area in front of the long garage was crowded with pricey automobiles belonging to guests celebrating the seventeenth birthday of the Duchatels' daughter. I added my humble Peugeot to the crowd.

Another armed guard appeared as I got out. This one I knew. Bernard Blondel, a local cop. Doing a bit of moonlighting. He grinned and shook my hand. ''Monsieur Chess said he'll meet you by the pool.'' He led me around the garage, toward the sound of hard-driving folk rock.

Behind the garage a four-piece band was working hard at one end of a large patio surrounding a good-sized swimming pool. All their numbers were American, of course. Like in half the bistros and on most of the radio stations. If you want to hear French numbers in France you've got to search around.

The area was screened from the house by more high hedges. There were about twenty-five young people—sixteen to twenty—amusing themselves around the patio. Dancing to the rock beat. Getting snacks and drinks from a long buffet table. Necking on the grass between flowering bushes. Slumped at small tables looking like they were fighting sleep. Or maybe just half-drunk. Or stoned and drunk.

The boys were dressed in summer formals. The girls wore

extravagant party dresses that shouted money and displayed ample amounts of cleavage and thigh. Some voices were nearing screech level, but most were still reasonably controlled.

I didn't see Dixon Chess. And then I did. He came plodding through an opening in the hedges, from the direction of the house. A big, bloated ball of a man with a long cigar in his fat mouth and a tall mixed drink in his pudgy hand.

He was wearing a panama hat with a gold-and-red band. Plus a loud checked sport jacket with a tieless black shirt and bright red slacks. High society accepted Dixon Chess any way he felt like dressing. Jet-setters aspiring to high profiles need the media to achieve star status.

Chess was from Tennessee and had been a pretty good war correspondent until he'd gotten badly wounded covering a street riot in Pakistan. He'd switched to writing about travel and restaurants, because he liked to move around and was passionate about good food. Especially if it was plentiful and free. Top restaurants led to top people. He now covered old money, new celebrity, and conspicuous corruption in a gossip column syndicated to thirty U.S. newspapers. A center of what's-in gravity for an invisibly walled world in which chic levels rise and fall with dizzying velocity.

I left Blondel and made my way toward Chess through a gaggle of revved-up dancers. He'd stopped at the buffet table to pick up a glass of wine with his free hand. He held it out to me when I reached him. "Here y'are, Pete—I guess you still like rosé."

I took the glass from him and we made it across the patio to a vacant table. I took a sip of the rosé. It was a little warm for my taste. Chess flicked ash from his cigar and raised his highball to his lips and tilted it. When he lowered the glass the level of liquor in it hadn't gone down more than half a millimeter. He did that a lot. And people talked about what a heavy drinker he was—every time they looked his way he was taking another swallow. Few noticed how long the same drink lasted.

I nodded at the children of the privileged. "Where are the grown-ups?"

"On the second patio. Other side of the house. Drinking and snacking and exchanging tidbits of social and financial news. In discreet separation. So they don't have to notice and disapprove of their spoiled offsprings' hijinks."

Dixon Chess attributed his detached view of the upper-crust to the fact he'd grown up in a family that never clawed its way out of dirt poor. He'd begun contributing to its in-come at age eight, hiring out as a ten-hour-a-day farmhand. By fifteen, Chess claimed, he could drive nails with his bare fists. Friends looked at what his hands had become and ad-vised him not to try it now.

"Stick around until dusk settles in," he said, "and you'll see some of these kids slipping off into the bushes together. Or into the guest house where they can do it in comfort. Might even get a group grope."

"Some've already started," I told him. "I spotted a cou-ple behind a hedge just before I parked."

"That must be the birthday girl and her new boyfriend." Chess did that trick with his highball glass again. "Since I don't see them here. I guess she was in need. Hasn't had any since this morning—when she parted from the fellow she spent the night with at the Negresco."

"Not her new boyfriend."

"Oh, no. He doesn't know where she was last night."

"But you do. Naturally."

"My ears never sleep," Dixon Chess said. "I bribe gen-erously at all the better hotels and restaurants."

"And you've got a fine memory for all the gossip you've ever heard."

"Have to, in my line. Got to keep track—who's up and who's down, who's in and who's out. It changes, and you want to know why, ahead of time."

"Tell me about Marius Lejon and his mistress, Ilona Szabo."

Chess immediately came alert: "Why? You come across some new dirt on the subject?"

"When I have something you can use, Dix, I'll give it to you. Like I have in the past."

"Sure—when it's not something that'd upset one of your clients."

"My job's got rules like yours has. Right now I'm the one after information."

"Okay . . ." When Dixon Chess squinted thoughtfully his eyes almost disappeared between balloons of overfed flesh. "Well, now—Marius Lejon is down of course. As in dead and buried. And Ilona Szabo, she's out because she got left out. It was a hot little story, for a short while there."

"I didn't hear about it," I said.

"That's because my column isn't printed over here. And you know how French journalism is played. Steering away from things that would embarrass people on the same power level as the media moguls. Which the Lejon heirs most definitely are."

"Spell out the hot little story for me," I said. "Euphemisms go over my head."

"It was an inheritance squabble," Chess told me. "Not too unusual an occurence in the heady universe of great wealth, as you're well aware."

"I've been involved in a few."

"I'll bet. Like divorce, it's a sweet source of income for both lawyers and private eyes." Chess looked at his cigar and decided he'd smoked enough of it. He dropped it on the patio flagstones and ground it out under his heel. "In most cases the battle over an inheritance is between the various children of the deceased. Juicier cases pit middle-aged offspring, by a former wife, against a widow who is usually much younger than them."

"If you're going to keep on with background I already know," I said, "I'll take a nap. Wake me when you get to the point."

He looked hurt. But not fatally. "Well, Marius Lejon only had one wife, and she died ten years before him. What gave the Lejon case a bit of extra spice was that it was a *mistress*, in her twenties, versus two sons and a daughter in their forties. Who were determined to prevent her from getting any crumbs from their late daddy's estate."

Chess refreshed his mouth with a sip of his drink, slurping it around through his teeth before swallowing. "Though nobody ever heard either Marius Lejon or Ilona Szabo refer to her as his mistress. It was always as just his private physical therapist. By whatever means, she made the old man's last years more pleasant. And he provided her with a nice Paris apartment, a sports car, clothes, some jewelry, and whatever money she needed."

Chess prepared to light another cigar. Then he decided to hold off a little longer, and returned the cigar to the breast pocket of his eyesore jacket.

"Unfortunately for Ilona," he resumed, "she does not appear to have been very practical about her future welfare. Marius gave her things—the apartment, the car, the jewels, etc.—but never got around to putting them in her name. And she wasn't grabby enough to insist. So, no legal transfer of goods. Lejon's kids contended that their late father merely lent those items to her. For temporary use. Ilona couldn't prove otherwise, and they wanted everything turned over to them as the legal heirs to all his property."

"I was told that Marius Lejon provided for her in an addition to his will."

"So she claimed. She said she was present when Marius instructed his attorney to add that extra provision. And that he later assured her it was done and signed. But the attorney swore the old man privately told him not to bother carrying out the instructions he'd given in front of Ilona."

"Had the late Lejon's attorney become the attorney for his sons and daughter by the time he swore that?"

Chess smiled at me. "You are such a cynic, Pete. And so right. Ilona Szabo hired a Parisian lawyer to defend her rights.

To prove the Lejon attorney was lying—that he'd destroyed that addition to the will in an attempt to defraud her. Her lawyer had a number of meetings with the Lejons and their attorney. He finally told Ilona she had no chance at all of winning her case."

"Since French lawyers aren't allowed to work on a contingency basis," I pointed out, "he wouldn't have reason to work very hard or long on a chancy case. No big chunk of the settlement if he did win it for her."

Chess smiled again. "There is that. The Lejons offered to let her keep some of the jewelry if she would settle for that, out of court, quickly and quietly. Her lawyer strongly advised her to accept. He pointed out that what she owed him was mounting rapidly, and that her only hope of paying it would be to take the jewelry and sell it. Which is what she finally and angrily did. Chalk up another victory for the virtuous families of France."

"Who was her lawyer?"

Chess shrugged. "He was never important enough a name for me to mention it in my column."

Another job for Fritz Donhoff.

"What's happened to Ilona Szabo since then?" I asked.

"Search me. Once she gave up the apartment, the sports car, and her hopes, she slipped beyond my ken. As far as I'm aware, she has never again been connected with the kind of people whose shenanigans earn me my living."

Chess looked away from me, across the patio. In the gathering dusk two boys were dragging a girl wearing an opulent brocade creation toward the swimming pool. She was struggling, but not convincingly. Her squeals of protest and shrill laughter were cut short by the big splash as the boys dumped her into the water. She came up sputtering, spread her arms wide, and bowed to the gathering onlookers.

"That dress she just ruined," Chess informed me, "is a one-of-a-kind confection that cost her parents twelve thousand bucks."

"Doesn't matter," I said. "She wouldn't be caught dead wearing the same dress to more than one party, anyway."

"True."

The two boys who'd tossed her in jumped into the pool to help her drag herself and her ruined dress out. A second girl was thrown into the water. A third jumped in, followed by a couple more boys. Everybody was getting the spirit.

I noticed the moonlighting cop, Bernard Blondel, standing by one end of the garage. He folded his arms across his chest and kept his face expressionless as he watched the sons and daughters of the rich at play.

I found myself telling Dixon Chess about Sonia calling the Riviera bimbo heaven.

He gave me a look of mock outrage. "*None* of these girls are bimbos, Pete. They may be feather brained, get drunk and throw up on the carpet, snort most of their allowance, and orgy the night away on occasion. But their daddies and mommies are *names*. You have to learn to distinguish between a party girl and an heiress who likes to party."

"A difference as wide and deep as a bank vault."

"Now you've got it."

"How do I get out of here?"

Chess shoved to his feet as I did. "I'll tell 'em to open the gate," he said, and poured most of the drink from his almost-full glass into a rose bush behind the table. Carrying the now almost-empty glass with him, he lumbered off toward the house.

I headed back to my car. Behind me the swimming pool was filling up. The band played on.

I stopped at a brasserie in Saint-Jean-Cap-Ferrat and used its phone booth to call my nearest neighbors. Judith Ruyter answered. Her husband was still at his oil company's Monaco headquarters. I asked her to check my answering machine for messages. The Ruyters had a key to my house, as I did to theirs; and they knew how to deactivate my alarm system.

Judith took down the number of the phone I was using.

Four minutes later she called from my house and told me there was a message to phone Antonio Odasso at his apartment.

Antonio picked up his phone on the second ring. "Klaus Troestler called about an hour ago," he told me. "The word around is that Brissac was tailing someone—nobody knows who or why—and got himself shot. Klaus says you should go to l'Escarène and see a doctor named Denis Millo."

"That where Brissac is?"

"I don't know. All Klaus would say was, from what Eric and him have heard, that's where you ought to try."

Dr. Denis Millo. In l'Escarène. The geography fit. The town of l'Escarène was on the Paillon River midway between the coast and Desiré Brissac's house. If he knew a doctor he could trust there, and if he'd been trying to get home but was too hurt to make it all the way . . .

If and if.

I could get Dr. Millo's phone number from information and call him to check first. But I didn't know the situation. The call might spook him. And Desiré too—if he was really there and in a condition to get out in a hurry.

More ifs . . .

I drove west from Cap Ferrat and turned north through the industrial ugliness behind Nice. Where that gave way to the beauty of the mountains there was a junction of two ways to get to l'Escarène. The wide, straight route, the N204, was choked with traffic. I switched to the D21—a longer and narrower but less used route. People drove it for the views it offered. With the last light of evening dying the view was shrinking fast.

It was entirely gone by the time I reached the lowest of the Paillon Gorges. I drove through its twisting depths in a darkness so dense my headlights seemed to be boring yellow shafts through spongy black rock.

THE LITTLE TOWN OF L'ESCARÈNE IS AT THE BOTTOM OF A bowl in the mountains, with the steep-banked river and a couple fast-moving streams cutting it into segments connected by bridges. None of the regional guidebooks pay it much attention. It's grown old without becoming picturesque. The going-to-seed look of its center is only beginning to lift with the restoration of individual houses here and there.

I parked under the big elm on its Place Carnot. Most of the space between the seventeenth century church and the tiny bar on the other side was filled with the parked cars of residents. The few one-lane streets through the jumble of stone houses between the *place* and the river get blocked up too easily.

The local phone book in the bar gave me Denis Millo's address.

It did not list him as being a doctor.

After consulting with the bartender I walked from the *place* through a twisty up-and-down street that tunneled under some houses and crossed a humpbacked stone bridge over a down-rushing stream. I'd turned up my jacket collar against the cold wind that funneled through the gorges. I would have liked to button the jacket, but I didn't. Holstered to my belt under it was the compact Heckler & Koch pistol usually stashed inside the Peugeot's back seat. I didn't want anything interfering with instant access to it if the need arose. I'd been of that mind since my encounter with Roland Mari.

The street was dimly lit and the curving alley I turned into had no lights at all. When the alley ended, atop a stream bank, the sudden moonlight seemed unnaturally bright. Across the stream some joined houses formed a wall rising straight out of the water. On my side to the right there was a grassy bank between the houses and the stream. I took a dirt path along it.

The bank grew higher. I passed the rusted wreck of a dump truck that had rolled down it and come to rest nose down in the rushing water. Beyond that the path climbed to a row of connected houses at that edge of the town. The houses presented their backs to the stream below. I followed the path as it curved around the near end of the row to cut past the stone house fronts.

All of these houses had been recently renovated. I seemed to be the only one around. Residents were inside for the night. Probably watching television, though no sounds escaped the thick house walls. It was murky along the front path. There were no outside lamps and all the window shutters were closed against the night wind. It was the same at Denis Millo's address: a narrow three-floor house. But a little light from inside showed through a chink in the shutters of the lowest window.

I knocked at his door.

After two seconds the light behind the shutters went out.

I sidestepped away from the door, instinctively and immediately. The H & K pistol was in my fist when I finished the step.

A moment later there was the start of a scream inside Denis Millo's house. Just loud enough to reach me through its stone walls before it was cut off. It had sounded like a man's scream; but hadn't lasted long enough for me to be sure of that. Though long enough for my insides to tie themselves into knots.

I worked at loosening the knots while I backed away from

Millo's house. Between the fourth and fifth houses, back in the direction from which I'd come along the path, there was a very narrow covered passage leading to a tiny garden overlooking the mountain stream. I went through the passage, through the garden, and over its railing. Below it the stream bank was high and gradual. With narrow stepped terraces that had once been cultivated but were now overgrown. When I eased down to the nearest terrace and bent my knees, my head was below the bottoms of the houses.

I pushed cautiously through the bushes, moving along the terrace toward the rear of Denis Millo's place.

When I was beneath it I stopped and listened. The only sound I could hear was from the stream below, battering noisily through fallen rocks. Just above my head a wrought-iron balustrade projected out slightly. When I straightened all the way, up on my toes, I could peer under its bottom rail.

Moonlight cast black shadows across a small tiled patio with two lounge chairs and some neatly arranged rows of potted geraniums and cactus plants. Only half the patio was open to the sky. The other half was covered by a three-walled loggia with a flat roof, sheltering two little tables and three chairs.

Across the patio from me was the rear wall of the house. Much of the ground floor wall was a big sliding glass door. It was halfway open. The moonlight was slanting from the wrong direction to show me anything inside but darkness.

I lowered my head and shifted along the terrace. When I straightened again I had the loggia's narrow end wall between me and that half-open glass door. Holding the pistol ready in my right hand, I gripped the balustrade with my left, got a toehold on a stone spur above my terrace, and hauled myself upright onto the edge of the tiled patio. The loggia's blind wall still shielded me from the lower part of the house. I looked up. The windows in the upper stories were shuttered. I climbed onto the balustrade's top rail and from there to the loggia roof, going flat the instant I was on it.

The shadow of the next house spread a dark patch across half of the flat roof. I stuck with the shadow, inching forward until I could see that sliding glass door again. That put me closer to it. But I still couldn't see anything inside.

I was watching and waiting for something to happen in there when it did. But I could only hear it: a sibilant noise, soft and short. Too mechanical to be a serpent's hiss. Just right for a handgun with a silencer.

There were several seconds of quiet after that—followed by an agonized grunt and the thud of somebody hitting the floor.

Then a stocky, heavy-shouldered man came darting out through the opened part of the sliding door. One side of his head was swathed in bandaging. What showed of his hair looked silvery in the moonlight. Whatever was under the bandages, it didn't slow him noticeably. He crossed the shadowed patio in a crouched, shifting run and vaulted over the balustrade.

He was followed by a short, muffled burst from the interior: a submachine gun or automatic rifle, equipped with an efficient sound suppressor. Some of the burst shattered the door's big pane of glass, flinging shards across the patio. A couple of the slugs spanged off the wrought-iron balustrade. But the target had already dropped out of sight beyond and below the patio.

I hadn't gotten much of a look at him. But it was unmistakably Desiré Brissac.

⊠ **12** ⊠

I DIDN'T CALL AFTER DESIRÉ BECAUSE I WAS TOO EXPOSED out there on the loggia roof and whoever was inside with the automatic weapon wasn't exposed at all. Lousy odds. But I was unlikely to be noticed as long as I remained silent and motionless. I was doing that when a figure began to materialize from the interior darkness.

It didn't materialize all the way. It was still in the dark when it stopped, looking out through the shattered door. The figure appeared to belong to a man. I couldn't make out the face or what he was wearing. All I could see of what he was holding with both hands was the glint of metal barrel. Too long for a normal handgun. The right length for a shortened version of an automatic rifle.

My own gun was aimed at the approximate middle of his chest. But I wasn't about to squeeze the trigger unless he spotted me and tried to shoot first. Because I still didn't know what the hell was going on. Desiré could have turned bad and that figure in there might be a cop. It is not wise to shoot at a cop in most parts of the world. Definitely not in France, where even speaking harshly to a cop can get you arrested and charged with the serious crime of "treating a government official with disrespect."

The figure turned away from the patio and was reabsorbed by the interior darkness. I saw him again, in sharper outline, when he opened the front door. The moonlight that leaked inside when he did also showed me the entire ground floor was a large living room. Nothing else between that front door and the shattered one to the patio.

He went out in a hurry, slamming the door shut behind him. The only thing new I got from that brief glimpse was that he wore an open topcoat that fitted loosely enough for him to tuck an automatic weapon out of sight under it.

I gave it a couple minutes. Nothing further happened. I lowered myself to the patio. Broken glass crunched under my shoes, so there was no use trying to make the next move slow and quiet. I dove into the living room, landing on my left side and doing some fast rolls across a carpet. The rolling ended against the bottom of a sofa. Nobody shot at me and none of the dark shadows moved. There didn't seem to be anything left in the house but me and the smell of freshly spilled blood.

I gave my eyes a little time to adjust. Being inside the dark of the living room was different from trying to look in from outside. Furniture shapes were strongly outlined against the moonlight out there. I crawled around the sofa to a lamp stand. Found its light switch. Held my breath and snapped it on.

There was a man sprawled on his back a foot away from me. Heavyset, dressed in jeans and a leather flight jacket. The lamplight gleamed on eyes that had no interest in me or anything else. He'd been about forty when he'd stopped aging.

His neck was very broken. That could be Desiré Brissac's work. I'd seen the delicacy with which his thick hands could manipulate flowers. I'd also seen the size of the rocks those same hands could lift out of the way to make room for planting.

Beside the dead man's right hand lay a pistol with a silencer. There was a hole in the back of the sofa near me, made by a bullet that had gone through and imbedded itself in the wall panelling.

It wasn't until I stood up that I saw the other dead man.

He was on the floor between the living room and a kitchen-dining alcove. Half-curled on his side. A lean man in his sixties, his face weathered and wrinkled, his head almost entirely bald. Wearing a white shirt with its collar open, brown slacks, and old-fashioned bedroom slippers with no socks.

A knife had gone into him just above the belt buckle, and ripped upward. The wound still leaked. There was a lot of blood around the slash in his white shirtfront, and much more on the floor under him. Whoever had put the knife into him had afterward wiped the blade clean on the man's white sleeves.

I wiped my thumbprint off the lamp switch and went up the stairway, turning on wall lights with the back of my knuckles. There was nothing of interest on the floor above. Just a bedroom and bathroom, both large. On the top floor, however, I did find something unusual. All of that floor was a library-study. One of the bookcases was hinged to the wall on one end. It had been left with the other end away from the wall. Behind it was an alcove that would be hidden when the bookcase was flat against the wall.

The alcove was just long enough and wide enough for the narrow cot inside it. There were a few small bloodstains on the pillow. Not like the blood downstairs. These were old stains that had been dry for at least a day. Under the cot was a doctor's medical bag.

I went back down to the living room. The urge was strong to keep going, out of that house, and fast. But I crouched and went through the pockets of the guy with the broken neck. He had a wad of about two thousand francs on him; but no identification of any kind. I moved on to the other dead man.

His wallet had all sorts of I.D. His name was Denis Millo, he was licensed to drive a car, this was his address, and he had two credit cards.

None of the I.D. said he was a doctor.

* * *

I left his house the way I'd come in. Across the patio and down along the overgrown stream-bank terrace. Up through the tiny garden and its narrow passage. I didn't find Desiré along the way. Before stepping out to the murky path I scanned it in both directions. Nobody seemed to be on stakeout, watching Millo's house. But that didn't relax me enough to take the same route back to my car that I'd used in coming from it.

Cutting away from the stream, I followed shadowed areas as I detoured around the town to the D21 road. Stopping in darker patches of shadow to restudy other shadows around me. Returning to Place Carnot, I slid my gun into my jacket pocket and kept my hand in there with it. And did some more careful scanning.

The only people in sight were at the two tables outside the bar. The light from inside it showed their faces clearly enough. None of them were Desiré or anyone else I recognized; and none appeared overinterested in me or my parked car.

Getting into the Peugeot, I took the Heckler & Koch from my pocket and laid it on the seat next to me. I checked the rearview mirrors as I pulled out onto the road.

A car parked near the church was starting up behind me. A four-door BMW sedan. I swung over to the side of the road, stopped, and picked up my gun. Holding it ready below window level.

The BMW reached the road. It had Monte Carlo license plates. There were two men in front whose faces I couldn't see. Nobody in back. The BMW turned away from my Peugeot and took the road leading up over the Col de Braus to Sospel.

When it disappeared I put the pistol back on the seat and drove out of l'Escarène in the opposite direction. Back down the same route I'd used coming up there.

I was down into the blackness of the lower Paillon Gorge before the car tailing me let itself be seen.

⊠ **13** ⊠

I FIRST SAW THE HEADLIGHTS A GOOD DISTANCE BACK WHEN I was entering the gorge. After that the car behind the lights put on speed and began closing the gap between us.

It could have been a reckless but otherwise innocent driver in a rush to get down to the Riviera coast. But I was pretty sure that wasn't it. Even before those headlights got much nearer and I saw it was the BMW with the Monte Carlo plates.

They'd chosen a good place for it. There were no other cars in sight. Not many would be using this route at that time of night. And the road was a narrow two-lane with no turn-offs through the whole twisting length of the deep gorge. No room for any evasion maneuvers, either. Not with a wall of rock on one side and a long drop down the other.

The BMW continued steadily to close the gap. The back-shine of its headlights reflected on a barrel the guy beside the driver was poking out his side window. Probably that same compact assault rifle, set for full automatic fire. They must have been hanging around Place Carnot, looking for Desiré and running out of hope. Then I'd showed up, and they'd decided bagging me would be better than reporting no results at all. Which meant that at least one of the two knew who I was. Also that new orders had been issued, to extinguish me if I was spotted nosing into the Brissac business again.

The things I could do, I did.

I tramped down on the gas and began taking the gorge's sharp, multiple bends at speeds just a shade this side of good-bye world.

The BMW kept gaining on me, gradually but definitely. It was faster than my Peugeot and a little better at holding the road. My knowing every twist in this gorge by heart was negated by the fact that the BMW's driver didn't need to know them. All he had to do was watch my taillights and do whatever I did.

I drove along the exact middle of the road, leaving no room for the BMW to come up alongside. The guy with the automatic weapon didn't fire at the rear of my car. He was content to wait. As soon as we came out of the bottom end of the gorge there'd be room for the BMW to maneuver. Room for me to do the same. But what I wouldn't be able to do would be to steer at that speed with one hand and fire a pistol accurately with the other hand.

The shooter in the BMW didn't have that problem. He had a driver and two hands. As soon as there was room for it they'd come up beside the Peugeot, stitching it from back to front with one long, sustained burst. While I'd be vainly attempting to drive and take steady aim at the same time.

Another thing I wouldn't be able to do when we came out of the gorge would be to stop, jump out, and find cover before the BMW was on top of me.

When I came into a rare stretch of straight road I took my right hand off the steering wheel, snatched the gun off the seat, and stuck it in the front of my belt. Then I held the wheel with my right hand while my left cranked my side window shut. The other side windows were already closed. I didn't want any of them open when and if I got the chance to work the gimmick I had in mind. But I would need more space for that. The BMW was sticking too damn close to my tail.

Both hands were back on the wheel when I reached the next tight bend in the gorge road. I turned into it going fast—

and then braked slightly halfway around it. The BMW coming around after me almost rammed into the rear of my car.

That scared its driver. If he collided with me at high speed, on one of those curves, there was no predicting which of us would slam into the cliff or go over the drop. Probably both of us. The BMW slowed, dropping back a little.

But not enough. I tapped the foot brake a couple more times, on sharp curves that followed. The sight of my brake lights going on alarmed the enemy driver enough to make him drop further back.

The space between us still wasn't as much as I would have liked. But it would have to serve.

The lower end of the gorge opened out with dramatic suddenness, its cliffs spreading away from each other with plenty of near-level ground between them. The BMW driver began shifting to the left, intending to race up along my side of the Peugeot. That would bring his partner's automatic weapon within inches of my head.

I floored the accelerator and got more space between the two cars. The BMW increased speed too, swiftly closing the gap again.

Up ahead to the right of the road, almost immediately after the opening up of the gorge, there was a cement company's quarry. Its machines had been gouging sand and gravel out of the cliff in there for years, spreading brown dust over everything for half a mile around it. I twisted off the road into the quarry's dirt truck lane. The Peugeot skidded on loose sand that the trucks were always leaking. I was prepared for that, adjusting for the skid before it happened.

The driver behind me wasn't prepared for the sand skid. The BMW spun around wildly and came to a near halt before the driver regained control. That put a satisfying amount of distance between us. The enemy car surged forward and began using its superior power to catch up to me.

That was fine. I wanted them to catch up—coming very fast—when we reached the right place for it.

I swung around a row of parked trucks, slowing to handle some more slippery sand spills. There was only one light inside the quarry area. Up ahead, near the ravaged cliff. It came from a shack next to a double line of cement mixers. That was the night watchman's roost.

He wouldn't come out to see what our two cars were doing invading company property. He was a sensible elderly man. His job, in case of trespassers, was to get on the phone to the nearest *gendarmerie*.

The action here, win or lose, would be over before the cops could arrive.

I hung an abrupt right and sped through the dark passage between the cement mixers.

When I came out behind them, a big hill of sand loomed directly in front of me. Waiting to be trucked away. It would need a lot of trucks and a lot of days to remove that much sand. The hill was higher than a four-story building. And would stay that high, no matter how much was trucked away, because more sand out of the cliff was always being added to it.

It was like a great dune in the desert. But much less stable.

The BMW came racing out of the dark passage no more than two car lengths behind me.

Perfect.

I floored the Peugeot and sideswiped the base of the sand hill with the right side of the car. The collapse began instantly. Sand thundered down on my car, pounding at the roof and hood, trying to get through the closed windows. The motor began to whine as the wheels spun in place, and for a moment I thought I wasn't going to make it. Then the tires found something solid to grip and the Peugeot lurched out of the collapsing hill.

Behind me the hill and what was happening to it caught the BMW's driver by surprise. He hit the brake hard and twisted sharply to the left. But there was too much loose ground sand for changes that sudden. His tires slid sideways as if they were on slick ice. The right side of the BMW

slammed into the collapsing sand cliff. The impact increased
the speed and size of the collapse, and stalled the car underneath it.

I used the ground sand to help me do a swift spin-around,
coming to a stop with my high lights trained on the big cloud
of dust spreading around the hill. I put the Peugeot in neutral
but left the headlights on. Then I was out of the car moving
in a low crouch with the H & K pistol in my hand. Getting
away from the car and its lights, into the darkness. As soon
as I was invisible I began circling swiftly to approach the
BMW from its rear end.

The dust cloud began to thin. The worst of the collapse
was over, though trickles of sand continued to slide down
the hill's gouged out slope. The entire right side of the BMW
was buried.

The front door on the driver's side hung open.

I froze in position, listening and doing a squinting survey
of the surrounding night shadows. I heard him first. The fast
slap and scrape of shoe leather. Then I spotted him, running
away toward the road.

Just one man. I watched until the night swallowed him.
Then I continued my circling. Until I could approach the
BMW from the rear. When I reached it I brought my gun up
first, before rising out of my crouch for a look through a
clear patch of the back window.

I didn't see anyone in there. What I saw was all the sand
that had poured into the open windows. It almost filled the
right half of the interior. Going back into the crouch I moved
around to the driver's open door.

An open hand and part of a forearm reached out of the
sand that had buried the rest of the second man. The hand
hung limp. The muzzle of the automatic rifle protruded from
the top of the sand, almost touching the roof.

I was acutely aware of time passing and the cops on their
way. But knowing who this one was might be of use. I slid
into the driver's half of the front seat and clawed away sand
where I judged the face belonging to the dead hand should

be. The first find was his other hand. Loosely gripping the fold-down stock of his weapon. I clawed some more and found his forehead. There was a swollen gash in it.

It had slammed against something when the car crashed. He must have been unconscious, unable to do anything about it, while he choked and smothered to death under that burial mound. And the driver hadn't done anything about it, either. He'd been too concerned with getting out and away.

The rest of the face came quickly. Eyes, ears, nostrils, mouth—all filled with sand.

Roland Mari's mean young assistant, Max-Emile, wouldn't be getting any more lessons in the professional management of menace and mayhem.

I WAS QUITE SURE THE ONE WHO'D GOTTEN AWAY WASN'T Roland Mari. First because Roland wouldn't run from a one-on-one gunfight with me. Second because if Roland had been in the BMW, he would have been the shooter. Max-Emile would have been doing the driving.

I returned to my car and got out of there. I drove south along the road until I came to the first dark house. Its carport was empty. I turned into it, cut my motor and lights, and waited. A few minutes later the *gendarmerie* car went past with its blue light flashing. Going north toward the quarry.

Driving back onto the road, I continued south. When I was below the junction of the D21 and the N204 I pulled over to an outdoor phone booth and made a call to the *gendarmerie* up in l'Escarène. A sleepy cop finally answered the phone there. I told him I'd heard screams and gunshots from Denis Millo's house. The cop was asking me to identify myself when I hung up.

I'd done my duty as an expatriate resident. Also, it might net me some new information, after the news media got the police reports on the killings up there.

Back in the Peugeot I executed a U-turn and drove north again. This time taking the N204. I hoped Mireille had something quick she could feed me, before I got her and her daughter out. Dinner was something I'd missed, and my insides were grumpy about it.

I was also in need of a good stiff drink. Not too small.

Mireille was busy in her workshop. She heard my car grinding up to the house and came out to meet me. The first thing she said was, "Did you get my message on your answering machine?"

"No," I said as we went inside together. "What's happened?"

"Desiré phoned—left a message for me in Lucéram."

"When?"

"A few hours ago. The wife of the bistro's owner came up and told me. She said she asked Desiré if he didn't want to leave a number where I could contact him. Or have her bring me back down so he could call me again. But he said no. Just to tell me he's involved in something and may not be able to phone again for a few days or more. But I'm not to worry, he's all right."

A few hours ago could mean he'd made the call before or after I'd seen him get out of Denis Millo's place. I said, "But you're still worried."

"Yes. Very. What *has* he gotten mixed up in?"

I softened it as much as I could: "All I know is that it might turn nastier than I originally expected. Maybe not—but there's some rough characters involved. I don't want you and Hugette around if they come here again. Go up and wake her, get her dressed and pack a bag."

Mireille stared at me. "I can't just leave. I have orders to fill, clients who might call. And what if Desiré comes back and doesn't find us here?"

"Leave a note for him on the entry table. Say you'll call the bistro regularly to check. There's a phone where I'm taking you. You can also use it to contact your clients."

"But . . ."

"Mireille," I said, "*I'm* not going home tonight. It could get that serious. I'll explain on the way down."

It was going to be a strictly censored account. She was worried enough.

Mireille looked at my face for a moment. Then she said, "I'll tell Hugette her father may want to call us direct in the next few days, so we're going where there's a handier phone. Where is it?"

"In Nice. She'll like it— only a block from the beach." But I wouldn't be letting them spend time on the beach without protection. "While you're getting ready," I said, "what have you got to eat? I'm starving."

"I can make a . . ."

"No time. Something that's ready."

"There's half a chicken in the refrigerator. And some seafood salad. And there's bread left from . . ."

"That'll do," I told her. She hurried up the stairs while I poured myself a glass of brandy from the living room cupboard. I took a healthy swallow and gave it a minute to begin doing a job on my nervous system. Then I had another and raided the kitchen.

Arlette and I had keys to each other's places. Her third-floor apartment was right behind the Negresco, that venerable queen of the Riviera's beachfront hotels. By the time we got there Hugette had used up her excitement over the unexpected night trip and had fallen back to sleep. I carried her from the car and settled her down in Arlette's bedroom. The bed was big enough for Mireille to share it with her daughter. I'd be sleeping on the fold-out couch in the living room that night.

While Mireille got Hugette undressed and under the covers I began phoning people who might have been trying to reach me. I wasn't about to risk sending either of the Ruyters down to check my answering machine. If someone had given orders to kill me, a bomb rigged to one of my doors would be one way.

First I called Antonio Odasso. But he hadn't heard anything further from Klaus and Eric. Nor had he been able yet to pick up anything else of use from other old soldier pals.

Next I tried the Paris apartment of Jean-Marie Reju, though it was unlikely he'd been trying to contact me. It was also unlikely I'd find him in. Surprise—Reju was there. I said, "How come you're not off baby-sitting some computer king or rock princess?"

"I'm taking a week off," he said in that somewhat morose voice I'd gotten used to over the years. "The doctor says I'll never get rid of this ulcer if I don't relax between jobs now and then."

"How about spending your week on the Côte d'Azur?"

"You're inviting me to stay at your place?" Reju's question held an awkward shyness that sometimes afflicted him when dealing with sentiments he wasn't used to.

"Not exactly," I told him. "It's a protection job. A woman and her child."

"Oh." Reju's tone returned to normal. "I told you, I'm on vacation this week."

"You can take the vacation after you do this one," I said. "And yes, I am inviting you to stay at my place—when this job is done."

"That is very nice of you," he said, very formal. He hesitated just a bit. "Well, all right—I assume you've explained to the client about my fees; and all expenses, of course."

Reju was serious about everything in life. As he was about death. But he was most serious about money.

"I'll cover your plane fare," I told him. "And I've got an apartment here where you can stay for free while you're on the job. As for your fees, my client hasn't got that kind of money. I'll have to help—and I can't afford your usual, either."

"I'm sorry," Reju said. "If it was for you personally . . ."

"The client is a close friend of mine, Jean-Marie. She and her child are in danger and I'm too busy getting them out of it to guard them full time. If you can do this for me I'd consider it a very important personal favor."

"I don't know . . ." Reju's voice had gone awkward again.

We settled for a third of his customary fee. He promised to come down on the first morning plane from Paris.

Then I phoned Fritz Donhoff. Before I got into telling him everything I'd done and learned since our last talk, Fritz had some news for me. About the yacht that Ilona Szabo had swum in from and back to:

"*La Dolce Vita*," he told me, "belongs to The Old Spider."

He added the real name of the boat's owner, but he didn't have to.

I knew who The Old Spider was.

⊠ **15** ⊠

RIVIERA CUTIES WERE ALREADY DECORATING THE CANNES beaches at nine-thirty the next morning. Early birds, reinforcing their summer tans before October cooled the Côte d'Azur. In hopes of invitations to hotter climes by November.

It would be a definite downer for them to show up at any of the status resorts that straddle the equator looking like they'd had to spend any part of previous months doing indoor work by day. Seamless self-assurance was as essential as pretty faces, energetic young bodies, and laid-back-fun dispositions.

I found a parking spot between the Martinez Hotel and its beach, and walked back along the Croisette to a choice five-floor condo. The small entry lobby had a simple elegance. The large security-doorman had nice manners and a quiet voice. I told him who I'd come to see. He asked for my name as he went to an intercom phone. I gave him the name of the firm that insured *La Dolce Vita* and said I was there about a problem involving that yacht.

He pressed a button and after a few moments he repeated my message into the phone. After another half minute he hung up the phone and nodded to a small elevator. "Top floor, monsieur." He didn't add an apartment number, so it occupied the entire floor.

When I got out of the elevator I was in a short corridor

with a Persian rug that showed just an edge of marble flooring. To the right a door with a bronze nameplate was flanked
by tall vases holding fresh long-stemmed roses. Yellow roses
in one vase, pink in the other. Off to the left end of the
corridor was a second door, unmarked. Probably a servant
and delivery entrance.

The main door was opened by a middle-aged woman in a
simple maid's outfit neatly tailored to her stout figure. An
unexpected touch was her pristine-white velvet slippers. She
pointed to a low, narrow stand just inside the doorway.
"Please leave your shoes here, monsieur. Madame does not
like having street dirt brought inside."

I removed my shoes and followed her across the furry
white carpeting of a drawing room with ebony-black furniture and scarlet walls and ceiling. It was a long walk—out to
a spacious curved balcony. "If monsieur will wait here, until
madame has completed her breakfast . . ."

The maid went away. The balcony, overlooking an inner
courtyard filled with small palm trees and big cacti, was not
crowded by its few furnishings. Three chairs and a table, all
of wrought-iron painted white. The chairs were arranged in
a semicircle facing the table. The morning sunlight was
strong on that side. A spotless white awning spread shade
across half the table and the empty part of the balcony on the
other side of it. I stood and waited.

She arrived seated in a straight-backed armchair carried
effortlessly by two burly young men wearing black leather
jeans and sandals. Their bared arms and torsos bulged with
weight-lifter muscles. So did their faces.

They set her and the chair down in the shade, facing me
across the table. Then they straightened and remained in
position. Behind and to either side of her. Each with a hand
resting on the back of her chair. Like a pair of dangerous
guardian angels. They were both handsome; and looked like
they had the brains of warrior ants.

The woman in the chair was something else. Thin and very
fragile. She looked somewhere between eighty and a hun-

dred and twenty. The elaborate satin-and-lace dressing gown she wore was lilac colored. The slippers on her tiny feet were black velvet. Her neat white pageboy was a wig. The skin of her clawlike hands and short triangular face could have been an overlay of cracking parchment.

Christelle Falicon—The Old Spider.

She'd caught the way I'd taken in her bare-chested guardian angels. "I'm a poor old woman," she told me in a voice that was faintly mocking and not at all fragile. "My legs have gotten shaky and my backbone has several fused vertebrae. Walking is hard, painful work, and I hate wheelchairs. The boys are my alternative." Her clawlike hands reached up and patted their muscular ones affectionately. "In addition," she added, "to providing a sense of security and the stimulating closeness of virile youth."

Her fragility didn't extend to the eyes regarding me, either. They had the look of graves where illusions are buried. Waiting with malevolent impatience for the next victim.

I gazed back at her. She was a legend, in several shadow worlds. Though not, in spite of her wealth, in the world chronicled by Dixon Chess. Her money was not old enough. Celebrity was something she'd always taken measures to evade. The various forms of corruptions that were her source of income had never been allowed to become conspicuous.

She said, "Sit down, young man."

I sat on one of the wrought-iron chairs. It was hot from the sun.

"Now," she asked, "what is this problem with my boat that has the insurance company worried?"

There was only the faintest undercurrent in the way she asked it. But it was enough. I said, "I'm not from the insurance company, Madame Falicon."

"Ah?"

"I assume you already phoned there and found that out."

"Naturally," she said—and then she just waited. As calm as a praying mantis embalmed in amber. Except for the malicious glint in those eyes.

I told her my name. She didn't show me the slightest re-action to it. A pro stonewall job—or she'd never heard my name before. Deciding which was about as difficult as spot-ting the difference between Snow White and the Evil Queen.

"I'm a private investigator," I said. "I have a client who is interested in some unsavory characters that he says have been seen around *La Dolce Vita*."

"Who is your client?" Madame Falicon asked. She didn't seem to be really interested in the answer. "And why is he—or she—concerned about my yacht?"

"It's these people my client is concerned about," I said. "I'm sorry, but professional ethics prevent me from men-tioning the client's name at this time."

"I quite understand," she assured me—though from what I knew she herself had always operated with the professional ethics of a rusty knife. Starting a long time ago when she'd been a high-priced hooker with a heart of greed. Progressing into a little blackmail—and then quite a lot of it. Which led into the profession she'd followed ever since. Information. Buying, stealing, or extorting it. Selling or trading it. Polit-ical information and business information, but mostly the latter. Industrial espionage is by far the more rewarding fi-nancially.

"To be honest," I said, "I'm not entirely convinced at this point that my client is right about the unsavory nature of the people seen around your yacht. Perhaps they're friends of yours, using it with your permission."

"Perhaps," she said, giving the word no meaning at all.

I tried two names on her. Roland Mari. And Desiré Bris-sac.

She just went on looking at me as though still waiting for me to say something of interest. Prying revealing responses out of this Old Spider was like trying to squeeze smoke.

But I'd known it would be this way. All I could hope for here was to stir things up. And note whatever rose to the surface. If anything did. Even Rumeal Robinson doesn't manage to sink every ball he shoots.

Persistence and mathematics, Fritz Donhoff had said. I prodded her: "Either name mean anything to you?"

"No." She raised her hands from the arms of her chair, turned them palms up, and spread her skeletal fingers wide—one of those gestures of utter helplessness that people who've never felt helpless are prone to. "But I must confess that the piling up of one's years does bring a certain amount of senility. My memory is not what it was."

"Maybe," I suggested, "these characters have stolen your boat."

"I doubt it," she said imperturbably.

The one thing I'd gotten out of Madame Falicon so far was her failure to ask any questions about the men those two names belonged to. That lack of even normal curiosity was out of character. She'd been making a living from prying out bits of information much longer than I had. It is habit forming.

"So *La Dolce Vita* hasn't been stolen," I said. "Where is it now?"

"I have no idea," she told me, with that faint ripple of venomous mockery. "I was never a sea lover. The boat was used for occasional business entertainment. But I don't care to go out of this apartment much these days. So I turned the boat over to my grandson—along with the management of my various business interests."

"Your grandson."

"Yes. Léon is the one who changed the boat's name to its present one."

"So he would know where it is."

"I would imagine so," Madame Falicon said. "Why don't you go ask him?"

"Where do I find him?"

"At this time of morning, almost certainly at home. That used to be mine, too. And there again, Léon has changed its name." An uncharacteristic indulgence crept into her tone. "The boy likes to put his own stamp on things. Quite natural."

"What's the address?"

She gave me that—and carefully detailed instructions in how to find it.

Kindly of her.

The Old Spider wanted to make absolutely sure I got there.

☒ **16** ☒

I RETRIEVED MY SHOES ON THE WAY OUT. MADAME FALICON had gotten me in and out of her presence in record time. When I slid back into my Peugeot the hands of the dashboard clock bit ten A.M. I switched on the car radio.

It was already set to Radio France Côte d'Azur. Its nine o'clock news broadcast had given me the police report on the so-far unexplained occurence in the quarry below the Paillon Gorge last night. It had contained less than I already knew. The dead Max-Emile didn't have any identification on him, and the cops hadn't found out who he was yet. The crashed BMW had been rented in Monte Carlo by a man using what proved to be a fake driver's license and credit card. The night watchman said there'd been two cars, chasing each other. He hadn't gotten the license number of the one that sped away from the scene, and wasn't sure of its make. For which I was grateful, though I would have been unpleasantly surprised if he'd managed to make my speeding Peugeot in the night.

The ten o'clock news led off with the two killings at Denis Millo's house in l'Escarène. Violent unexplained deaths are not unknown along the Riviera and its backcountry. But they are unusual enough to rate front-page headlines and detailed coverage.

The lean man in his sixties who'd been knifed was Denis Millo, the news announcer said. He'd been a doctor and for some years had served as a medical officer in the French army. Eight years after leaving the army Millo had been found guilty of performing abortions, before those had become legal. For that he'd spent a year in prison, in addition to losing his license to practice medicine. The police now suspected that Millo had continued to operate as a doctor, illegally. That came from their discovery of the hidden alcove in his house, with the bloodstained cot and a fully equipped medical bag.

The cops had recognized the other dead man in Millo's house—the one with the broken neck—as a local thug. His name was Jean-Patrick Gally, and he had a nasty record. In and out of jails since he'd been seventeen. Suspected of involvement in a couple of gang murders, unproven.

The fact that Gally's body, like the one in the quarry, had no I.D. on it, indicated a possible connection between the two events. The police had no explanation for either, but would pursue leads vigorously, etc.

I switched off the radio, drove to the nearest post office, and made a phone call. Then I headed east out of Cannes and went to visit The Old Spider's grandson.

Léon Falicon's place—formerly his grandmother's—was between Cannes and Nice on the Cap d'Antibes. It was in one of the plush enclaves of small estates out near the sea end of the cape. Shortly after I curved past the Hotel du Cap one of the private security cars that patrol that area day and night came up beside me. It slowed while the man in front next to the driver looked me over briefly. No doubt he'd already marked down my license number. Then it picked up speed and turned into a side road going toward the Eden Roc.

Seconds later I reached the driving entrance to the enclave I wanted. It was barred by a closed gate, with TV cameras perched on either side of it aimed at my halted car.

There was a small cabin on the left side, covered by untrimmed growths of mimosa. A guard came out of it and asked politely if he could be of assistance. I told him who

I'd come to see and gave him my name. He went to a phone almost hidden by the mimosa near the cabin door. After speaking into it he turned back to my car and said, "He'd like you to come to the phone."

I got out of the Peugeot, took the phone and said, "Monsieur Falicon?"

"Yes. Henri, the gateman, said your name is Sawyer, have I got that right?" His voice on the line had a quiet control, and an edge to it that I guessed could turn harsh pretty quick. I said that was my name. He said, "I'm sorry but—do I know you?"

"Didn't your grandmother call you about me?"

"When?"

Maybe The Old Spider was into practical jokes. I said, "I've just come from her apartment. I'm a private investigator. There were some questions I thought she might be able to give me answers to. She couldn't, but she thought perhaps you could. She suggested I come here to see you. I assumed she would phone and let you know I was on my way."

Léon Falicon's laugh was merry but short. "My grandmother—she has become *so* forgetful in her old age. The last time she invited me to her place for dinner—less than a week ago, that was—I arrived to find she'd gone to bed early. Completely forgetting about me."

I believed all this the way the Soviet Politburo believes in Santa Claus.

He waited for some response from me and when he didn't get it he said, "Well, never mind. Would you just turn so I can get a better look at you through this TV hookup?"

Keeping the phone to my ear, I turned enough to look up into one of the cameras. After a moment Falicon said, "You appear to be respectable enough. All right, give me back Henri. I'll have him let you through." He added instructions to his place that echoed his grandmother's final directions.

I handed the phone to the guard and climbed back in my car. The guard listened to Falicon, hung up the phone, and vanished inside his cabin. The gate swung open and I drove through. High walls on both sides of the paved, winding driveway. I passed a closed entrance to one estate. Then another.

The gate of the third one I came to was open. Another of those TV cameras eyed me as I turned in past it. The gate swung shut behind me. Its oiled hinges were almost silent, but the click of the lock was sharp.

The parking area was immediately inside, to the left and right, hidden from the rest of the Falicon estate by bushes that had been allowed to grow wild. On the left a Rolls-Royce Silver Cloud and a Jaguar XJ-S convertible sheltered under a carport. I parked in the open area on the right, next to a shiny red Aston Martin Volante. As I climbed out two men approached along an orange-brick path that curved through the wild garden. One man in the lead, the other walking three paces behind.

The one in the lead, a large man in his forties, wore a silk sport shirt, faded jeans, and thong sandals. The thick wrist of the hand he extended to me in greeting had a silver Navaho bracelet with a large blue stone. On his other wrist he wore one of those deceptively plain looking Patek Philippe watches that cost more than most people's automobiles.

"I'm Léon Falicon," he announced, and shook my hand while his hard, intelligent eyes sized me up. His grip was firm without trying to test his strength against mine. He looked like he had plenty of it, and kept it in fighting trim. The hint of latent brutality in his blunt-featured face was softened by a quiet smile as he asked, "What kind of gun are you carrying, Monsieur Sawyer?"

"None," I told him.

"Really? I'm disappointed." Falicon's tone had the same small vein of mockery I'd gotten from his grandmother. "Television has led me to believe private detectives wear guns at all times."

"Not in this country. It's against the law, unless you get a special permit from the government. Which requires filling out forms explaining what emergency situation requires the carrying of a gun. It takes a lot of time to go through all the bureaucratic red tape, and the permit is only good for a very short period. Usually it's not worth the effort.''

"And you never transgress that law?''

"Never,'' I lied. But I wasn't lying about not having a gun on me at that moment. It was back in its hiding place inside the Peugeot. If this meeting turned unpleasant—and I expected it would—I didn't want Falicon to have any grounds for a countercharge that I'd come onto his property and threatened him with a weapon I had no legal right to walk around with.

I figured he knew as much about that law as I did.

"Come,'' he said, "let's go to the house, get comfortable and have a drink while we talk.'' Falicon walked me past the other man without bothering to introduce us.

He was a short, dumpy man in his fifties. Dressed in a light-gray business suit that did the best it could with his figure. A neatly-trimmed sandy mustache failed to add much character to a soft, fleshy face. Most of his personality was in the dark eyes watching me walk past him. They regarded me like a butcher looking at a newly arrived beef carcass. Deciding on the best methods of carving it up.

The butcher waited until Falicon and I were a few steps beyond him along the brick path. Then I heard him begin to follow. I got a crawly feeling thinking of those eyes on my back. It took willpower not to turn my head and look at him.

Falicon said, "Sawyer—that is surely not a French name.''

"My father was American. So am I.''

"Ah, I like America. I was there only two weeks ago, as is happens. Boston. The Leahy Clinic, for my annual checkup. Its medical staff and equipment are unquestionably the best one can find anywhere.''

Also, it was a good place to get to know business and government executives from all over the world who used the Leahy for *their* yearly full-physicals.

"Do any business while you were over there?'' I asked.

Falicon smiled and shook his head. "Not a drop. I am a man of many sins, but working very hard is not one of them."

"Your grandmother told me you handle most of her business these days."

"Her notion of a joke, I imagine. The fact is, there's very little of her business left, for either of us to handle. The few shreds that remain are managed, quite easily, by a part-time accountant."

"What happened to the business?"

Falicon shrugged. "My grandmother became too old to run it. And since I don't care to, there was no reason to continue with it. She has more than enough money to last out her days. And, thanks to her generosity, so do I."

I decided he was enacting some kind of private comedy. One he'd performed many times in the past. With people who had taken his role seriously. I didn't. He had too much of that look you see among serious players at the head of any big enterprise. The look of the carnivore. Forever hungry no matter how much they catch and eat.

Pleasure wouldn't distract this man from prey.

The building at the other end of the path took up most of the space inside Falicon's estate. From outside it appeared to be one of those large, old Provençal farmhouses that are wrapped around big central courtyards, showing only a few small windows to the exterior world. But it wasn't more than thirty years old, with the rustic look of the tiled roofs and thick walls professionally applied.

We walked through a wide passage between the walls. When we reached the open inner space surrounded by the wings of his house, Falicon paused and nodded at it. "Why would any sane man break his head with work, when it is unnecessary and there is so much here to enjoy?"

The place now had the look of a luxurious Roman villa. The court area had arched shade arcades on three sides, supported by stone columns and floored with blocks of white and brown marble.

Most of the unshaded area was filled by a black marble

free-form swimming pool with a narrow border of new-mown grass. In the middle of the pool a young redhead with a spectacular body lay spread-eagled on her back across a blue rubber raft. Her fingers, toes, and the ends of her long hair trailed in the water. Her eyes were protected by dark sunglasses. The rest of her had nothing at all shielding it from the hot caress of the sun.

Dazzling.

Falicon looked at my profile and chuckled. "These up-market houris seem to gravitate to my Shangri-la. No effort on my part. Only simple hospitality."

There was another of them in the shade of the arcade off to our left. Her glossy green, stretch-material bathing suit was a high-thigh job, scooped to the waist. She sat on a table edge. Her bare feet were on the arms of the chair of a scrawny, scholarly-looking guy in his mid thirties. He had on baggy swim trunks and steel-frame glasses. She appeared to be telling him an amusing story. At least, it amused her. He listened with rapt attention while a manservant in a white jacket and black tie refilled their champagne glasses on the table beside her shapely right hip.

In the middle arcade a plump middle-aged man, a German financial wizard I recognized from his newspaper pictures, sat watching a third beauty chin herself on a bar attached to two columns in front of him. She had on a skimpy red halter and a *cache-sexe*. Her biceps and shoulder muscles bulged and relaxed, taking her up and down with the ease of an Olympic champion. The financial wiz, enthralled with her display of strength and energy, leaned forward, gazing intently at the way her tummy hollowed and went flat, hollowed and went flat. . . .

"I am not selfish, you see," Falicon said. "I like my friends to enjoy, too."

"How do I get to be one of your friends?"

"We may get around to discussing that, too, inside." He led me around the court through the long arcade on our right. The creepy guy with the butcher's eyes was still trailing us.

"I appreciate the sight-seeing tour," I told Falicon, "but you could have answered my few questions back where I parked."

"No, no . . . You are my first private detective. I'm curious to hear about your profession." Falicon nodded at the louvered door ahead.

The first room we entered had creamy walls and a decorated ceiling. White-painted columns flanked two tall alcoves containing stone statues. A *Belle Epoque* nude, and an athlete that might have been from ancient Greece. Much of the room was taken by a mahogany billiard table with the red ball and two white balls waiting on the green felt of its playing surface.

"Do you like billiards?" Falicon asked.

"Part of my youth was misspent as a pool player," I told him. "Fair but not brilliant."

"Perhaps we'll play a game after our talk." Falicon couldn't seem to relinquish his private little comedy; the one for which only he was supposed to be an aware audience.

He led the way along a marble-floored corridor to a wing extending from the rear of the villa. And through that into a richly furnished library with red velvet lining its walls. On entering he flicked a switch that turned on all the room lamps. It was necessary, unless you wanted a nap on the leopard-print sofa. Little daylight came through the single window facing out on an old, tall hedgerow that had grown almost as dense as a wall.

Falicon crossed the Aubusson carpet to a Louis Quinze desk while the butcher stepped in behind me and shut the thick oak door. It was a relief when he strolled past me toward the desk. Falicon settled himself into the Chippendale armchair behind it and gestured at a Versailles chair facing the desk. "Please sit down, Monsieur Sawyer."

I sat. The butcher took an at-ease stance next to the desk, looking at me. His dark eyes weren't at ease. Their speculative expression still made my flesh creep.

"Place your hands on the arms of your chair," Falicon

told me. The brutality in his face had become more than a hint. "Then glance behind you—but with care."

I sighed, gripped the chair arms, and turned my head.

A closet door had opened and a tough-looking guy in his mid twenties had stepped out of it. He held a long-barreled .22 revolver with both hands, aimed at the back of my head.

When I looked at Falicon again he said, "Now I advise you not to move in any way again. The gentleman behind you is an expert marksman."

He didn't have to tell me that. A gunman who depended on a weapon of that small a caliber had to have absolute confidence in his ability to put each shot exactly where he intended.

I took a sneak peek at my wristwatch.

Falicon opened a desk drawer and took out a Colt .38 with a silencer screwed into its short barrel. He rested his right hand on the desk top with the gun in it pointing at my chest. A bit of macho theatrics that wasn't at all required. Not with that .22 already aimed at my skull. Just showing off, mostly for his own benefit. I guessed Falicon liked to feel he was up to real savagery, not just the kind that goes on in quiet business conferences.

He reached under his desk and pressed something. A steel shutter came down the outside of the room's window and shut us off from the world. Heavy draperies closed across the inside of the window. Louis Quinze would have been impressed with what modern technology had added to his furniture.

Léon Falicon said: "Now we will talk."

◪ 17 ◪

"LATER," FALICON SAID, "WE WILL FIND OUT IF YOU ARE really not armed. But armed or not, you will keep your hands where they are while you answer my questions."

The man with the butcher's eyes spoke up for the first time, revealing some kind of Middle East accent. "We'll have no way of knowing when he is lying," he told Falicon. "With my way we will know."

Falicon smiled at me. It wasn't a smile that gave comfort. "Zayid is another of my experts. In extracting answers from the reluctant. Nothing crude. Zayid places his faith in electricity. A technique he learned from American specialists. Part of your assistance program for backward Third World countries."

"It is a technique," Zayid said, "that never fails."

Now that I knew what he was I understood that look in his eyes. I said, "Yes it does. Sometimes you keep giving the shocks until you wind up with a vegetable on your hands, and no answers. Or a heart attack—and no answers."

"Very rarely," Zayid assured me softly. "Only with a few subjects who are crazy, holding out beyond the point where the brain and nervous system are finished."

"It's not necessary," I told Falicon. "Ask your questions. If I know the answers I'll give them to you."

"First, where is Desiré Brissac?"

94

"If I knew that I wouldn't be here. I hoped you might know. Or have something that would give me a lead to him."

"Don't try toying with me," Falicon said harshly. "What led you to me and my grandmother?"

"I've spread word around that I'm looking for Brissac. I got a phone call. A man who wouldn't identify himself. He said to try asking your grandmother. And she sent me to you."

Zayid spoke up again: "He may even be telling us the truth. But how can we be sure? My way it's sure."

Falicon gestured for him to stop interfering. "Later, you will have your chance. It will be interesting to compare what he says, now and then."

"If I knew why you're looking for Brissac too," I said, "I might be able to put some things together that would give us what we're both after."

"Brissac," Falicon told me, "was following—some people I employ. I want to know why. I want to find out what he knows about my affairs. I want to find out what *you* know. Everything you know. Nothing held back. Just tell it. I don't like the way you play with my questions."

"All right," I said. "It starts with the fact that Madame Brissac hired me to find out what's happened to her husband. He'd gone missing—and she still hasn't heard from him. She was scared he's deserted her for another woman. When Roland Mari and that kid Max-Emile showed up at her place asking about her husband she got scared it's something worse."

I paused just long enough to let Falicon break in if something in what I'd just said puzzled him.

He didn't.

"I hadn't had any luck up to that point," I went on. "But she got scared enough to pay me extra to keep looking. So I spread word around, with everybody I could. And then I got that phone call I mentioned."

Falicon's eyes stayed on mine, unblinking. A trick I think

they teach in the first year at business schools. He said, "You asked my grandmother about *La Dolce Vita*. Why?"

"The anonymous character who phoned me. He said he'd seen Roland Mari around the yacht, and that it belonged to your grandmother. Well, since I already knew Mari was after Brissac, I went to see if your grandmother could tell me anything. I threw in Brissac's name, along with Mari's, just to see how she'd react. It didn't get me much. Just her advice to come here and talk to you."

"And what took you up to l'Escarène last night?"

Max-Emile would have told the driver who'd gotten away who I was. And the driver had told Falicon. No other way he would have learned about my being there.

I said, "One possibility was that Brissac hadn't called his wife because he was badly hurt. A friend who's an old former soldier told me Brissac used to hire out as a mercenary. I asked him if he knew any doctor who'd take care of someone like Brissac without telling the cops. The one he knew of was Denis Millo, a former army officer in l'Escarène. And that's all of it."

"You haven't told me anything useful," Falicon said.

"I don't have anything else to tell."

He glanced at Zayid. "Very well. Your turn."

Zayid almost smiled. I watched him go to a gilt-encrusted cabinet between bookcases against one wall. He opened it and poured what was probably water from a pitcher into a large glass. Then he took a small bottle from his pocket and unscrewed its cap. He began dripping liquid from it into the half-filled glass, silently counting each drop.

"Don't worry," Falicon told me. "It's not poison. Just something to put you to sleep. So we can move you out the back way and around to your car, without you doing anything to disturb my guests. When you wake up you'll be in another place."

"Where your expert there can turn me into a vegetable with his electric jolts."

"Not necessarily," Falicon lied smoothly. "Not if you

can persuade me that you've given me complete and accurate answers—before you are too damaged. We might even get around afterward to discussing whether you would like to enter my employ.''

"Sure," I said. "We might even get around to playing that game of billiards."

"It's possible."

No it wasn't. And he'd already given me much of what I'd come there to find out. I'd been pretty sure of it when I'd left The Old Spider's apartment. But pretty sure isn't entirely sure. Now there was no question of it: Falicon and/or his grandmother had sent Roland and Max-Emile after Brissac. Max-Emile, his driver, and the broken-necked man in Millo's house had gone up there for the Falicons. Hunting for Desiré Brissac.

I still didn't know why. Just that Léon Falicon was worried that Desiré knew about something he shouldn't. But the details were obviously something I wouldn't be able to dig out here.

I also didn't understand Ilona Szabo's part in whatever was going on. But I hadn't mentioned her to the grandmother and I wasn't about to with the grandson. She was still my client. One of them.

And time was running out, with the situation here getting too hairy.

Zayid recapped his little bottle, stirred the mixture with a cocktail swizzle stick, and put the bottle back in his pocket. He walked over to a small table near the Louis Quinze desk and set the glass on it.

"Zayid," I told Falicon, "will have to miss his fun and games today. The police know I'm here. One of them is waiting right now for me to come out and meet him. If I don't show they won't believe I've suddenly decided to sneak off and start a new life. If I have a fatal accident they won't believe that either. They'll come at you with grounds for crawling all over whatever you're mixed up in."

"That must be one of the oldest and stalest bits of fakery

there is," Falicon said. "I would have thought you could come up with something new and better."

"I thought it was pretty good," I said. "It happens to be true."

Falicon raised his gun off the desk top and aimed lower, looking down the sights to get it exactly where he wanted it. "You will stand up—carefully. Remembering my marksman behind you. You will walk over and drink what is in the glass. All of it. Or I will smash your knee. I am an excellent shot myself. If you persist in being difficult I will smash the other knee, as well. Then we will force-feed the drink to you."

I looked at my watch again. Without moving my head enough to upset the guy with the .22 revolver. I began to worry.

Taking as much time as I dared, I got up out of my chair. I took more time going to the table where my drink was waiting. That wouldn't irritate Falicon. It was natural for a man walking to his doom to do it slowly.

Zayid backed away from the table as I approached. Sensible of him. I looked down at the glass, hesitated, looked from it to Falicon.

"Do I really have a chance of coming out of this in any kind of reasonable condition?"

"Of course," he said. "Drink it."

I looked at the glass again. I picked it up. Each move a separate effort.

Falicon took aim at my knee again. "Drink," he snapped.

I started to raise the glass to my lips, and then put it back on the table and looked at him again. "All right, there is something I haven't told you about."

"I'm listening."

"Brissac was hidden in Millo's house when the people you sent went up there."

"I know that," he said impatiently.

"What you don't know," I told him slowly, "is that while he was there he wrote a letter. Giving some details of your operation. He didn't know too much. But what little he did know he wrote down. He mailed the letter to me. It says that the information business you and your grandmother . . .''

The phone on Falicon's desk rang, saving me from having to keep stalling with more gibberish.

He looked at the phone but didn't reach for it. He looked back to me and rasped, ''I told you to drink. I think you're lying but we'll find out later.''

His phone rang again.

I said, ''You'd better answer it.''

⊠ **18** ⊠

My tone and expression bothered Falicon.

On the fourth ring he snatched up the phone and barked, "Yes?" And then: "Who is this?"

He didn't like the answer he got. It slugged him into an emotional somersault that must have been painful. His lips stretched thin, parting to reveal a nice set of clenched teeth. After a long moment he spoke more politely into the phone: "Yes . . . Certainly . . ."

He held out the phone to me. "It is for you." He was struggling not to snarl it. "The *Police Judiciare*. Commissaire Juy."

I took it from him and identified myself.

"What's going on?" Juy's voice asked.

"At the moment," I told him, "Léon Falicon and a couple of his employees are holding me at gunpoint and trying to make me take a drugged drink. I think they're planning for me to have a terminal accident or commit suicide."

"Is this your way of cancelling a lunch date?"

"I'll be there in twenty minutes," I assured Juy. "If they let me go in one piece. Here, I'll let you talk to Falicon about it."

I gave the phone back to Falicon. He drew a slow breath before speaking into it: "Commissaire? . . . No, of course not . . . A joke. He is quite a joker. . . . Yes, of course."

He slammed the phone down and stared at me, working

his way out of shock. "Get out of here," he said through those nice teeth.

General Patton slunk over to smell my leg for identification when I came into Le Chantilly. I patted his big head and then kissed Louisette, the restaurant's owner. The German shepherd she'd named after the American she most admired slunk away. Louisette pointed toward a rear table where Commissaire Juy was just being served his luncheon order: a big bowl of bouillabaisse.

I walked through to join him, passing a number of other high-level plainclothes cops. Le Chantilly is near Nice's central commissariat on Avenue Foch, and Louisette is a fervent police buff. I told Vivi, the waitress, to bring me what Juy was having. Except for the wine: he had a bottle of white. I asked for a demi-bottle of rosé.

"Did I get you out of trouble?" he asked as I sat down across the table from him.

"Not really. It was more of a joke." I didn't want to owe him more than I would have to by the time we left there.

Both police and private sector detectives, like journalists, operate on a system of favors given, owed, and repaid. You can't function well as an investigator unless you've built a large stable of people who are obligated to you—and a reputation for redeeming your own debts on demand. My situation with Commissaire Juy was different than with Dixon Chess. Chess had owed me a couple; now he only owed me one. Juy and I were even. Every bit of aid he gave me would have to be returned eventually, perhaps in ways I wouldn't like.

I watched him pluck a large shrimp out of the steaming soup and peel away the shell very carefully so he wouldn't lose any of the flesh inside. He popped it between his teeth and chewed with open pleasure. After swallowing it he looked across the table, studying me with those cold blue eyes.

"I think I got you out of trouble," he said. "I think you

knew you were going into trouble. That's why you asked me to phone there and remind you of this lunch. Which you said you'd buy.''

I'd gotten to know enough about Commissaire Juy to understand that he was two different men. Josette—a woman who knew him much better than I did—had told me the other Juy liked practical jokes and sang in a church choir and played a harmonica. She'd said that with close friends he was affectionate and full of boyish humor.

But outside that circle of close friends—and I wasn't one of them—he was a suspicious-minded, cold-eyed cop.

"I invited you to lunch," I said. "So of course I'm buying."

"I can pay for my own lunches, Sawyer. How big a favor do you owe me?"

In addition to being very bright, Commissaire Juy was quite a handsome man—in spite of the fact he was going bald. He was thirty-seven, with a strong face and a trim build. He had won police pistol championships, shooting with either hand, but had never shot anyone. He was also into the martial arts and could handle most kinds of trouble without a gun.

I said, "I'm about to owe you more than one."

Juy nodded slowly. "I'll keep count."

"I never doubted it," I told him.

At that point my own meal arrived. We didn't speak again until we were finished eating. Juy had as much respect for a nourishing bouillabaisse as I did.

"That old bitch has been at it for more years than I've been alive," he said. "The amount of confidential business information the Falicon operation has leaked from one company to another, and the technology that it's given to spies from other countries—it boggles the mind. Not to speak of all the political and military secrets she's passed around."

We were on our after-lunch coffees. Commissaire Juy

didn't know anything about Roland Mari. I'd asked him to tell me what he knew about the Falicons.

"You know how she started her business?" he asked me.

"With some whoring and blackmail, from what I've heard."

"Sure, but that only made her enough to buy the kind of apartment, clothes, and jewels she needed to con upper circle types into taking her for a legitimate, successful business woman. Along with teaching her how dumb some men can get—men who're smart and careful in every other way—if you hit them with the right girl. I'm talking about how she got her first really big bankroll."

"I don't know that one," I said.

"She persuaded a small group of investment bankers that she was producing a movie. And she let them meet a bunch of pretty, young actresses who were competing desperately for parts in the movie. The actresses were actually hookers—ones intelligent enough to pretend to be what The Old Spider needed. Those investment bankers could have had any of them for a thousand francs. But these guys weren't into paying hookers for what they wanted. What they did like was the notion of screwing around with glamorous actresses in exchange for promising them roles in the movie. They invested millions in the movie for that thrilling privilege. One of them went to prison for embezzling funds from his company after plans for the film collapsed. Two others just got fired. But by then Madame Falicon had her big bankroll. And nobody could prove she knew it was embezzled money."

"A neat con," I acknowledged.

"And the Falicon operation still uses honey traps as its come-on. Not hookers anymore. Just action girls, that like a good time with the chance of nice presents from smitten males. Jewelry and high-fashion clothes and trips in first class to exciting places."

Commissaire Juy's cold eyes had real anger in them.

Juy was square—for him the line between good and bad was sharp and clear. "In most cases," he said, "I don't think these girls know what the Falicon operation is using them for. Aren't aware how often what's said and done between them and the victims is being bugged and filmed."

"I saw some of them today," I told him, "at Léon Falicon's place."

Juy nodded sourly. "Sure you did. The Falicon business really boomed when she moved down here from Paris. She did it after Sophia Antipolis got organized. And there's more industrial secrets to be found in there than almost anywhere in Europe."

Sophia Antipolis, in the hills just behind Antibes, was named after the original Greek settlement there, four hundred years before Christ. It's a modern industrial development that's drawn high-tech research facilities from companies all over the world. Firms like IBM and Dow Chemical and Minoru of Japan. Along with their commercial directors, scientists, technicians, and defense contractors. With the number of big businesses that have established their research facilities there nearing the five hundred mark, Sophia Antipolis was getting close to rivalling California's Silicon Valley.

As Juy had said—a hive of secrets, waiting to be plundered by bribery or blackmail.

"Just look at the kind of people who work there," Juy said. "Inexperienced, most of them, about anything outside their narrow sphere of expertise. Eager as puppies for some fun—because that's how the companies persuaded them to shift to here. Skiing in the mountains above Sophia Antipolis, sunning and swimming and boating just below it. And fabulous women all over. They're ripe for the plucking. Boasting about what they're doing to the kind of girls the Falicons let them meet. Needing more dough to have any hope of going on seeing them. Or ready to roll over and beg for mercy at any price, after they get a look at their indiscretions in living color.''

"According to Léon Falicon," I said, "the family business isn't that active anymore. He says his grandmother's gotten too old for it, and he'd rather amuse himself than carry it on for her.''

"Léon Falicon," Juy told me, "likes to act at being a playboy. With nothing else on his mind and a lot of toys to play with and a willingness to share the playing with those he chances to meet and like. Harmless, gregarious, and generous. It attracts the kind of people he wants to attract. But the family business is very much alive. Growing, in fact. The old bitch is still the directing brain, but Léon is responsible for expanding it into new areas.''

"Would the new areas include furnishing mercenaries?''

The subject didn't surprise Juy. "That and arms dealing. Which grows out of knowing so much about what is going on. Selling weapons to well-financed terrorists. Selling information on the terrorists to interested parties. Supplying advanced weaponry to rebels in Third World countries. Then telling the governments of those about the rebels and selling them what they need to counter the rebels. The weaponry and the mercs.''

That was interesting. With much else he'd told me. Things that had been puzzling began to come together.

"Also," he added, "I'm sure the Falicons supplied some of the technicians and materials for both that Syrian atomic installation and the Libyan poison gas plant.''

"You know so much about them," I said, "it's surprising you haven't been able to nail them.''

"I'd love to," he told me heavily. "It's too late to get Madame Falicon—her lawyer could probably delay any trial until she's dead. But nailing Léon would hurt her even worse. He's the only one left in the whole world she cares for. Her son and daughter-in-law were drowned when the grandson was a kid. She's the one who raised him. I *had* the evidence, once. But it went down the drain. Like all the attempts by other cops before me to nail either of them went down the drain.''

"How come?"

"What do they deal in, mostly? Information. Who else lives off information? Our secret services." Juy's tone had acquired a biting contempt. "The Old Spider trickles just enough of it their way. Every time she feels the law breathing too close, she gives the DST some more. Usually information she's already been paid for. And people they're looking for and that have stopped being useful to her. And the word comes down the line—from the top, in Paris—for the cops to drop what they've got and back off. For high political reasons.''

"It's the same all over," I said, trying to soothe his feelings about France doing it. "Look at the CIA—protecting the biggest dope merchants in the world, for political reasons, while street cops bust their balls arresting the small-time pushers.''

"I have looked." A dark sadness had entered Juy's cold blue eyes. "We live in a time when integrity has become negotiable.''

"Not for everybody," I said, looking at him directly.

He looked at his watch. "I've got to get back to work soon. Anything else?''

He didn't have anything further on the Falicons that was helpful, so I said, "There's a yacht called *La Dolce Vita*. Madame Falicon owns it, but it would be Léon who uses it. I'd like to know where it is right now. You could probably find out faster than I've been able to.''

Commissaire Juy nodded. "If it's anywhere along the Côte d'Azur.''

"I'd appreciate it.''

"Yes," he said, "you will." And with that he got up and went out of Le Chantilly, trailed to the door by General Patton.

I used the restaurant's phone to make a couple precautionary phone calls. Then I paid Louisette for Juy's meal and my own. So at least I didn't owe him for that. The worst thing about what I did owe him was that he'd be the one who would decide how the debt should be paid off.

My car was down the block. I got in and went to see how Mireille and Hugette were getting along with Jean-Marie Reju.

🔳 19 🔳

I FOUND REJU SITTING ON THE BEACH IN FRONT OF THE Negresco with Hugette. Mireille was off in the sea taking an extra-long swim. Making up for lost time. She'd always been half fish. Daily swims were one thing she missed now that she lived up in the mountains.

Reju sat with his back to the sea. The long peak of the fishing cap he wore was pulled down to shadow his face. So the sun wouldn't interfere with his vision no matter what direction he had to turn in a hurry. But when I hunkered down with them I could see his eyes, their size shrunk by the thick lenses of his glasses. He was sizing up every newcomer that descended the steps from the Promenade des Anglais to the beach. His eyes moved to give further study to any of them who settled down nearby.

He was in his early thirties, wide across the shoulders but the rest of him lean. The fishing cap was one of the extras I kept at Arlette's apartment. So were the espadrilles and terry cloth robe Reju was wearing. The robe was partly open, showing he was also wearing my swim trunks. But it wasn't open enough to show where he was carrying his big Colt .45.

My guess was that he had it holstered under his left arm, in a shoulder rig. Reju never had the problem I did in getting a permit to walk around armed. He'd been with the government's V.O. service—assigned to bodyguarding French min-

isters on trips abroad and foreign politicians visiting France—
before he'd gone for the bigger money of private enterprise.
High government officials who could afford the tab still asked
for his services, and they'd sliced through the red tape for
him. Reju had that rarity: a permanent carry permit.

Hugette sat beside him in her wet bathing suit, with his
traveling chess board open across her knees, trying out opening moves. She jumped a knight over a pawn and looked to
Reju to find out if she'd done it correctly. He nodded. She
looked up at me happily. "Monsieur Reju is teaching me to
play chess!"

This was a new facet to Reju; at least to me it was. "You're
lucky," I told Hugette. "He's one of the best players I know."

Good enough to beat Fritz Donhoff two out of three—to
Fritz's incredulous irritation.

"She is unusually intelligent," Reju informed me in his
usual grave tone. "And she remembers quickly."

Hugette beamed at him adoringly.

He smiled. A small smile, but a real one.

I tried to remember if I had ever seen him smile at anyone
like that, and I couldn't. Reju had difficulty relating to people
in a normal manner. But I had never seen him with a kid
before. Certainly not one like Hugette.

"All quiet?" I asked him.

He didn't answer immediately. He was watching someone
walk past behind me. When he was satisfied the person posed
no potential threat, he told me, "No sign of trouble so far."

"Good. But get them back to the apartment when Mireille
comes out of the water. I don't want them out in the open
too long."

Reju started to nod—and then stopped it. His attention
became fixed on a point a distance behind me.

I said softly: "Something?"

He was silent for about six seconds. Then he said, "It
could be."

We discussed it in terms that wouldn't alert Hugette, whose
head was bowed over an experimental move with the black

bishop. I bent over enough to hide the shift of my compact pistol from its belt holster. When it was stuffed up inside my jacket's right sleeve, muzzle down, I straightened and walked back across the beach. Up the steps and along the Promenade.

Twenty feet away I stopped at the railing to gaze over the beach. Joining the other males who were lined up there studying the array of exposed pulchritude between us and the water's edge. I couldn't make out Reju's face at that distance in the shadow of the fishing cap's peak. He scratched his right knee and then gave his attention to Hugette and the chess board.

I directed my own attention to a shapely topless blonde giving her left side its dose of tan. After thirty seconds I detached myself from the other spectators and walked on.

A block later I stopped at the railing again. This time to retie my shoelaces. It took time to get the bows just right.

My Peugeot was parked half a block from the Promenade, in a side street two blocks from the Negresco. The Mercedes that had been parked behind it was gone. In its place was a Rolls-Royce Silver Cloud. I stopped and looked at Léon Falicon seated behind its steering wheel.

He looked back at me and said thinly: "Come here."

I went over and bent down, resting my elbows on the bottom of his open window and looking in. Falicon held the gun with the silencer that I'd seen before on his right thigh, pointing up at my face.

Close behind me a whispery voice said, "No sudden moves, Sawyer."

Without straightening from the Rolls window I turned my head. It was Roland Mari and his tight smile. And his Luger.

None of the people passing by, on their way to and from the Promenade, noticed it. Roland had a jacket draped over his right hand and forearm. The view of the Luger's snout was just for me. I looked back to Falicon.

He smiled at me. "I had a friend in the police find out where Commissaire Juy was lunching. Then we came and located your car near the restaurant. I had two boys on motorcycles take turns following you when you left there. One came back and told us where you stopped, while the other kept track of you on foot."

He was tickled by his cleverness.

I was not tickled by my own carelessness. I said, "I don't see your motorcycle boys around now."

"They're not needed anymore," Falicon said.

"Yes they are," I told him. "But they still wouldn't give you enough backup."

Falicon was irked by my seeming so cool with two guns aimed at me. "Get in the back with Mari," he rasped.

"So you can take me where you've got Zayid waiting to get on with his work."

"And this time no one will know about it," he said with vicious pleasure.

"Zayid," I said, "is going to have to swallow a second professional disappointment in one day. There are too many people around and this Rolls is too memorable for either of you to shoot me here."

Roland Mari warned me softly: "Don't bet on it."

I looked over my shoulder at him. "I am betting on it, Roland."

Jean-Marie Reju walked up behind him and said, "Stand easy, Mari."

Roland turned his head. Reju stood there with his right hand down inside the deep pocket of my beachrobe. It was obvious from the size and shape of the bulge that his hand was not the only thing in there. Roland didn't try to bring his Luger around. He'd heard the quiet authority of Reju's voice, before he recognized who it belonged to.

Gunmen in Europe made a point of knowing Reju on sight. It was the only way to avoid the fatal error of trying to get at someone he was bodyguarding.

"You can console yourself with a point of pride," I told Roland. "You're getting well known in some circles. He spotted you up there on the Promenade."

From inside the Rolls, Falicon demanded, "What is this, Mari? Who is he?"

Roland ignored him, looking at Reju. "I didn't recognize who you were, down on the beach."

"That's good," Reju said, dead level. "Please lower what you're holding."

Roland lowered his right hand, just short of having the concealed jacket spill off the Luger. A good sergeant has a keen awareness of what can and cannot be done. Against Reju, he knew it was no contest. Roland was a solid, journeyman gun for hire. Jean-Marie Reju was simply the best in Europe. I had seen him prove it once, in Venice. Roland would have heard about other examples.

He looked from Reju to me. "So you got scared enough to rent protection."

"I didn't hire him for this," I said. "We're friends, and he happened to be around."

He looked at Reju again. "I didn't know you had friends," he said, and didn't mean it as a joke.

"A few," Reju told him soberly.

"Mari . . . ?" That was Falicon again, shaky now.

I looked in at him. He was staring uncertainly at Roland Mari, unable to understand what had taken the spine out of his killer so suddenly. I dragged my right forearm across the bottom of his window. The pistol slid out of my sleeve and into my hand. It was aimed at his chest when he registered it.

He made no move to interfere when I reached my left hand in and took his gun away from him. I stuck it in my belt, under my jacket. Falicon tried a tough smile to show he could cope with setbacks. But the smile was sick.

I straightened up and turned to Roland. That brought us close enough together for me to switch his Luger to my belt under the other flap of my jacket. I said, "Good-bye, Roland."

He was still looking at Reju. "Stick with Sawyer," he told

him, "and you'll find yourself going up against more fire-power than even you can handle."

Reju didn't react at all. On someone else his expression might have been taken for a look of boredom. But boredom, like amusement, was not part of his makeup.

Roland's own face was expressionless when he got into the front seat of the Rolls next to Falicon. Falicon said something to him, too softly for me to hear it. Roland gave him a dirty look and said something back. Just as quiet but apparently short and sharp. Falicon started his Rolls.

Reju and I watched it go up the street and turn out of sight around the next corner.

"Get Mireille and Hugette," I said. "Bring them back to the apartment. We're going to shift the three of you some-where else. Probably Crow's place near La Turbie."

"All right." Reju knew Frank Crowley, the best Ameri-can friend I had in Europe. They'd both once teamed with Fritz Donhoff to help me pry a girl out of a death contract put on her by an Italian mobster.

Reju strode back to the beach. I went into a service alley and stuffed the guns of Roland and Falicon down in a garbage can. Then I headed for Arlette's apartment to phone Crow.

We were close enough for either of us to ask a lot of the other. We'd begun as war buddies. The war that wasn't a war. Years after Vietnam Crow had come over from the States to spend a week's vacation as my houseguest. His week on the Riviera had stretched considerably after I'd introduced him to Nathalie, the woman he married.

I got him in at his working studio in the old part of Nice and told him my problem.

"Easy," he told me. "There's the two beds in the guest room for Mireille and the kid. The sofa bed in my study for Reju."

"It'll crowd you some. I'd have asked Nathalie first, but I heard she's off on business somewhere."

"Rome. She'll be back tomorrow evening. But don't worry, you know she likes Mireille."

Nathalie, now chief of merchandising for her mother's fashion firm, had been part of the same beach gang as Mireille when they were in their teens.

I thanked Crow and hung up as Reju came in with Mireille and Hugette. Twenty minutes later they'd repacked the few things they'd brought here and we were on our way. Mireille and Hugette with Reju in the car he'd rented when he'd arrived at the airport from Paris. Myself tailing them in my Peugeot.

When we reached the port on the eastern edge of Nice, Reju turned up along the route to the Grande Corniche and Crow's house. I'd told him where to find the emergency key to it that the Crowleys kept hidden in their garden. By the time we'd reached the port area I'd made certain we weren't being tailed by someone else. I turned around and drove to the car rental agency on the other side of the port. When I left it my Peugeot was parked two blocks away from there and I was driving a Fiat Uno.

I went east out of Nice along the Lower Corniche—to find out if anybody had gotten around yet to rigging a bomb in my house.

⊠ **20** ⊠

THERE WERE TWO MEN WAITING FOR ME AT MY HOUSE. THE one I didn't know sat at my patio table having a drink from a bottle of my wine and admiring my view of the Mediterranean. A handsome, solidly built black guy of about thirty. He wore a T-shirt, baggy white canvas trousers with a lot of pockets, and high-top orange-red sneakers. There was a metal suitcase on the patio beside him and the doors to my living room behind him were wide open.

When I arrived he turned his head and called into the house. Antonio Odasso came out with a bottle of beer and told me, "The place is clean. No booby traps."

One of my precautionary phone calls from Le Chantilly had been to Antonio. The other to Judith Ruyter, telling her to let him use my spare house key and instruct him how to turn off the alarm system from outside.

I looked at the other man. "You're sure?"

He took another swallow of my wine and smiled at me. "I didn't overlook anything."

Antonio introduced him to me as Grosjean. "He used to be a demolition and bomb disposal specialist with the GIGN." Gesturing at the metal suitcase he added: "He took some stuff with him when he left it."

GIGN is the acronym for the French military's crack anti-terrorist unit. Grosjean didn't need more credentials than that.

"Your phone was ringing when we got here," Antonio said. "Stopped before Grosjean could make sure your front door wasn't wired to explode."

"Anything since?"

Antonio shook his head and drank from the bottle.

I went inside to the study, rewound the answering machine to the last call, and put it on play.

"Monsieur Sawyer, this is Ilona here." Her voice came through hurried by a jumpy urgency, but it was unmistakably Ilona Szabo.

"I'm in a dress boutique in Cannes," she said quickly. "The back dressing room. It's the only place with a phone I can use without any of them knowing about it." She rattled off the phone number there. "Please call me if you get this in time. I can't stay here trying things on for more than an hour. Just ask for Ilona."

The message had clocked in almost fifty minutes ago. I switched off the machine and dialed the number in Cannes.

On the fifth ring a woman with a stagy solemn voice answered with the name of the boutique and her own name: Madame Chaplet. I asked for Ilona.

Two seconds later she was on the line, speaking fast but keeping it low: "Thank God—I've already bought two outfits I don't really. . . . Did you give him my letter?"

"I haven't found him yet," I told her. "I'm close but I can't get closer unless you and I get together—today—and talk about these people you're afraid of."

"I can't. Why is it so hard to find him?"

"One thing I know is he's been hurt. Probably by these same people. So if you care about Desiré you'll have to meet me and . . ."

She interrupted anxiously: "But he is not—he will recover?"

"I think so. This time. But if they get a second chance at him the odds are they'll kill him. I can prevent that, but only if I see you and . . ."

She interrupted again: "No. I can't and it *won't* happen again. I'm going away this evening. After that he won't be able to interfere and they won't have reason to . . ."

I was the one who interrupted this time: "Wait a minute. Where are you going? You can't just take off without seeing me and paying me for the work I've done for you."

"I should be back within a week," Ilona said, and her voice had become warmly persuasive. "It will be over then and I will have enough to pay you and redeem my ring."

"That's not good enough," I told her harshly. "I've trusted you too long as it is. If the job's finished we meet and settle the account."

"Then *sell* the damn ring. Keep whatever you think I owe you. That's all that jewelry was ever good for, anyway."

She hung up on me before I could switch to warm persuasion myself.

I disconnected at my end and then redialed the number. It rang longer this time before being picked up. Madame Chaplet again.

"I'm the one who was just speaking to Ilona," I told her. "Could you put her back on the phone, please?"

"I'm sorry, monsieur. She has left."

"She bought two dresses. Didn't she have to pay for them and have them wrapped first?"

"The gentleman who was waiting for her outside in the car came in and took care of that before your call. Then she had an afterthought and was back in the dressing room trying on something else when you phoned. Now if you'll excuse me, I have some clients. . . ."

"The gentleman," I cut in, "that must be my friend Léon." I described Falicon.

"Oh no—this man was an elderly gentleman. Foreign, I believe. But quite cultured and handsome."

"Of course," I said. "Léon's uncle. I'm his attorney, Madame Chaplet. I called back because I forgot to mention a problem that's come up to Ilona. Did he pay with a check— or a credit card?"

"Neither, monsieur. With cash."

That put paid to one way of learning who he was. I tried for it, for something on Ilona Szabo, another way: "I believe Ilona and Léon's uncle have been frequent customers at your boutique?"

Another miss: "No, this is the first time I've seen either of them. And now I really must . . ."

I let her terminate our fruitless conversation. Hanging up my own phone, I cursed quietly. I'd just lost one client. That left me with only Mireille wanting me to find Desiré Brissac—and no leads to him. I rewound the answering machine to the start and put it on play again.

There were no messages on it except Ilona's. That worried me. There should have at least been one from Fritz Donhoff by now. I'd called him twice today. Neither time had he been in. Each time I'd left a message on his machine for him to call me.

Picking up the phone, I tried his Paris apartment again. And got his machine again. I told it: "Where the hell are you off to, Fritz? I'm at home now. Call me, damn it!"

I hung up and brooded. My brain felt like parts of it were on strike and my gut was too tensed. I went back to the patio and asked Grosjean how much I owed him. He told me. His services didn't come cheap. My expenses on this case were going to add up to every franc Ilona Szabo's ring was worth if it went on like this. She might not be my client anymore, but she could afford the tab easier than Mireille.

"I'll make you out a check," I told Grosjean. "Later. I need a swim. Badly. I'd like you to stick around and make sure I don't have a surprise waiting when I come back. I'll add your charges for that to the check."

"Glad to," Grosjean said. "I wouldn't mind a swim myself. But I didn't bring a bathing suit. Should have."

"I've got an extra you can use. After I have mine."

"Marvelous. The swim lowers my charges."

Antonio took a last swallow of beer and set the empty on the table. "I wish I had time for a swim, too, but there are clogged drains waiting for me.'' He shook hands with us and hiked off up the drive that corkscrews down from the coast road and ends at my place. I'd seen his car parked off the road outside the driveway. You can't drive in without a key to the gate.

Grosjean refilled his wine glass and admired my view again. ''A man can really relax in a place like this.''

''It helps,'' I admitted.

If you've got to have problems like everybody else, the Riviera's at least a nicer place than most to have them. Certainly better than being back on the force in Chicago, busting into dope wars around Forty-fourth and Greenwood between kids of fourteen armed with the latest in compact submachine guns.

Motioning Grosjean to follow me, I went back into the study and unlocked the drawer where I kept my house handgun. A Beretta. In France you do have the right to keep guns at home. ''Protection of domicile.'' I gave Grosjean the Beretta and a spare ammo clip, and unlocked a closet. From that I took a pump-action shotgun and a box of shells, putting them on my desk.

Grosjean looked from the Beretta in his hand to the shotgun on the desk. ''Think I'm going to need them?''

''Probably not. But recent events have jangled my nerves. I'm not in a mood for repeats.''

''Sure,'' Grosjean said calmly. He was checking out the Beretta with professional care when I went to change into swimming trunks.

I made my way down the wooded slope and into the cool sea and swam for a full hour. When I came out I felt better. I climbed back up to the house and found Grosjean on the patio having another sip of wine. He had the Beretta in his belt and the shotgun leaning against his thigh.

''Any calls?'' I asked him.

''None.''

''Merde,'' I whispered—and there went some of the good feeling the sea had given me.

I gave Grosjean the spare trunks. He was down having his swim when my phone rang. I carried the Beretta and the shotgun inside with me when I hurried to answer it.

The call wasn't from Fritz. It was France Hennies, calling from her office services agency in Nice. She'd just received a fax for me from Milan. One of Sonia Galeazzo's photos of Ilona Szabo. I told France to make a few pocket-sized copies and said I'd pick them up later.

I went outside and began a drastic pruning job on the ivy that clung to too much of the house. Just to be doing something while I waited for Fritz to call. But the job did need doing. Ivy growing up stone walls looks pretty. But over the years it gets too much and too heavy. Its branch roots support the added weight by digging deeper into the mortar between the stones, breaking it loose. It would take a long time for ivy to do any real damage to walls that thick. But these walls had been there for as long as the big olive tree, some five hundred years. I liked to think I had done my part toward their continuing to stand there five hundred years after I was gone.

I do get notions that strike other people as strange if not downright weird, now and then.

I'd accomplished a satisfactory amount of that chore when Grosjean came back from his swim. There'd been no phone calls and no further surprises from Falicon. I told Grosjean he could go home. While he showered and dressed I made out his check. He left me his phone number, in case I ever needed him again, and went up the drive with his metal suitcase to catch a bus.

The swimming trunks I was still wearing had dried in the sun and gotten wet again from perspiration during the pruning. I cleaned and oiled the pruning shears and took a shower and put on jeans and a T-shirt. Then I brewed some strong coffee and drank it and brooded some more. Mostly about what could have happened to Fritz. But also over what Ilona Szabo had said: that she was going away somewhere this evening.

Evening was not far off.

I made myself an early dinner. Rare steak and a bowl of salad, with *pain de campagne*, goat cheese, and black olives. I decided that if I didn't hear from Fritz by nightfall I was going to take a plane to Paris and search for him. Other matters would have to go on hold. I was getting that concerned.

Fritz could usually take care of himself better than most. He hadn't lost too many of the qualities that had earned him a scary reputation in the Resistance, after the Nazis had made him mad enough to quit the Munich police and escape to France. But there was no getting away from the fact that he wasn't that young anymore.

I phoned my nearest neighbor up the drive. Judith Ruyter answered and I asked if they'd mind taking phone messages for me when I was out. With two young children, one of the Ruyters was almost always around their house.

"I'll be glad to," she told me. "But if you're going to keep demanding secretarial services of me perhaps I'll ask my husband if you shouldn't start paying for them."

"If your secretarial services include my seeing more of you, tell him you can charge whatever you want."

She laughed softly. "I don't think I'll tell him that. He might go down and beat you up."

"I withdraw the suggestion," I said, and told her I would phone and check for messages from time to time.

Then I recorded the new message on my machine, telling callers to phone the Ruyter number.

Two minutes later the phone rang. I snatched it up before the machine could take over.

It was Fritz Donhoff. Finally.

⊠ 21 ⊠

"THE TONE OF YOUR LAST MESSAGE," FRITZ TOLD ME, somewhat stiffly, "was hardly polite."

"I was worried about you," I told him. "Where have you been all day?"

"Out working." His stiffness eased a bit. "I can't always carry my part of our partnership with telephone calls. In this case it required a good deal of leg work."

"What have you got?"

"Fatigue." Humor brought his own tone back to its normal warmth. "A heavy case of fatigue."

He paused. Fritz's pauses often meant a teasing stretching out of the suspense before he hit you with something juicy he'd turned up. I waited—refusing to let myself be drawn into asking what it was he'd found. A small reprisal for my afternoon of worry. Unreasonable but human.

When he spoke again I could hear that he was still holding off the juicy part: "I had a discussion with the lawyer who represented Ilona Szabo's claims against the heirs of Marius Lejon. He gave me nothing useful. Except that he dislikes her. He says her expectations were unreasonable, and that he had to threaten to take her to court before she would sell most of her jewelry to pay what she owed him."

"Think he was in collusion with the Lejon attorney?"

"Almost certainly. Which would explain his dislike of her. A common emotional response to wronging someone. A transformation of one's guilt into righteous anger—until the guilt is buried deep and forgotten.''

Fritz paused again. I waited again.

"I had a much different time," he said, "with the doctor Ilona Szabo worked for before she went off with Marius Lejon. He speaks of her with remembered fondness. I believe he was infatuated with her.''

"A lot of men would be.''

"So I gather. The doctor took her out to several dinners. At the time she was sharing a small apartment with two other young women. He was able to remember their names. The first one I found hasn't seen or heard of our Ilona Szabo since she quit their shared apartment.''

Another pause. This time I gave Fritz the satisfaction of my prodding him: "But the other one has.''

"A lovely woman. Her name is Suzanne Fayard. I have a feeling she was somewhat smitten by my elderly but appreciative charm.''

I didn't doubt it. There were few people, male or female, young or old, who were impervious to Fritz's brand of old world charm when he wished to turn up the voltage. That was one quality age hadn't dimmed at all.

"She happened to run into Ilona Szabo again only two weeks ago,'' Fritz went on. "In a Paris restaurant. With a distinguished, good-looking man of about sixty. Ilona introduced him as Raymond Hayes. An American, but he spoke fairly good French.''

It sounded very much like Madame Chaplet's cultured, handsome foreign gentleman. "The name doesn't say anything to me," I told Fritz. "Should it?''

"Not yet," he said, with a certain relish. Fritz was a man who enjoyed his work; especially when it paid off. "I made enquiries about Raymond Hayes. He is a retired businessman from Atlanta, Georgia. Not a big businessman. He owned two department stores. After the death of his wife he sold them for a good profit. And decided to spend his remaining years here, because of a love for France. He was one of the

American soldiers involved in the liberation of Paris in the Second World War, and back in America he made efforts to continue learning the language.

"He has a spacious apartment in the sixteenth arrondissement. But he hasn't been there for the past ten days. His local acquaintances believe he went off to the Côte d'Azur. None of them know exactly where. Nor do they know of Ilona Szabo and his relationship with her. And," Fritz added, "there is something else none of them know about Mr. Hayes."

Fritz had done a good job and I was fond of him and he was entitled to his little satisfactions. So I said, "But you managed to dig it out, somehow."

"I contacted several people at the American embassy here. And learned nothing useful about Raymond Hayes—except that one of them seemed rather edgy about the subject. So I got together with a woman I know quite well. A high secretary with the embassy's security people. She told me that for a year—two years ago—they had an intermittent surveillance on Mr. Hayes. She doesn't know why. Only that they stopped it, finally, as what they called 'unproductive.' So I phoned Atlanta."

"Your friend in the police there," I said. "The one you got to know at that international lawmen's conference."

"Yes. And he consulted some people who knew Mr. Hayes quite well when he lived there. Mr. Hayes is part of an extensive family. He has many nephews and nieces. Most of them with different last names, since Mr. Hayes had only one brother but four sisters."

This time Fritz's pause was not to entice me into impatient prompting. He was only setting himself for the punchline: "One of Raymond Hayes's nephews is named Barney Kavanagh."

"Ah," I said.

"Yes," Fritz said. "That Barney Kavanagh."

That Barney Kavanagh was a hard-driving financier in his forties who had manipulated his way to the head of a consortium controlling a number of Texas banks. Three years ago he'd been arrested and charged with milking the banks of almost a billion dollars and hiding most of it in Swiss number accounts. Along with laundering money for big dope merchants and bribing government officials to let him get away with it.

His lawyers had broken through the prosecution's objections and gotten Kavanagh released from jail while awaiting trial. He'd put up bail of two million dollars. Considering the amount of money he'd looted, that was a pittance to pay for his freedom.

Two weeks before his trial came up, Barney Kavanagh had vanished.

For a couple years after that the hunt for him had been pursued implacably—almost desperately—by American law officers, insurance detectives, and Interpol. The effort had slackened when they'd all finally run out of leads. But they still wanted him.

There were rumors that he was dead and other rumors that he was living the rich life hidden in some part of the world. But no evidence to support either rumor.

"Somebody," I said to Fritz, "is hunting him harder than the law."

"Perhaps," Fritz said. "I have heard those rumors, too."

Those concerned other conspirators who'd been in on the banking swindle with Barney Kavanagh—and whom the law hadn't been able to corner. People willing to pay a fortune to anyone who could find Kavanagh and kill him—before he was found by the law and gave evidence against them to save his own neck.

"I think," I told Fritz, "that one pair of hunters have gotten close to turning up Kavanagh." I gave him an account of my own long day. With detailed attention to what I'd learned from my encounters with The Old Spider and her unpleasant grandson.

"You are leaping too far ahead on unsubstantial evidence," Fritz said judiciously. "But—the leap may be in the correct direction."

"It would make what's been happening down here much clearer."

"However, the Falicons would not be the only extralegal types who have thought of trying to locate Kavanagh through his uncle."

"Sure, but they all finally gave that up, like the U.S. law did. Because none of them detected any sign that Hayes was in contact with Kavanagh. Maybe the Falicons tried and gave up, too. Until their information mill happened to turn up something new. An indication that Kavanagh has gotten in touch with his uncle—probably only recently."

"It is a possibility," Fritz admitted.

"And what follows fits the way the Falicons operate. Léon goes up to Paris and sees to it he gets to know Raymond Hayes. I'd say Léon Falicon can be extremely ingratiating when he wants. And he'd always have plenty of exciting and available women around him. Spreading his lures. The male target's likely to get interested in one or another of them. This particular target—Hayes—went for Ilona Szabo. After that all she has to do is stick close to him as much as possible."

"And report back to the Falicons on everything Hayes says or does in her presence. Until she comes through with something that gives them a lead to his nephew."

"If the Falicons get their hands on Kavanagh," I said, "they'll milk him the way he milked those banks—in exchange for not giving him to the police. And when they're finished milking him, they'll kill him for the payoff from the other conspirators."

Fritz heaved an unhappy sigh. "I hate to think of Ilona allowing herself to become part of something like that. From all I've heard of her, I had formed an impression of someone I liked."

"She almost certainly doesn't know much about what the Falicons intend to do to Kavanagh. Just that he's their target.

Not Hayes, the man who's fallen for her. Remember, after what the Lejon heirs did to her she has no reason to feel any sympathy for people who have too much money and not much conscience. On the record, Barney Kavanagh fits both categories.''

''True. The desire for revenge, even by proxy, would be a natural, if somewhat exaggerated, one. I imagine the Falicons could have played on that. However,'' Fritz added in a tougher tone, ''now you have me leaping to conclusions without a sufficient basis. And we have not yet dealt with Desiré Brissac's part in all this. Judging from the letter Ilona wrote to him, they have passionate feelings for each other.''

''The way it reads, he broke off their relationship—at some time in the past. Then he must have seen her again, probably when she came to the Riviera with Raymond Hayes, and found he couldn't handle the break emotionally anymore. He started following her around, and discovered some of what the Falicons are up to.''

''Please,'' Fritz chided, ''one step at a time. We don't know that he discovered anything. Merely that Léon Falicon is afraid that he might have.''

''It comes to the same thing. Either way, Falicon wants him dead. And Mireille wants me to bring him back alive. Which I can't unless I find him. Before Falicon does.''

Fritz said, ''If Brissac has recovered enough from his wound to move about . . .''

''From what I saw at Denis Millo's house,'' I interrupted, ''he's definitely recovered enough.''

''Then he is likely to be wherever Ilona Szabo is. Or trying to get to her.''

''And she's likely to be with Raymond Hayes. Now that I know about him.''

''I will continue with my efforts, here in Paris, to locate him.''

''Fine,'' I said. ''But if Hayes is down in this area now, I'll probably do better.''

"I have something that may help you," Fritz told me. "I was inside his apartment an hour ago."

"With the help of your favorite locksmith, I imagine."

"Yes. There was nothing else of use there, but I did find a photograph of Hayes. Fairly recent. I've also obtained the last known photograph of his nephew, Barney Kavanagh, from a journalist friend. I'll messenger both pictures to France Hennies's agency in Nice first thing in the morning. You can get them when you go to pick up Sonia Galeazzo's photo of Ilona."

"Fritz," I said, "you're a wonder."

"I know," he said, with more modesty in his tone than in the words.

I remained seated before the phone after hanging up. Considering the most efficient ways to go about tracking down Raymond Hayes. Who might be in the company of Ilona Szabo. Who in turn was a magnet for Desiré Brissac.

If Hayes had been romancing someone like Ilona on the Côte d'Azur he'd have taken her to one of the better hotels and showed her off in the swankier restaurants. No one could get answers out of those places, anywhere along the Riviera, quicker than Dixon Chess.

The answering machine at his apartment said to try the Monte Carlo Beach Club. I tried there and was told that Chess had left to have dinner somewhere but was expected back. I knew his two preferred dining places in Monte Carlo. If he wasn't having a gourmet meal in the Hotel de Paris he'd be at Flashman's, a pub with a French cook who made British-type food better than you could get in any pub in England. Flashman's also served the best American-style cheeseburgers to be found in Europe, and Dixon Chess sometimes got homesick. I tried there first and got him.

Chess was willing to try locating Raymond Hayes but felt the attempt should pay off the favor he still owed me. I held out for discharge of the obligation based on results. We argued about it. Chess was usually a tough bargainer. But his third cheeseburger arrived in the middle of our argument and he let me win so he could get off the phone and eat it before it got cold.

I was considering who else I should enlist in the hunt for Hayes when my phone rang.

It was Commissaire Juy at the other end, with more troubled ferocity in his voice than I'd ever heard from him. He gave me an address in Nice and told me: "I'm waiting for you. Get here fast."

"What is it?" I asked him.

"You'll *see* it," he snarled, and broke the connection.

🔲 22 🔲

The hotels near the Nice railroad station used to be fashionable. That was back in the days when the wealthy came to the Côte d'Azur by train, accompanied by servants and four or five big steamer trunks loaded with clothes for gala occasions. Nowadays most of the people with enough loose change for galas arrive by jet; and the international airport is on the sea, minutes from the beachfront hotels. The train station is only ten blocks from the beaches, but the area around it feels as remote as Brooklyn from the doings of the jet set. Some of the hotel facades there retain a certain faded elegance, but the accommodations behind the facades are now strictly for visitors of limited means.

The hotel that belonged to the address Commissaire Juy had given me was a couple blocks from the railroad station. It was getting dark out when I left my rented Fiat at the station's parking area and walked the couple blocks. The hotel was off Rue Paganini, in a side street that got little activity after business hours. There was a small café across the street that was open, but the hotel itself hadn't been open for seven years.

It had been partially gutted by an enterprise that intended to convert its interior into apartments. The company had gone bankrupt before the gutting was completed. The outer walls with their boarded-up windows remained standing, dark and empty, waiting stolidly for someone to finally come along and resume the building's reconstruction or complete its demolition.

A police car and two unmarked cars crowded the hotel's short, curved driveway. The chain across its entrance door had been removed and a gendarme stood guard there. I told him my name and said the commissaire was expecting me. The gendarme had been advised about that. He gave me a flashlight and directions.

The flashlight was needed inside. The big lobby was dim and full of rubble. Heaps of timber, bricks, and plaster. And some large broken tiles; but not many of those. They were Art Nouveau tiles, and any the wreckers had been able to pry off the walls intact had been sold to antique dealers. Weeds sprouted from mounds of plaster dust. An incredibly tall, skinny wild fig tree grew out of a hole in the flooring, reaching for one of the gaping holes in the lobby's high ceiling, searching desperately for the sun.

A couple plainclothes inspectors were prowling through the debris with flashlights. Looking for clues and not looking as though they expected to find any. One of them gestured for me to go on around a wide central staircase that had only six steps left, leading up to nowhere. I circled past it and into a corridor with most of its flooring gone. A cop in the uniform of the city force was outlined by strong light coming out of a doorway with no door behind him. He asked if I was Sawyer and when I said yes he called into the lighted room.

Commissaire Juy appeared in the doorway as I reached it. "You were quick," he said. "The medical examiner only beat you by a couple minutes." The rage firing his phone call had been locked away and he was back in his flawless envelope of cold calm. He turned and motioned for me to follow him inside.

The room was lighted by two big battery lamps. Whatever the room had been originally, it had apparently last been used by the wreckers. They'd left a heavy wooden workbench behind. A pair of fingerprint men were working their way around the walls. The police doctor was probing what was on the workbench with delicate fingers.

"Half of the bones have been smashed," he said. "At least half. By some kind of blunt, heavy weapon."

A police photographer was moving around the workbench taking pictures of what the doctor was examining and trying very hard not to look at what he was photographing. The doctor looked toward the commissaire and said, "Death not more than two hours ago. But he was alive when most of this was done to him."

Juy ignored him, concentrating his attention on me. "You mentioned a man named Roland Mari at lunch today. Is that him?"

I looked at what was on the workbench. "I can't be sure," I said after a time. "It could be."

I looked at the clothes on the floor. "That's what he was wearing, the last time I saw him."

"The identification in the wallet left with the clothes belongs to Roland Mari," Juy said. "But his fingerprints will tell for sure—if they're on record anywhere."

"You'll find Mari's with his military dossier," I told him. "He used to be an army sergeant."

I made myself look at the workbench again. Roland Mari—if that was him—had been stretched out on his back with his hands and ankles nailed to the thick legs of the workbench. The tall, thin figure could be his, though it was badly distorted and darkly discolored by the mass of swollen bruises. The doctor pressed where the left shinbone should have resisted his fingers. It looked like he was probing Jell-O.

The face had taken the same pounding. Nothing recognizable was left. But the hair and hairline belonged to Roland Mari.

A knife had carved five letters on his chest. The letters had filled with blood but the word they spelled was still readable. LÂCHE—coward.

Roland Mari was no loss to the world. But nobody ought to die like that. If I hadn't taken his Luger away from him he probably wouldn't have. They would have had to kill him quickly, or not at all. Maybe.

Maybe and probably—and I wasn't responsible for the way he'd ended. He should have been more careful about the kind of people he worked for.

I looked back to Commissaire Juy. "I think the finger-prints will prove it's Mari. If it is, Léon Falicon is the one who had this done."

His cold blue eyes studied me. "We can step outside for our talk. If what's in here bothers you that much."

"Not necessary," I told him. "I've seen worse."

The worst had been a lieutenant with all of his face burned off, down to the skull. Worse, because he'd still been alive. And conscious. On bad nights he sometimes came into my sleep. Making the same sounds he'd made while Crow and I had lifted him into the rescue chopper.

Juy said, "We'll step out, anyway." I followed him into the corridor. He gestured and the cop on duty there walked off to the corridor's other end.

Juy turned and faced me in the light coming out of the doorway. "I got a call, at my apartment. Not many people know my number there but this man did. He wouldn't say who he was and he was disguising his voice. He said if I came here I'd find a present waiting for me. And for my friend Sawyer—that's how he put it. You think he was Fali-con?"

"I'm sure of it."

"And now you're going to tell me why you're so sure." Juy fastened a hard, flat, cop stare on me as he said it.

I just stared back, the same kind of stare. I'd been a cop, too. You don't forget how. I didn't want to lie to him any more than I had to. But I had my license and a client to protect. Two clients, even if one had quit me. It was her ring that would be paying my expenses on this case, after all.

"You helped me humiliate Falicon this morning," I told Juy. "At least, he's the kind that would consider it humili-ating. He was looking forward to having some of his thugs question me, the hard way, and then kill me. Your phone call forced him to let me go. He didn't like it. And then I humiliated him again, when he tried to grab me later in the day."

I told Juy about my second encounter with The Old Spider's grandson—and Roland Mari. Leaving out the part about my carrying a gun at the time. Giving all the credit for my rescue to Jean-Marie Reju.

"From what I've seen of Falicon," I said, "he's not used to life's little setbacks. And he can't handle it like most of us can. Because we've learned you have to take a certain amount of crap in this life."

Unexpectedly, Commissaire Juy said, "Not like it—and not forget it. Just accept it."

I knew he was thinking of the time he'd been ordered to drop his case against Falicon and The Old Spider. I nodded. "But he can't. He's got to get the humiliation out of his system, right away. So he has his thugs do what they did to Roland Mari in there. Punishment for failing him. That's how Falicon would regard Mari's not being able to stop me from walking away from his second try at grabbing me. Wouldn't surprise me if Falicon helped his thugs work on Mari. He fancies himself one of the rough boys under that veneer."

"He does indeed," Juy said softly. "And he'd get a sick kick out of making sure we both came here to get the full shock of seeing what he'd done. A way of getting even with each of us."

Falicon might consider that it evened matters between him and Commissaire Juy—but I doubted that he'd feel it finished settling his score with me.

"All right," Juy said, "I was very nice at lunch and didn't press you to explain your interest in the Falicons. Now I press. Tell me why he wanted to get his hands on you. What's going on between you and them?"

"It's very simple—from my end at least. A young, good-looking woman who said her name was Helene came to see me. She wouldn't tell me her last name. She thought she was being followed and she wanted me to stop whoever was following her—long enough for her to get out of this area. That seemed easy enough, and she paid enough for it, up front. So I tailed her and watched for someone else doing the same.''

"You took a client and don't even know her name?"

"I know her first name. If she told me the truth about that. And I told you, she didn't give her last name."

It was a relief to be able to tell Juy the truth, about something. He hadn't asked if I'd gotten her last name any other way.

"And it didn't seem to matter," I went on, "for a job that short and uncomplicated. I figured it was just some husband or lover she was trying to shake off. Well, I did spot someone else tailing her. Roland Mari. I managed to grab him from behind, before he could get his gun out. And I held him till she jumped into a cab and disappeared. I think she went to the airport and caught a plane, but I'm not sure."

Commissaire Juy's eyes weren't believing any of this. "Mari must have been sore about you doing that to him," he said stonily.

"He didn't like it," I agreed. "And then, this morning, I got a call from Léon Falicon, asking me over to his place. He said he had a job for me. Coming right after what had happened with Mari, I guessed there was a connection. That Mari worked for the Falicons. Which turned out true. I was curious. But I've heard enough about them to know they can be bad news. So I arranged for you to call there, just in case. I do owe you a big one for that."

"What did Falicon have to say to you?"

"Not much. He wouldn't tell me anything about the woman, but he did want to know my connections with her. And he didn't believe my simple story. He was sure I must know something about his business. He wanted to know what it was and how I'd learned it. There's a pet torturer he keeps around the house. Zayid is his name, all I know of it. Falicon was about to turn him loose on me when you phoned. After that, I was naturally interested in learning whatever you knew about the Falicons.''

Commissaire Juy's expression had remained patiently skeptical. ''You haven't told me a single thing I can use against the Falicons. Knowing Roland Mari worked for them gives me an excuse to question them. But that won't get me anywhere. I can't prove they know anything about what happened to Mari.''

''And,'' I added, ''you can't do anything about Falicon trying to grab and torture me. You've only got my word for that, and Reju's, against his.''

''And that isn't good enough, Sawyer. I had much more on them before, and couldn't make it stick.'' Juy grimaced. It almost looked like a smile. He leaned toward me slightly. ''I think you're holding out on me.''

''Nothing that would be of use to you at this point,'' I told him. That was fairly true.

''I think you're holding out on me,'' he repeated evenly. ''If I become sure of that you'll suffer for it. You know that.''

''I know it,'' I agreed.

''On the other hand, if you've come across something in whatever you're really up to that results in squashing Léon Falicon, I would like it—and you—very much.''

I considered it. ''Would you also figure it paid off the various favors I owe you?''

Commissaire Juy nodded.

''Barney Kavanagh,'' I said. ''The guy that took a bunch of Texas banks for a billion U.S. dollars, give or take a few million.''

''You don't have to explain to me who Kavanagh is,'' Juy snapped. I had his full attention.

''The Falicons—Old Spider and grandson—are hunting Kavanagh,'' I told him. ''I think they're very close to finding him. I think they're going to sell him protection—from themselves and everyone else. For a price that'll drain him dry while they keep him hidden, as their prisoner.''

''Where did you get this from?''

"Sources. Good ones. I'm not going to tell you who they are."

"Fritz Donhoff?"

I didn't say anything.

I watched Juy tasting what I'd just told him. The taste obviously gave him pleasure. "Interpol is after Kavanagh," he said reflectively, almost dreamily. "The American government is after him. International insurance firms and financial institutions are after him. If the Falicons get involved with him, our secret services couldn't protect them. Not this time."

"They wouldn't even try," I said. "Not against that much outside pressure. Not with the news media all over the world jumping on the story."

"You intend to pursue this?" Juy demanded.

"Oh yes."

"Because I can't. I'd get stopped before I got near to sinking my teeth into the Falicons." Juy was silent for a time, and then he added: "I can't even go aboard Léon Falicon's yacht, to see if I can find drugs or evidence of smuggling or anything else I could hurt them with. Not without first applying for official permission, which I can't justify and wouldn't get if I could."

"You've found out where the boat is."

"In the Garavan marina," Juy told me. He raised his hands a bit and looked at them. Maybe he wanted to use them on someone he knew he couldn't touch. He lowered his hands and said, very softly, "I want to see the Falicons squirming on a hook nobody can pull out of them. You have no idea how much I want that."

"Yes I do," I said. "I had made cases yanked out from under me, too."

"You can leave now," he told me. "I think you know why I'm letting you go."

"I'll try my best," I assured him. And meant it. What I'd seen inside that room wouldn't get out of my head.

"Do that," Commissaire Juy said, and went back into the room.

When I came out of the building it was night. A low cloud cover had come in over the city and there was a sharpening wind, but the air was still warm. The light from the front window of the café on the other side of the street shone on four men seated at one of its sidewalk tables.

It wasn't until I reached the pavement in front of the gutted hotel that I saw one of them was Léon Falicon.

He smiled as I walked across the street toward him.

⊠ 23 ⊠

ONE OF THE THREE MEN AT THE TABLE WITH HIM I ALREADY knew. The young guy who had enough confidence in his speed and markmanship to use a .22 caliber handgun.

The other two were muscle. Not the kind of muscle displayed by the two beauties who carried The Old Spider around and kept her company. These two were heavy slabs of bone and beef, with dull expressions and slime for brains. Members of the same subspecies as the storm troopers who'd beaten old men and kicked pregnant women for the greater glory of the Third Reich. Incapable of experiencing any stronger emotions when smashing a human being than the brief pleasure they'd get out of crushing a beetle under a boot heel. Their eyes told you all about them. You can't outstare men with eyes like that. You can only avoid them or grab a club and pound them back into the dirt.

Léon Falicon's smile was bland. "What a surprise, meeting you again—here of all places." His voice wasn't bland. It was clogged with gloating mirth. He was back to being an actor in his own malignant comedy.

I stood and looked down at him until I was sure I could keep my own voice normal. "Come to watch the show you arranged?"

"Whatever do you mean?" Falicon asked with mocking puzzlement. "We're here because I have an appointment with

Roland Mari and this is where he suggested we meet. I intend to fire him," he added. "But he doesn't know that."

"No," I said tonelessly, "he doesn't."

The tough young marksman spoke up: "It was past time to get rid of Mari. He got old and scared. Turned to jelly soon as Jean-Marie Reju braced him."

I looked at him. "And you're not scared of Reju."

"Reju's got a reputation," he said, "but it was made when he was younger. It's a business for young pros. Like tennis. After thirty you're on your way down, fast. Reju ought to retire, before somebody retires him."

"Hang on to that thought," I advised him. "It reassures me that you won't reach thirty."

Falicon said, "This is an interesting discussion. Won't you sit down and join us?"

"I have a squeamish stomach," I told him. "Just standing this close to you makes me nauseous."

"I'm sorry you feel that way, Sawyer. Because I'm sure we'll be meeting again." The vindictive tenor behind Falicon's quiet words came through sharp and clear.

"Count on it," I said, and turned away from him.

The two hulks at his table had their hoggish eyes fixed on me, but I didn't have anything to say to them before I left. I didn't think they'd respond to any known human language.

I walked to the railroad station and got into the Fiat. After taking a number of unnecessary turnings, to make absolutely sure I wasn't tailed, I drove the Fiat to the car rental agency by the port and traded it for a Renault 5. I didn't think anyone had followed me from Falicon's table to the station, but couldn't afford to overlook any basic precaution from here on.

Drops of rain were beginning to leak out of the low night clouds and spatter the windshield when I drove the Renault east out of Nice. I turned on the windshield wipers and headed for Garavan to see what I might find inside Falicon's boat, *La Dolce Vita*.

The likelihood of finding anything there that I could use

was small. But another thing I couldn't afford to overlook now was any possible weapon that might come in handy against the Falicons.

I did not intend to spend the next weeks and years looking over my shoulder and worrying about ending up the way Roland Mari had.

There are some old, tired clichés around that can suddenly come to life on you. Like prevention is easier than cure. And the best defense is an immediate offense.

Get them before they get you.

You can't go any further southeast along the French Riviera than Garavan. It's a suburb between the town of Menton and the frontier. After that you are in Italy. That's why so many Italians stash their boats in Garavan's marina to escape the notice of their income tax snoopers. Locals call it the Italian yacht garage.

The rain had become a thin windy drizzle when I swung down the turnoff from the coast road into the marina below it. The loud ringing of hundreds of wind-whipped sailboat riggings rose to meet me. There was no sign of human activity on or around the rows of docks and the multitude of boats moored to them. The rain blurred the dim lights from the little dock lamps, leaving larger areas of heavy shadow than usual. I parked and got a cap and a windbreaker from my overnight bag, putting them on before starting my search of the docks.

Each one took time, though I only checked boats of the right size and shape. After touring five of the docks my jeans were wet through and my socks were getting soggy. Rain dripped off my cap and leaked inside the windbreaker's turned-up collar. The rain was warm but the drops that worked their way down my spine felt unpleasantly cold.

I didn't find *La Dolce Vita* until I was on the long breakwater that shields the marina from the sea. I stopped in darkness against the breakwater's high wall and observed it for a time. It was fifty feet long, built wide and solid. I couldn't hear anything from it through the clatter of all the rigging in the marina. But there didn't appear to be anyone aboard. The stern gangway was up, the flying bridge was a patch of dense shadow under its overhang, no light showed from inside the pilothouse and long cabin.

I moved through the breakwater shadows to it with my pistol in hand. Using my free hand, I pulled one of the yacht's stern lines until its transom was close enough. I stepped up onto its aft gunwale and down into the cockpit, from its transom bench to its rain-slick deck, instantly sinking into a crouch.

I stayed low as I went along the cockpit to the closed hatch to the pilothouse and cabin. When I reached it I felt for its lock to determine how much of a job it was going to be to pick it—and got a surprise. It didn't require any work with my lock pick. Somebody had been there before me and broken the lock open.

Break-and-entry burglars aren't a rarity at any marina along the Côte d'Azur. Anyone who'd come to rob this boat wasn't likely to be hanging around afterward. But I brought my gun up at the ready before sliding the hatch open with my left hand. I peered into the shadowed pilothouse and the inky blackness down in the main lounge. There was a small flashlight in a pocket of my windbreaker but I wasn't ready to use it yet. If anyone was in there it would only make me a better target. What was needed first was some exploration in the dark.

I was raising up to venture through the hatchway and down the steps when someone dropped from the flying bridge above me and landed heavily across my shoulders. A thick forearm locked across my throat and an enormously strong hand got a clamp on my gun wrist.

His weight twisted me off balance. We tumbled together down the steps inside, past the pilothouse to the carpeting of the lounge. I lost my gun hitting one of the steps on our way down. But the impact when we struck bottom broke the attacker's lock on my throat and wrist.

I clubbed him across the ear and broke all the way loose, surging to my feet in the interior darkness. He was up in the same instant, hands finding my neck and closing like a vise. I got both my forearms up inside his, broke his hold, and hit him in the midsection as hard as I could.

It was like hitting a thick board of hard oak, but he grunted and fell back a step. I went after him and ran into a heavy fist. It struck my temple and staggered me sideways with my brains ringing louder than all that rigging outside. He came after me, grabbing for my neck again. I twisted inside his arms and drove an elbow upward. It collided with the underside of his jaw. His murky figure stumbled backward and his feet tangled and he fell, hitting the floor hard, half inside the forward cabin.

He was trying to get his legs under him when I closed in. I got set to kick him in the head before he could rise all the way. Then I caught the flash of white on that head and stopped myself.

He was coming up off the floor at me when I snarled, "Hold it, Desiré! It's me, Sawyer. . . ."

⊠ 24 ⊠

THE NEAREST PLACE OPEN WAS THE GALION, OFF BY THE parking end of the marina. The walls and ceiling of its restaurant and bar were done in luxury imitation of an old-time wooden sailing ship. Two big tables in the restaurant had been pulled together to accommodate a group of late diners. Hard-drinking insurance men from the German part of Switzerland, down for a Riviera convention. The bar was a separate room and we were the only ones in it. The bartender had brought the drinks to our table and gone off into the restaurant to help the only waiter still on duty. I sipped my brandy and watched Desiré Brissac read the letter Ilona Szabo had written to him.

He held the page as though it were brittle and might disintegrate in his powerful fingers. His heavy shoulders hunched forward and the creases deepened in the tough, wide-boned face. It was a long time since he'd read Hungarian. His lips moved as he silently pronounced the words to himself.

He wore a too-large watch cap that hid most of his thick white hair. It showed only an edge of the bandaging. The surgical tape holding it in place had gotten dirty.

His dark-green zipper jacket, heavy-duty dungarees, and work boots had shed most of the rain. My own windbreaker had done a pretty good job and I'd gotten dry trousers, socks, and shoes from the car, changing in the Galion's washroom.

The brandy was helping to restore the inner man and lull the aching bruise on one side of my head while I watched Desiré and waited.

He must have reread the letter a couple times. Finally he folded it carefully and slipped it back into its envelope. He put it down beside his untouched pastis and gave me a troubled look. In my business you meet too many people with mild faces and dangerous eyes. Desiré had the opposite combination. Much less common, except among professional boxers.

"Do you know what's in the letter?" he asked me.

"I know she's worried about your safety and will love you forever but wants you out of her life. A Hungarian friend translated it for me."

"What did Ilona tell you about—us?"

"Only that she didn't want your wife to know about the letter—or about her."

He nodded to himself and seemed about to sink into some inner dialogue. I nudged him out of it: "Mireille's pretty good at holding on to her nerves, but she's badly scared. If you're going to leave her for this woman you ought to tell her what's going on and get it over with. And soon, before your daughter gets scared too."

"I have no intention of leaving Mireille," Desiré said.

I studied his craggy profile. "But you want it both ways. You're not going to take Ilona Szabo's advice. About getting out of *her* life."

"No." Desiré shook his head slowly, like an aggravated bear. "I have already done too much of that."

I got a feeling I'd had before. Only this time it was stronger. An intimation that I'd been going on false assumptions.

"You'll lose Ilona anyway," I told him with deliberate harshness. "Right now she's got a rich old guy taking care of her. She may be crazy about you but in the long run you'd need real money of your own to go on screwing her. Maybe she's not exactly a hooker but she is play for pay."

I saw the way his expression changed as his hands began

clenching into fists. "Calm down," I said in a gentler tone. "I'm not an enemy. According to my information your family name in Hungary was Kormany. Is that true?"

Desiré knew what I was getting at. He looked down at his fists and worked at getting them unclenched. The fingers wouldn't uncurl entirely. He placed his palms flat on the table and pressed his blunt fingertips against the wood. Without looking up he said: "Kormany—yes."

"But Ilona Szabo *is* your daughter."

His hands finally opened all the way. He picked up his pastis and took a swallow. Then he set the glass down slowly and said it:

"Yes. Her mother took back her own family name some years after I left—though she never divorced me."

"You cannot comprehend what it is like to be forced into a choice like the one I had to make," Desiré said after a time. "The pain of the decision. The guilt after carrying it out. A guilt you never get rid of. No one can understand that. Except other exiles who have deserted their families because it was the only way out of prison. That is what Hungary had become, in that time. A prison. And the worst of it was that I was one of the prison guards."

He took another drink from his glass. "I told you once about being part of a unit trained to deal with guerrillas, riots, and insurgents. In fact I was a sergeant. But we didn't get much to do except more training operations. There were no real guerrillas around. And no riots or insurgency. The country was tamed, on the surface at least, after the Russian tanks broke the attempt at limited independence in 1956.

"One day we were assigned to handle a demonstration in Budapest. By people who wanted permission to leave the country. A peaceful demonstration—but our orders were to break heads. Two of the demonstrators died and most of the rest had to be hospitalized. Our commanding officer reported me for failure to carry out the orders with sufficient enthusiasm. I was punished by being sent to join the patrols guarding the Hungarian frontier with Austria.''

''According to the news,'' I said, ''Hungary is now tearing down the barbed wire along that frontier.''

''Something no one could have envisioned happening at the time I was there,'' Desiré said grimly. ''The regime was steadily tightening its grip back then. A lot of that wire carried electrical currents of lethal voltage. There were alarm systems all along the frontier, in addition to our patrols. Sometimes we were ordered to shoot anyone we spotted trying to cross over. Other times we were told to capture as many as we could. So they could be taken to prison. And tortured into giving names of other dissidents.''

He finished off his pastis before continuing. ''I saw one escaper I'd helped to catch, a year later. One of those they'd released, as a warning to others. He was disfigured and his mind was vague. He'd keep forgetting whatever he was saying and break down into incomprehensible stuttering. . . .''

Desiré grabbed up his glass and looked puzzled when he found it was empty. He stood up and stomped over to the restaurant doorway and shouted for another pastis. The bartender came in and made him one at the bar, and looked at me. I shook my head. The bartender went back into the restaurant. Desiré returned to our table with his pastis. He took a very small sip and put it aside.

''I had a wife,'' he said, looking at the table more than at me. ''Her name was—and is—Klara. We had a daughter. Ilonka—she was seven at that time. I told Klara I wanted us to get out of Hungary. I knew that frontier well enough by then to have figured out ways it could be done. But Klara wouldn't hear of it. Her father was a party functionary. My desire to escape was treason in her eyes. She told me that if I ever brought up the subject again she would report me to the police.''

Desiré told me that as though he still remembered her exact words.

''So you escaped alone,'' I said.

He nodded. "Leaving my wife and child behind—forever. I thought of taking Ilonka with me. But that would have been like kidnapping her. She wasn't able to make the decision for herself yet. Also, a child that young belongs with its mother. And I didn't know what my life would be, in the west. Whether I would be able to take care of her, make a decent living at some totally new occupation . . ." His hands were clenching again. "At any rate, those were my excuses—for leaving Ilonka in Hungary with Klara."

"And taking the guilt with you, instead."

Desiré got out a pack of cigarettes and lit one. His thick fingers were trembling a little.

"I stayed in Austria for a time," he resumed, "doing odd jobs. But I wasn't comfortable in spirit there. It was too close to what I'd left, perhaps. And too full of unrepentent Nazis—worse in their beliefs, even if unable to act them out, than the kind of people I'd run away from. So eventually I came to France. And applied for political asylum. Officials in Paris considered my request—and my background. Finally they told me I could have what I wanted, plus French citizenship, if I joined the army. And passed on everything I knew about Hungarian antiguerrilla and counterinsurgency methods."

Desiré crushed out his cigarette and looked at his pastis but didn't touch it. "After my years in the French army were over I began searching again for some sort of profession. I tried a number that didn't feel right for me. Until I came down to the *Midi* and went to work for Mireille's father as a gardener."

"And fell for Mireille," I put in.

He almost smiled. "Yes."

"But you never got around to telling her you already had a wife and child."

His smile faded. "You don't understand. My life in Hungary—that had come to seem like another life to me. Almost unreal. Except for the shame I still felt for having deserted my family. A shame I didn't want to reveal, to anyone. I told you, only those that circumstances have pushed into the same kind of shameful actions can ever understand.''

"That may be,'' I admitted.

"Also,'' he added wryly, "I was afraid. I was in love with Mireille and she was pregnant and I wanted to marry her. I didn't want her to know that I was—had been—a man capable of deserting his wife and child. The past was long ago and far away and it didn't seem possible any part of it would ever reach out to touch us. And I was afraid that if I said or did anything that delayed our marriage, Mireille might change her mind.''

"You were a damn fool. Mireille wouldn't have gone into shock if you'd told her the truth. She would have helped you work it out. The two of you still can.''

Desiré was studying his fists again. "What could I tell her? That she has never really been my wife, because I already had one when I married her? That our life together has been a lie and that our daughter Hugette is an illegitimate child?''

"You're living in a different century, Desiré,'' I told him impatiently. "Let's reserve your sense of guilt for another day. I need to know what's going on now. Ilona showed up in France, fully and spendidly grown, and you saw her. When and how and what the hell have the two of you gotten mixed up in?''

⊠ **25** ⊠

"SHE CAME OUT OF HUNGARY A FEW YEARS AGO. HUNGAR-
ians don't have to sneak across the frontier anymore. They
apply for permission to make a holiday visit to another country. Usually it's granted. Once out they can stay out; or go
back. As they wish. Ilonka wanted to see what life in France
was like. And, she wanted to find me—to see what I was
like. So she asked for and got the permission, and took a
plane from Budapest to Paris. That simple."

A trace of bitterness had come into Desiré's voice: "If I
had known things were going to change like that, perhaps I
would have been patient and waited all the years between.
But probably not . . ."

I prodded him back to the subject: "How did Ilona know
you were in France?"

"Shortly after I first arrived in Paris I sent Klara a letter.
Trying to excuse what I had done, and giving the address I
was living at then. In case she wanted to answer my letter.
She didn't, and I never wrote her again. Ilonka says her
mother tore up my letter and threw it in a wastebasket. After
Klara left, Ilonka took out all the pieces and kept them. She
still had them with her when she came to France. When she'd
saved enough from her earnings in Paris she hired a private
detective to find me. Starting with my original address I suppose it was fairly easy for him to follow the course of my
life, from my arrival in France to now."

"He didn't have to go to all that trouble," I said. "Ilona would have told him your Hungarian name. The change from that to Desiré Brissac is on file in Paris. Once he had the right name he could get the rest in half an hour. Your current driver's license and vehicle ownership are on file too. With your present address. I doubt if the whole job took him more than a day."

"This detective told Ilonka it took him more than a week," Desiré said. "He charged her for eight days' work."

"Not all private detectives are as scrupulously honorable as I am."

Desiré managed a slight smile. "She came down for a visit to the Riviera a few months later—this was a couple years ago. She rented a car and drove to Lucéram. People there gave her directions to my place and said I probably wouldn't be back there until late. I was doing a landscaping job at an estate near Vallauris at the time. Ilonka drove up our hill and waited off the road near the bottom of the track to the house.

"When I came back from work late that evening and drove up to the house she saw me and what I was driving. She didn't follow me to the house. Ilonka wanted to see me alone. She knew I'd married again—though not that I'd never gotten a divorce from her mother."

Which meant her detective was slipshod, on top of being a crook. A little more work would have shown that the records on Desiré Brissac—formerly Dezsö Kormany—contained no reference to a previous marriage or subsequent divorce.

"The next morning when I drove down to work," he said, "Ilonka was waiting near the bottom of the hill road. I didn't notice her car following me. Just before Vallauris I stopped and went into a bistro to get myself fully awake with a strong *café noir*. She came in and stood at the bar near me and ordered an *orange pressé*. And kept looking at me while she drank it. She said later I hadn't changed much from the father she remembered. But I didn't have any idea who she was.

"I smiled at her, the way you do when any good-looking

woman shows an interest in you. And I tried some of the usual remarks about the weather. She didn't say a word—and then suddenly she told me who she was. Just like that. 'I am your daughter, Ilonka.' And immediately turned away and walked out.''

The emotions of that moment came back and choked him. He had to take a couple deep breaths before continuing:

''I was stunned. By the time I ran out after Ilonka she was inside her car, waiting for me. I got in beside her and for a while we sat there and didn't say anything. Just looked at each other. Then she asked me why I had run away and left her. Klara had only told her I was a bad husband and father. Apparently that didn't humiliate her as much as my opinion of the government's oppressive policies. I explained to Ilonka, as best I could, what the circumstances had really been, back then. In the middle of my explanation she kissed me and began to cry. I took her in my arms and cried with her.''

Desiré choked up again. His eyes got a wet shine. I picked up his pastis and handed it to him. He took several small sips, and then sighed.

''We Hungarians,'' he said, ''are so horribly sentimental. Much more than the French. Even worse than Italians. As for your Americans, they would be too embarrassed to make a display of such feelings.''

''You'd be surprised how often that stereotype breaks down,'' I said. ''Did you level with Ilona about being a bigamist?''

''Not then. Later. I took a long break from my work in the middle of that day and had lunch with her in Juan-les-Pins. And Ilonka asked when I had gotten a divorce from her mother. I had to tell her the truth—to explain why I couldn't let her enter my life as fully as I wanted to. I would have had to tell Mireille who Ilonka was. And I—just couldn't. It tormented me, but Ilonka said it was all right. That she had her own life to live and that it would be enough if we simply met from time to time.''

''She sounds more adult than you,'' I said.

"Probably . . ." Desiré smiled tenderly. "Mireille says I never had my childhood—until after marrying her."

"How much did you see of Ilona after that?"

"We met a few times. When she came to this area. She would phone the bistro in Lucéram and leave a message for me, making it sound as though it was about work. We had lunch again twice. Once I wasn't on a job and we spent the entire day together."

"Did she talk about what she's been doing with her time in France?"

"Not much. Just that she did the same kind of work here as she had back home. As a physical therapist. And that she met more interesting people doing it here than she had there."

Apparently she hadn't told him about her old tycoon, Marius Lejon, and being cheated out of her part in his will. I finished off my brandy and put the glass aside. "All right, that fills me in on the background and brings us up to date." I gestured at his bandaged head. "What happened?"

"I didn't know she was back in this area until four days ago," Desiré said. "I had spent the day finding out what landscaping work was available along the coast. It was evening and I was driving back on the Lower Corniche, ready to head for home. Traffic was slow both ways. This Rolls-Royce went past me going in the opposite direction. You always look at a Rolls. Ilonka was in the front seat beside the man driving. I think she saw me at the same time. She had sunglasses tucked up on her head and she suddenly pulled them down over her eyes. But if she was trying to keep me from recognizing her it was too late. I recognized the character who was driving, too. Somebody I know and don't like. It worried me, seeing Ilonka with a man like that."

"Léon Falicon."

Desiré shot me a startled look. "That's right. How . . . ?"

"He the one you got your mercenary jobs through?"

He looked surprised again; but not as much this time. "A

couple of them, yes. In the Congo and Oman. Not the last one I ever went to. Morocco—I got that job through somebody else, a man in Marseilles.''

"The same one who sent Klaus Troestler and Eric Savart to Morocco?"

Desiré nodded. He was getting used to the fact that I knew more about him than he'd expected.

"Do they know Falicon?" I asked him.

"I don't think so. They always get their merc assignments from the same man in Marseilles."

That eased one thing that had bothered me. Klaus and Eric hadn't betrayed Desiré to Léon Falicon. If they'd contacted their man in Marseilles, they would have learned he didn't know where Desiré was. So they'd checked among their merc friends about a doctor and come up with Millo in l'Escarène as a possibility. A lot of Falicon's employees were mercenaries. They'd come to the same possibility in the same way.

Desiré said darkly, "I stopped having anything to do with Falicon after I got to know some things about him. His other businesses. And what he uses women for—in addition to his own pleasure. And the kind of men who work for him on a permanent basis. As evil as Falicon. You think I have old-fashioned attitudes, I know. But there *is* such a thing as evil."

"I wouldn't argue against that," I said. "I guess that makes me old-fashioned too."

But then, most cops and ex-cops are. They get that way from coping with the nightmare levels of humanity. It teaches you too much about what it is that lurks in the hearts of some men, and some women.

"I was able to turn my van around before the Rolls-Royce was out of sight," Desiré told me. "I followed it here. It went to the boat where you found me tonight. I stopped just before the breakwater and stayed inside my van, watching. Ilonka went aboard the boat with Falicon. Two other men got out of the back of the Rolls-Royce. One a very big man I don't know. The other I do. A man named Zayid."

"I've met him," I said. "A professional interrogator."

"When Falicon got me the assignment in Oman, he sent Zayid there too. That's another reason I never went back to Falicon. I saw some of the results of Zayid's methods."

Desiré wiped a hand across his mouth, trying to get rid of that memory's taste. "Zayid and the other man carried supplies from the Rolls-Royce to the boat. Enough food for a few days, I suppose. Then they returned to the breakwater and cast off the mooring lines when Falicon started the boat's engines.

"I didn't know what I should do. I'd neglected my responsibilities to Ilonka too long to suddenly claim the rights of a worried father now. But I couldn't stand the thought of her being with someone as bad as that man. She can't know *how* bad he is."

I pointed at her letter on the table. "That says she does know."

"She can't," Desiré insisted, "or she wouldn't be with him."

"Maybe she didn't know, at first. And when she did find out she was already too involved in Falicon's schemes—and too afraid of what he would do to her if she tried to quit."

"I finally decided that must be it, too. But by then Falicon was steering the boat out of the marina. Nothing I could do. Ilonka was standing out on the deck looking back along the breakwater. Toward me. I'm sure she knew I was there—that she saw and recognized my van. The boat went off west along the coast. Zayid and the other man got into the Rolls and drove out of the marina."

"And you followed them."

"What else could I do? I didn't have a gun, and one of them might have. So I kept them in sight and waited for a chance to get one of them alone. So I could make him tell me what Falicon had Ilonka involved in and where he was taking her. So I could go there and try to help her."

"You push your luck too far," I told him.

"I deserted her," he said angrily, the anger directed entirely at himself. "And she is my daughter. I do have some obligation to her—finally."

I gestured at his bandaged head again. "And what did it lead you into—finally?"

Desiré had tailed the Rolls to Falicon's estate on Cap d'Antibes. Zayid and the other man took it inside. They came out in another, more modest car, and Desiré had tailed them again. To a restaurant in Golfe-Juan. After their dinner there they split up. Desiré followed Zayid, into an apartment building a few blocks from the restaurant. Zayid had unlocked one of the apartment doors and was opening it when he heard someone coming up behind him and turned and saw who it was. Desiré clobbered him, threw him inside, and went in after him. He was dragging Zayid off the floor and asking him where Falicon had taken his yacht to when a man came out of another room.

"A young guy," Desiré said. "With a pistol. A .22, it looked like."

"I think I've met him before, too," I said.

"I lifted Zayid all the way off the floor, trying to use him as a shield. But this young guy fired anyway. It couldn't have missed Zayid's head by more than an inch." Desiré's hand went up to touch his own head. "But it didn't miss mine."

That told me something. The boy with the .22 was probably almost as good as he thought he was.

"Definitely a .22," I told Desiré. "Anything bigger wouldn't have just gouged your skull, it would have broken it wide open."

"It was bad enough. I came to on the floor and couldn't remember falling. Though I couldn't have been out long. Zayid was still trying to get up off the floor where I'd dropped him when I was shot. The guy with the pistol was bending over me asking who I was. I hit him."

"Jesus . . ." Brave is one thing, foolhardy is another.

It had worked though. The .22 had gone off again, but missed as the shooter was knocked away and sprawled over Zayid. But Desiré had been dazed and awkwardly positioned when he threw the punch. The guy didn't drop his gun, and he was shaking his head to clear his vision when Desiré went out the door.

"I don't know how I made it the block and a half to where I'd left the van," he told me. "I was plowing through fog all the way."

"Fear," I said. "The greatest adrenaline booster there is."

"That's probably it—I was scared enough. I dragged myself into the back of the van and passed out. I don't know if they came out looking for me. According to my watch it was over two hours before I came out of it. I got into the front seat and went to get my head taken care of. Not a hospital; they'd notify the police and I couldn't explain because I didn't want Ilonka brought into it. I don't know what she's involved in or how deeply."

So he'd driven up to l'Escarène. He'd met Millo, the former but still secretly practicing doctor, through an ex-soldier he'd taken up there after the man had been hurt in a knife fight. He'd had to stop often along the way to fight off that fog trying to swamp his head. But he'd made it; and hidden his van behind bushes just out of town. And made it the rest of the way to Millo's house on foot. And fallen unconscious when he was let in.

"When I woke up it was morning and my head was cleaned, stitched, and bandaged. I wanted to use Millo's phone to call Mireille and tell her not to worry about me. But Millo wouldn't let me. He was afraid of his phone, sure it was tapped. That's how they'd gotten him for illegal abortions. But I did get him to call her for me, from an outside phone."

He'd slept through most of that day. When he'd wakened it was night and there were angry voices downstairs.

"I went down as quiet as I could and took a peek around the corner. There were two of them with Millo. One was another of Falicon's bunch. A hood named Gally. The second one was an ugly kid. Redhead. He had an automatic rifle, compact version. Gally was holding a pistol with a silencer. Millo was telling them he'd never heard of me, and if they didn't get out he'd yell for the police. They wanted him to show them through the house. He tried to get indignant and refuse. The redhead pulled a knife and threatened to slice his face up if he didn't cooperate.''

That was the moment when I'd come along and knocked at Millo's door. Gally had switched off the lights inside and seconds later Millo had screamed. He must have tried to use the sudden darkness to escape them. All it bought him was a knife in the gut.

Desiré slipped upstairs and felt through Millo's drawers for a gun. Not finding any, he sneaked back down. The two were still there, arguing in whispers. Gally was afraid the knock had been the police. Max-Emile, the redhead, said the police would have kept knocking. He thought it had been a visitor who'd given up and gone away, and that they ought to search the rest of the place before leaving.

"I couldn't make out where they were in the dark," Desiré said. "So I just ran straight through the living room, toward that open patio out back. I bumped into somebody and a silenced gun went off near me. Somebody grabbed me and I got hold of his head and twisted it, hard, and he went down.''

Gally—of the broken neck.

Desiré had gotten back to his van and driven to the apartment of the friend he'd once taken to Millo after a knife fight. He'd spent the night with him, and in the morning the friend had gone out and found him a small revolver. It had been in his pocket when he'd come to the Garavan marina to see if Falicon's yacht had come back.

"It had, but Ilonka wasn't on it. Nobody was. The door to the inside was locked. So I went to Cap d'Antibes and tried to watch Falicon's place from down the road. But the guard patrol came along and made me go away.''

He'd returned to the marina, and when it was dark he'd

broken into the boat and prepared to wait for someone to come along and board it. Someone who could tell him where Ilona was. If they came in numbers he had the gun. But the one who'd come along had been me—though he hadn't recognized me in the rainy darkness.

"At least," I said, "you didn't use that gun on me."

"I thought I could handle just one man without it. I wanted to question, not shoot."

"I'm glad that was your thinking," I said, and touched the bruise over my ear. And wincked.

Desiré winced too, in sympathy. "I'm sorry—I couldn't see it was *you*."

"Don't add me to your pile of guilt," I told him sharply. "You cannot be responsible for all the misery in this world. Nobody can."

"No," he agreed, "not even God."

"I think He may have finally quit trying," I said. "Just walked off a while back and gave us all up as an error in programming."

⊠ 26 ⊠

I TOOK DESIRÉ TO A DISCREET DOCTOR I KNEW IN BEAULIEU. She cleaned his wound, pronounced the stitches to be intact, and put on a new, smaller bandage. She promised not to notify the authorities and I promised her a healthy check. We left her and spent the night in one of Nice's medium-priced hotels.

I had offered to take Desiré to Crow's place so he could see Mireille and Hugette. He didn't want to. He wasn't ready to talk to Mireille about what he'd been doing. And why.

"I still don't know what I'm going to say to her about that," he told me nervously. "My mind isn't clear enough to handle that yet. It won't be until Ilonka is safe. I owe Ilonka that much, at least. To find her and help her, first. I need your help for that, I realize now. Whatever it costs, I can raise it. Falicon isn't the only merc broker around. It will take time, but I'll pay you."

I told him we'd talk about what he owed me and how he would get the money after I got results. Ilona's ring hadn't used up all of its value yet, though it was getting close. And I had my own reason for wanting to find her. I hadn't discovered anything aboard *La Dolce Vita* that I or Commissaire Juy could use as a weapon against the Falicons. That left Ilona as one of the only two potential weapons I could think of.

The other being Raymond Hayes. Her current aging lover.

Uncle of fugitive billionaire Barney Kavanagh. And she was the route to both of them.

I phoned the Ruyters from our hotel room. Bill answered. He said there'd been no messages for me; and added pointedly that he and Judith were just about to go to bed. I promised not to call again until a reasonable hour in the morning.

Desiré passed out as soon as he finished a bath and stretched out on his twin bed. I didn't. I lay on my bed for an hour and stared at the dark ceiling. Putting together a probable—or at least possible—timetable for Ilona and Léon Falicon and his yacht. I decided it could go like this:

La Dolce Vita had gone west from the Garavan marina, along the coast. Past my place, most likely. However far they'd gone, Falicon would have taken the boat into some other marina when night came. Maybe late. He'd make a phone call from there, either that night or next morning. To his estate headquarters. Just to check on developments. They would have told him about Desiré Brissac trying to find out where he was with the boat. It couldn't be the first time the Falicons had had to deal with people trying to spy on what they were doing. He would have given orders to search for Desiré, find him, and bring him in for questioning. Or, if that couldn't be managed, to simply kill him.

Ilona was either around him when he made that phone call, and heard part of it, or he told her a little about it afterward. Not knowing she was Desiré's daughter.

Falicon wouldn't have been too worried at that point. It would still have seemed an easy problem to solve. He wouldn't have been in a rush, when he sailed back east along the coast. And there was no way Ilona could send a warning to her father—until Falicon had anchored off the cove below my place.

I'd give odds that Ilona had persuaded him to stop there. And done a determined job of relaxing Falicon enough for him to fall asleep. So she could swim ashore and write the letter for me to deliver.

It all felt right. Experience had taught me how often things that felt perfect just before you fell asleep turned out to be very wrong. I was pretty sure, however, that I wasn't far off this time.

After breakfast next morning I phoned the Ruyters again. This time I got Judith. She told me Dixon Chess had phoned their number an hour after I had last night. "Waking us up," she added, not at all pleased.

I said I was sorry about that, and she gave me the message. Dixon Chess had asked that I call his apartment this morning—but not before eleven.

It was nine-thirty. I called him anyway. He came on the line sounding groggy and grumpy and said to call him back later.

"No," I told him. "I can't. Tell me what you found out and I'll let you go back to sleep."

He made a martyred sound and said, "Wait. . . ." He went off somewhere and when he came back on he sounded a little better: "Your Raymond Hayes checked into a pricey hotel suite in Cannes two weeks ago." He named one of the best hotels there. "With a young woman. Whose first name, according to what one of my spies there overheard, is Ilona. Would that happen to be the Ilona Szabo you were so interested in? I do suspect that."

I didn't say anything, and after a bit he went on: "Mr. Hayes left the hotel four days ago, but did not check out. He kept his suite and young Ilona remained there awaiting his return. Hayes came back late yesterday morning," Dixon Chess finished. "I'm told that he and Ilona had a lengthy and probably passionate lunchtime siesta in their suite to celebrate his return to her. However, you can't always put your faith in gossip. Have I discharged my debt to you?"

"Yes—thank you, Dixon."

I was getting ready to hang up when he said, "In that case I must tell you that Raymond Hayes and his Ilona checked out of the hotel last evening."

I registered the undertone in that. "But you know where they went."

"Yep—because Hayes made the arrangements through one of my people at the hotel's travel desk. Who won't tell you a thing, because I said not to. I imagine you can find out where they went some other way. But it will cost you time and effort."

"You are a son of a bitch, Dixon."

"You betcha. And I got you by the balls, sweetheart. If you want me to tell you where they took off for, it'll be your turn to owe *me* a favor. A big, fat, juicy one. Agreed?"

"Agreed," I said.

He told me where Raymond Hayes and Ilona Szabo had gone.

⊠ **27** ⊠

BY NIGHT OR DAY THE MEETING PLACE OF THE DEAD—THE Djemaa el Fna—pulses with a noisy, crowded exuberance that has a tang of ancient mystery and intangible danger behind its merriment. Times Square and Piccadilly Circus at their busiest are sedate and underpopulated by comparison. It is almost a thousand years ago that Marrakesh emerged as the terminus for the long caravans from the south: coming out of the Niger jungles, across the Sahara, and over the Atlas Mountains to the greatest marketplace in Africa. Djemaa el Fna is the heart of the labyrinthine old city.

The freshly severed heads that Moroccan warrior-rulers used to stick up on poles around that vast, irregular square are gone. But the throngs of natives and travelers from all of northwest Africa—Berbers, Arabs, Senegalese, Tuaregs, Sudanese, and odd mixtures of any of these—still congregate there. The tourists from Europe and America get engulfed by that multitude.

The Residence de Laplace, on one edge of the Djemaa el Fna, isn't a hotel for Europeans or Americans. Some do occasionally find their way up its confusing stairways to the hotel's rooftop restaurant, the Fleur de la Place. This night Desiré and I were the only ones.

A slim man in a black nylon suit and crisp white shirt shared the roof-edge table with us. Captain Hafidi, an intelligence officer Desiré had gotten to know during his stint as a mercenary in Morocco. Desiré was not sure if Captain Hafidi's authority derived from the police or the military. Or both—in Morocco the two often merge, as they do in France.

"It would be difficult," Captain Hafidi said, taking a sip of his orange juice and looking up from the two snapshot-sized photos I'd placed on our table before him. Sonia's picture of Ilona. And the head-and-shoulders shot of Raymond Hayes that Fritz had sent me. Hayes matched the descriptions I'd gotten of him. Distinguished looking and rather handsome for his age. The face firm, without excess fat. Salt-and-pepper hair and an engaging smile.

"They arrived late last night on a Royal Air Maroc flight from Nice," I said. "They had reservations at the Hotel Mamounia. Connecting bedrooms. They checked in under their true names. I've printed those on the backs of those photographs."

I took a long swallow from my own glass of orange juice. The heat this far below the Mediterranean coastline kept drying me out. Captain Hafidi politely refilled my glass from the big pitcher on our table, and I thanked him. Desiré hadn't touched his glass. He seemed as unaffected as the intelligence captain by the heat. He sat with his fists on the table, holding his impatience and worry under stoic control.

"Late this afternoon," I went on, "Hayes rented a car through the hotel. A new Volvo 440. White. They went off in it." That would have been about the time the flight carrying Desiré and me had arrived at the airport outside Marrakesh. "Hayes told the hotel to hold the rooms for them, because he wasn't sure when they would be back. Perhaps tomorrow, but it might not be for three or four days. That means the two of them have left Marrakesh." I gave Captain Hafidi a slip of paper. "This is the license number of their car."

"I would be interested," he said, "to know what your business is with these two people."

Desiré told him heavily: "It's not business. It is a family matter. She is my daughter."

"Ah," Captain Hafidi said gravely, "I see." He glanced again at the two photographs. The elderly man. The lovely young woman. Not married, since they didn't have the same last name. The man probably rich, since they had rooms in the most expensive hotel in the country.

Captain Hafidi looked back at Desiré with respectful concern. "I am sorry to learn this, my friend. I would wish to help you, if I can."

He meant it. Matters involving family honor are even more important to Moroccans than money and power. For centuries tribes warred against each other for wealth. But entire tribes had been slaughtered over incidents as small as a man looking overlong at a pair of inviting eyes above an unmarried girl's veil.

"But," he added, "it *would* be difficult."

"You have a description of their car and its license," I said. "There aren't that many roads for normal automobiles this far south. And even fewer good hotels outside the city—of the standard Raymond Hayes is used to. All you'd have to do would be to ask your police in this part of the country to make routine checks."

"It would involve much time and effort." With studied carelessness, Captain Hafidi threw away the punch line: "Not to mention the expense."

"We expect to compensate you for expenses," I told him, and added firmly, "Within reason, of course. We are not rich men."

"That is unfortunate. A misfortune I share."

An underplayed swerve into haggling over his price. Moroccans get a kick out of hard bargaining, win or lose. A day spent working for profit is boring unless spiced by frequent duels of wits and wills that you can recount, in detail, to friends over an evening's mint tea.

"Contact your colleagues at the Moroccan embassy in Paris," I said. "Have them get in touch with my partner there. He'll assure them that your expenses will be paid. Within reason," I repeated. "My partner's name is Fritz

Donhoff. If your people in Paris don't already know of him, they should. A little checking around will convince them he is a man to trust. Also that he is an extremely valuable man to know.''

"You are lucky. A partner like that can be more useful than immediate gain.''

"True. And not only as a partner.''

Captain Hafidi thought about that. "So—we will postpone discussing my expenses until after we see what develops.''

An extraordinary concession.

He put the photographs in his pocket as the waiter came out of the kitchen with our dinners. The same for all three of us. Couscous with *méchoui*. Captain Hafidi had recommended it. He had good taste. It was superb. It had to be. Most of the customers of the Fleur de la Place were natives who knew the difference, not tourists.

While we ate Captain Hafidi talked about the barrier being completed along the Southern Military Zone. A sand wall, more than a thousand miles in length, equipped with the latest antipersonnel radar and seismic sensors. He thought it would prove an effective shield against Polisario Front rebels, making most of the antiguerrilla tactics Desiré had taught unnecessary. Desiré thought the long barrier would be about as effective as the French Maginot Line had been against the Nazi blitzkrieg. Small talk. I let my attention wander to the outsized square five stories below our table.

Little lights flickered in its spread of darkness. The kerosene lamps of outdoor tooth-pullers, barbers and soothsayers, of acrobats, dancers and snake charmers. Smoke rose from a dozen cook-fires turning out quick, cheap snacks for the nightly mob. Thousands of murky figures milled around on the square's hard-packed dirt, raising a haze of dust that mingled with the smoke. Taxis, camels and donkeys detoured slowly around them.

From somewhere in Djemaa el Fna's darker areas came the booming of African drums and the tinkling of watersellers' bells. Up on our well-lit roof the restaurant's cassette player went from a Charlie Parker number into Dave Brubeck's *Time Out*. Morocco is a land of contrasts that somehow blend rather well. Through the open kitchen door I could see the woman who was washing the dishes. She had a tattooed forehead and wore a veil, T-shirt, and stretch jeans. Our waiter was a fair-skinned, sandy-haired man with eyes like black olives. Captain Hafidi had a very dark complexion and green eyes.

We were having our mint teas after the dinner when I told him, "There is somebody else I'd like you to check on for me. His name is Léon Falicon. If he comes to Marrakesh I want to know about it."

An hour and a half later I knew.

The Old Spider's grandson was already here.

I GOT THE FIRST PART OF THE NEWS FROM COMMISSAIRE JUY, way off on the other side of the Mediterranean. There was a message to call him waiting when I came back alone to our hotel, the Ibn Batouta just off Avenue Mohammed V. I made the call from the room I shared with Desiré. It took almost half an hour to go through.

"Léon Falicon took a plane out of Nice International a couple hours after you did," Juy told me when he came on the line. "He flew to Marseilles and changed to a flight going to Marrakesh via Casablanca."

He read me the names of other men who'd been on the same two flights—Nice to Marseilles, and Marseilles to Marrakesh. None of the names meant anything to either of us. But some of them were certain to be Falicon employees. I was equally sure that other men working for him would have already reached Morocco before him. Perhaps coming on the same plane that had brought Ilona Szabo and Raymond Hayes.

If Hayes was here for the reason I thought, Falicon wouldn't have let him wander around unwatched.

I phoned Captain Hafidi with Juy's information. Thirty-five minutes later he called me back with the rest of the news: Léon Falicon had rented a car on his arrival at the airport outside Marrakesh. A blue Peugeot 605, the big four-door luxury sedan for top executives. Captain Hafidi read its license number to me, and said: ''According to the agency employee who rented the car to him, this Falicon drove off in it together with four other men who arrived on the same flight. At this point he has not checked into any of our Marrakesh hotels. Unless he used a false passport.''

''Falicon's not in Marrakesh,'' I told him. ''He's gone off to wherever Raymond Hayes and Ilona Szabo went in their Volvo.''

''I am checking into that,'' he said. ''I am also thinking about this Falicon you are interested in having arrived in my country with four men described to me as dangerous looking. And I am wondering if this may develop into something of which I should take official notice.''

''If it does turn out that way,'' I promised him, ''I'll let you know.''

''Do that,'' Captain Hafidi said mildly. ''Because if you do not—and if it *is* something like that—you will find it difficult to leave this country. And our prisons, I regret to admit, are not pleasant.''

From what I'd heard about them, that was not a threat to be taken lightly.

I left the hotel and went around the corner to Avenue Mohammed V, the city's longest and widest street. The stretch between Place El Hourria and Place Abdel Mouman ben Ali runs through what is still called the European section, because the French who used to run most of Morocco lived there. It's a favorite stroll for Moroccans who have absorbed some Western ways. I walked through the wide, square-columned arcades and sat down at a sidewalk table.

It was outside a café named Le Petit Poucet—Tom Thumb. That was where Desiré and I had agreed to meet, if what he'd gone off to do didn't take him too late into the night. He was out hunting through the city for certain items that we might find ourselves needing. And for a special kind of man that we definitely would need.

The waiter came to my table. I ordered a tall glass, a bowl of ice, and a pitcher of orange juice. The pitcherful that I'd had most of over dinner had oozed out of me and evaporated. I was dehydrated again. The Sahara was off on the other side of the Atlas Mountains, but the land around Marrakesh was desert enough. The air was dry and sandy.

My orange juice arrived. I drained the first glass without putting it down. Then I settled for occasional sips while I watched the night's passing parade.

You see things on this stretch of Mohammed V that you don't often find out in the open elsewhere in Marrakesh. Young Moroccan women in native gowns altered to be figure clinging. Others in stylish Western dresses or butt-hugging Levi's and revealing blouses. You might even see some groups of men sharing their tables with their wives. Or a young married couple strolling along together—though never holding hands. In Muslim countries men only hold hands with other men or small children.

I had emptied my pitcher when Desiré joined me more than an hour later. He waved away a hovering waiter and told me, "All I want now is some sleep." He did look exhausted—but more from his unrelieved anxiety than the late hour.

"Did you get the things on our list?" I asked him.

"All of them. They're locked inside the trunk of our car, and the car is in a garage where nobody's going to touch it."

"You're sure about that point."

"Very sure," he said. "I paid the right price to the right people to make sure of it."

"What about the other thing. Somebody who is familiar with the country around here and to the south."

"There is one man who would be perfect. We got to know each other when I was here before. And according to people I've talked to he is definitely somewhere here in Marrakesh now. A Berber smuggler named Hammou ben Rehamna. There are not many corners of southern Morocco that he hasn't been in and out of. I haven't been able to locate where he is tonight. But I think I know how to find him in the morning."

"I hope," I said, "that he knows some useful people in all those corners he's been in and out of."

"You can be sure of that," Desiré said. "A smuggler cannot operate without that."

He was up and out very early next morning. I woke up only long enough to note his going. Then I went back to sleep for a while.

I was having breakfast in the room when he phoned later. "I have him," he said, and told me where to come.

I put through a call to Captain Hafidi's office first. He came through with a sleep-drugged voice and told me he'd just arrived for work and still didn't have any news for me. Both statements annoyed him.

I finished getting dressed and left the hotel.

Desiré and his Berber friend were waiting for me inside the extensive ruin of the sixteenth-century El Bedi Palace.

Hammou ben Rehamna wasn't anything like what I'd expected. When Desiré had last seen him he'd been in his late thirties, and he couldn't be much more than forty now. He looked an unhealthy sixty. Painfully thin, with sparse gray hair and weary eyes in a haggard face.

Desiré noticed the way I looked at Hammou ben Rehamna, and explained that the Berber had been caught during a smuggling venture and had spent a year and a half in the Marrakesh prison across from the European Cemetery. Hammou looked to me like he'd spent that year and a half in purgatory. It made me think uneasily of Captain Hafidi's warning to me.

"Don't worry about how I look," Hammou told me with a crooked smile that revealed missing teeth. "Desiré has explained what it is that you may want of me. Of that I am still capable. I know this land better than anyone else you could find—though I am not a smuggler any longer."

Now he worked as a guide at El Bedi, and most of his income depended on tips from the sightseers he showed through the ruins.

There were no sightseers around this early. The three of us walked alone over the broken mosaic tiles around one of the long basins that had once been filled with water to reflect palms and fruit trees and exotic songbirds in elaborate gilded cages. Above us storks flew to and from the big, untidy nests they'd built on the crumbling ramparts.

"You must understand something, however," Hammou ben Rehamna told us. "I can be your guide—but I won't do any fighting. For that my nerves are no longer steady enough. And my fear has become too strong."

Desiré patted his shoulder in sympathy. "But you can pick up others who have not suffered a similar affliction—if the need for such men should arise."

"In most areas, certainly. We Berbers are born warriors, hunters, and smugglers. But," Hammou added unhappily, placing one hand flat against his heart, "*I* am not what I was. I am ashamed to admit this, but it is so. We Berbers are used to open spaces. Too long in confinement crushes the spirit. Forever, I fear. It is like pulling the wings off a bee."

He looked away from Desiré, to see if I understood him too. I nodded. Hammou ben Rehamna was not the first bee I'd seen with its wings gone.

"You must understand something else," he told me in a different tone. "I have nine children. And a wife. Mouths to feed. I must not lose this job. I have to continue to work here until the moment that you actually require my services. Because I have to be sure they will take me back, afterward. Not be angry with me. When you do require me I will tell them that I am sick, and be able to stay away for a few days. But not before then."

We discussed the price for his services. Hammou started by demanding a sum well above anything he expected to settle for. It seemed reasonable enough to me. But I bargained him down, just a little, so he could feel he was back among the living—not someone I regarded as a charity case.

When we'd reached agreement I said, "But you do realize

that our need for you may come at any moment, quite suddenly.''

"That will not be a problem," Hammou ben Rehamna assured me. "I am able to get sick very suddenly. And very convincingly."

A hawk had appeared in the sky, high above us. It began swooping lower, looking for a chance to make a meal of a baby stork whose parents it could chase from a nest.

Four big storks launched awkwardly off the ruined ramparts. They were not at all awkward once they were in flight. They rose in formation and began to fly in a circle together below the hawk.

The hawk tried to dive down through that circle. One of the storks broke formation and sped toward its tail. The hawk whirled to counterattack and the stork flew away from it—while another executed the next feint at the hawk's rear. Again the hawk whirled in mid flight, and the second stork flapped away from it. By then the first stork had rejoined the circle and a third was taking its turn at attacking the enemy's rear.

I stood still in the middle of the courtyard of El Bedi and watched the coordinated hit-and-run tactics of the storks with clinical fascination. No stork is a match for a hawk. But each time the hawk turned on one tormenter there was another on its tail. Finally the hawk tired of it and flew off in search of an easier meal. The four storks kept circling up there, waiting to repeat the performance if the hawk came back for another try. It didn't.

I would have liked to believe I could outnumber Falicon like that, when the time came. I wished I wasn't so sure it was going to be the other way around.

Our need for Hammou ben Rehamna came two hours past noon that day. Captain Hafidi had received information about where Ilona, Hayes, and their rented Volvo could be found.

🞳 **29** 🞳

I DROVE SOUTHEAST OUT OF MARRAKESH AND UP INTO THE
High Atlas range via the Tizi n' Tichka, a long and arduous
route pioneered across the mountains by the ancient caravans. It's a paved road now, but you don't drive it at any real
speed. And you don't do much daydreaming about all the
gold and slaves, ivory and peacocks, that the caravans once
brought over that route. You try not to let yourself get hyp-
notized by the thought of how long it would take your car to
fall to the bottom of the incredible depths below each climbing hairpin turn. You concentrate on the road ahead as it
twists and climbs, twists and climbs.

When we reached the route's highest point there was snow
on the peaks rising higher to the east and west of us. Far
below to the south we could see the reddish-yellow mixture
of dust and heat haze that hovered over the Sahara Desert.

I began the descent toward it. The route down wasn't any
easier than the way up had been. But the four-door sedan
we'd rented, a two-year-old Lancia Thema, continued to handle it well. Hammou ben Rehamna was up front beside me
to give directions. Desiré was seated behind us. Our gear
was stowed away in the locked trunk. A practical car for our
requirements. It had gotten rough treatment from some previous renters and wasn't the fastest thing around. But on
roads like this one a Formula-One racing car couldn't have
made much better time.

175

We came down out of the mountains, onto the route's approach to the Sahara. The stark terrain became relatively level and there weren't enough vehicles using the road in either direction to be referred to as traffic. I was able to put on more speed.

It was a glaringly bright, blisteringly hot eight P.M., with a couple hours of daylight left, when we reached Ouarzazate. A low sprawling frontier town. Flat roofs and dusty streets of cement-hard dirt. A big sandy square full of people in robes and turbans wandering between the parked camels and trucks and the awning-shaded stalls of its open market. The town was a junction for the only four real roads in this region. One we'd just come south on. Two diverged further south into the desert. Hammou directed me to cut left and take the fourth one.

It led east, between the northern fringe of the Sahara and the rugged granite fingers reaching out of the southern flanks of the Atlas range. The land on both sides of us was red— from dark blood to golden pink in the lowering sun. In places the red was broken startlingly by the bright green of palm and fig groves.

In over an hour of driving this road I saw just one other car and an aged bus. There was living movement in different forms, though. Goats and sheep grazing at patches of dried-out weeds. Donkeys plodding along with heavy sacks tied across their backs, accompanied by men and women in traditional robes. Most of the women had tattooed faces and hands. None of them wore veils.

All of them were Berbers, Hammou informed me. South of the Atlas the country is sparsely inhabited; but what population there is, is predominantly Berber. Hammou was at home there. He sat up straighter beside me, taking deep breaths of the arid air, smelling something in it that I couldn't. He began to look younger.

"We are almost there," he told me.

I slowed a bit. "I want to stop before we're in sight of it," I reminded him.

"I will tell you when," Hammou said. "No problem." He watched the country ahead.

So did I—but I wouldn't recognize the landmarks that would warn Hammou before El-Kelaa-des-Mgouna appeared.

The road curved between low, almost barren hills. When we were past that I spotted a little Kasbah village in the distance off to our left. At first I mistook it for part of the long hill-slope against which it was built. The village and the slope were the same reddish brown. Like the few other villages we'd seen from this road, this one was made of sun-dried bricks fashioned out of mud from the ground around it.

"That's not El-Kelaa," Hammou told me. "Nobody lives in that one anymore. Very old. Too much of it began falling down." He gave a little shrug. "Time and weather. Erosion."

That explained why it had been especially hard to distinguish this village from the hill-slope at that distance. The buildings were dissolving back into the mud from which they came into being. When that happened in this part of the world people just moved out. It's easier to construct new adobe villages than to reconstruct old ones. And the building materials cost nothing.

Hammou pointed ahead. "Turn off there, to the right."

I didn't see it until we got there. A wide path led away from the road. I took it, following its meandering route to a low rise. There it curled left between small hills of red clay with spurs of stone protruding from them like cracked bones. The car churned up a trail of dust cloud behind us.

The paved road was out of sight when we came to a hill that was wider than the others, with a flattish top. It wasn't until we were very close that I saw this hill had once been a group of connected buildings. Only a few things near the top gave it away. Some broken rafters, a timber window lintel, part of a square tower's corner. Its base was a shapeless mound.

The path took us around it. On the other side a long, low hump of wall extended from the base. Behind it, in what had been a wide courtyard, were half a dozen low palm trees. Directed by Hammou, I drove through a break in the wall hump and parked under the palms.

"It will be safe to leave the car here," Hammou told me as he climbed out and stretched. "No one in this village steals. Besides, I will find a man who will guard it."

Desiré and I got out with Hammou. "Where is the village?" I asked him.

He pointed down a slope, toward where I judged the road should be. But the low hills blocked our view of anything down there.

Hammou pulled the hood of his old robe up from behind his neck to protect his head. It was almost sunset now, but the power of the sun remained intense.

"Don't worry if I don't come back quickly," he told us. "I know what must be done." He went off down the slope, at ease among his fellow Berbers. He knew El-Kelaa, and many of its inhabitants.

I unlocked our car trunk. Desiré and I lifted out our gear. One large sack for each of us, containing the items he had obtained from the Marrakesh black markets. The sacks were made of canvas, with leather straps. The kind many Moroccans from the countryside carry on journeys. Our sacks were old and worn from use and ingrained with years of grime. The first things we took out of them were two holstered pistols. Both were Lugers—making me think of Roland Mari, and what had been done to him by the people we were about to tangle with.

We fastened the holstered Lugers to our belts and took the next items from the sacks. *Djellabas*—hooded, loose-fitting robes of the same kind that Hammou wore. Like our canvas sacks, these too were old and much used, but fairly clean.

We put on the robes and changed our shoes for used leather sandals. When we pulled the hoods over our heads to shadow our faces we could pass, at a little distance, as a couple of natives. The citizens of El-Kelaa wouldn't be misled by the masquerade. They'd spot us for strangers. But it wasn't the people who belonged here that we had to be concerned about.

It was more than half an hour before Hammou returned. He had a man with him. The man was a full head taller than I am, and whipcord lean. He had a dark, weathered, ageless face with the profile and eyes of a hawk. There was a long sword in a leather scabbard hanging down his back from a shoulder thong. Its two-handed hilt stuck up past his ear.

"This man guards the village at night," Hammou told me. "He will see to it that no one goes near the car."

Every country village had someone like this to patrol it at night. So did most isolated hotels. Partly to keep out thieves from other areas. But mostly it was a hangover from the old days. When sudden, bloody attacks between tribes could be expected at any time. Tradition. With a tinge of nostalgia for a time when warfare was the national sport.

I asked the village guardian how much he wanted for his service. He looked at me in expressionless silence. Hammou said, "He doesn't speak any French." That became more common the further south you went. I told Hammou to ask the man for a price.

"I already have," he said, and named the price. "That is what he expects to be paid—not his bargaining offer. I have taken care of the bargaining for you."

Hammou was beginning to reveal a spirited initiative that our first meeting inside the ruins of El Bedi hadn't led me to expect. Maybe the ramparts around El Bedi reminded him too much of the walls of that prison.

I gave the swordsman half of the amount he wanted, and told Hammou, "I'll pay him the other half when we leave. Plus a bonus if the car hasn't been harmed in any way."

Hammou spoke rapidly in a Berber dialect. I didn't understand a word of it. The swordsman smiled and nodded. He drew a rag from inside his robe and began polishing the dust off our car as Hammou started back down the slope, motioning us to follow.

We slung our sacks over our shoulders and went after Hammou. Trying to look like part of the normal scenery.

"The hotel," Hammou said when I caught up with him, "is across the road from the house I am taking you to. You can watch it from there. The house belongs to a very old man named Youssef. I have known him a long, long time. He was once rich. He is not poor now. His house is very big. Most of his children live there. And their husbands and wives. And Youssef's grandchildren. But there is room enough for us, too, if you wish us to stay there tonight. Many, many rooms."

"How much does Youssef want for taking us in?"

Hammou named a small sum. "But he does it more for the excitement. You understand? He used to lead an interesting life. Now he is too old to go anywhere. All he can do is sit and watch his grandchildren grow. Your visit is something new and unexpected. A bit of spicy tonic for his old blood."

Desiré came up on Hammou's other side. "Is my daughter in the hotel?" he asked tightly.

"I think so," Hammou told him. "I went across the road and spoke a little with a man there named Salim, who is one of Youssef's sons-in-law. He works at the hotel as its night manager. Nine at night to nine in the morning. Salim told me Raymond Hayes is registered there—with his wife. A young, pretty woman. I showed Salim the picture of your daughter. He says it does look like the woman registered as Monsieur Hayes's wife."

"Is she at the hotel *now*?" Desiré demanded.

"I don't know. Salim was busy, he couldn't speak with me long enough."

I asked Hammou if Salim had mentioned other men being there with Ilona and Hayes.

"No, but you can both ask your questions of Salim yourself. Soon he will make an excuse at the hotel and come to

Youssef's house. But not for long. He will have to get back to his job.''

Desiré gave Hammou a thankful look. ''You deserve a bonus for this. A big one, I promise you that.''

I said, ''Save the promises until we're sure we'll be around to fulfill them.''

''*Inch'Allah,*'' Hammou said—if God wills it.

30

Sunset came while we were negotiating a chestnut grove that spread out behind the village. The daylight began to fade quickly after that, as it does in all desert areas. Hammou drew his hood back away from his head. Desiré and I did not.

A couple pretty women with colorful robes saw us as they came from their work in the grove. They lowered their baskets and watched us with open interest. Both smiled as we passed them, and one gave a little wave. Berber women have an independence and assurance you don't find among most other Muslims. It comes of their having the right to inherit property and divorce their husbands since long before the Arabs conquered their country. Berber origins go back into a dim past when the gods were female.

Hammou waved back at them and led us into the rear of the village through a series of high-walled alleys that grew dark as the last daylight went. When we emerged from the last alley a flashlight snapped on ahead, guiding us to the rear door of Youssef's house.

The flashlight was held by a tall, slender boy of about fourteen. One of Youssef's grandchildren, Hammou said. The boy opened the door and lit our way up an interior stairway. Inside, Youssef's house turned out to be several houses that had become interconnected. Corridors led off in different directions. Some into darkness, others toward areas glowing with the light of oil lamps and candles. Youssef's grandson took us through the maze to the entrance of a large reception room.

We left our sandals and sacks outside it. I took a small pair of powerful binoculars with night lenses from my sack and put it in a pocket of my robe before going in with the others. The few windows were wide open to let in the cooling night air. There was plenty of light from a scattering of oil lamps. Small rugs and large cushions were spread over the floor. A low divan stretched the length of one wall. Before it was a large round table, the same height, of hammered brass, with a big teapot and small cups on it. The room had no other furniture.

Two women sat on cushions against the wall across from the divan, regarding us with inscrutable expressions. They were old. But Youssef, sitting on the divan with his back supported by orange and yellow pillows, was much older. I guessed at ninety. He was of average height and had once been fat. The flesh had melted, leaving his skin drooping in empty folds. But his eyes were clear. He studied us with a childlike curiosity.

Hammou made the introductions in Berber. He'd told us that Youssef had once understood a good deal of French, but had forgotten most of it in his old age.

Youssef smiled brightly and spoke in the same dialect, looking at Desiré and me, spreading his hands wide. Hammou translated it to us: "He says you are welcome guests. He says that friendly foreigners on mysterious missions are a stimulation for the mind, and his house is yours."

"Tell him," Desiré said, "that we are honored and grateful for his hospitality."

Hammou translated and Youssef beamed. The old man pointed to the teapot and cups, and motioned for us to join him on the long divan. But when Hammou spoke to him again, his tone regretful, Youssef nodded and said something else.

"Fresh tea will be brewed," Hammou translated, "whenever your mysterious mission allows you time to rejoin him. He says it would give him pleasure to hear whatever you feel free to tell him about it at that time. New stories of intrigue reach his ears so seldom these days.''

"Tell him," I said, "that it will give us equal pleasure to tell him this story—when we know its ending.''

Youssef beamed again when told this.

The boy with the flashlight was waiting outside the room. We followed him along a corridor, up a short flight of steps, around a corner to a small, unlit room with a single window and no furniture other than a carpet and several cushions. The boy left us there. We crossed the dark room to the window.

It looked across the paved road at the new hotel that the government's ministry of tourism had built. Unlike most modern tourist hotels in all parts of the world, this one had the look of belonging in its setting. Except for its mint condition it could have been part of a native Kasbah. Three stories high, with a solid spread to it. Thick red-brown walls, crenellated turrets, surrounded by palms. Night had closed in fully now, and the hotel's lights were on. Electric lights, though no power lines reached this village.

"It's got its own generator," I said.

Hammou nodded. "But all the rooms have oil lamps and candles, as well. They turn the generator off at midnight. Earlier, if they don't have many clients.''

Desiré was looking at the parking area at one end of the hotel. "I don't see any white Volvo," he said tensely. "There is a big Peugeot but I don't think it is the right color. I can't make out the license number.''

I took out my binoculars and focused on the parked cars. He was right: the white Volvo Raymond Hayes had rented wasn't among them. I found the Peugeot—and its license plate. "No," I told Desiré, "it's not the one Léon Falicon took off from the airport in.''

"If Ilonka is *not* there we'll have to . . .''

"We'll know in a few minutes," I cut in. "You can't figure out the next move until we're sure."

He grabbed the binoculars from my hand and began using them for a slow scan of the hotel windows.

A short, slim man in a dark blazer and white trousers came out of the hotel's entrance and crossed the road in our direction. Hammou said, "That is Salim."

Desiré turned from the window to leave and meet him. But Hammou stopped him. "Wait. The boy will bring Salim to us, here."

While we waited he told us about Salim having gone to France to study engineering. "But when he came back he learned that Morocco has too many young engineers. And not enough work for them. Since he understands some German and English, as well as his perfect French, the hotel chain offered him the job here. He had to accept, but he has never been happy with it. He says it makes him feel like people's servant."

We saw the boy's flashlight before we saw him. He arrived with Salim, a handsome, dignified man in his early thirties. The boy left him with us and went back into the corridor to wait. Hammou introduced us to Salim. Desiré broke into the middle of it:

"Has my daughter gone away? The young woman Hayes registered as his wife?"

"No," Salim told him. "She is there. In the hotel."

Desiré turned quickly to look across at the hotel again.

I asked Salim, "*Where* in the hotel?"

"In the suite her husband took, I believe. Probably with those two friends of Mr. Hayes. The two who remained behind with her when the other friends went away with Mr. Hayes." Salim hesitated uncertainly. "At least I assume they are all friends. But they have acted strangely."

"How many friends are there altogether?" I asked him.

"Nine. The first four arrived only shortly after Mr. Hayes and his wife. They took two rooms. The other five arrived late last night."

"And seven of them went away with Hayes," I said. "When?"

"Very early this morning. It was still dark. Only two hours after midnight." Salim hesitated again. "Another strange thing is the two men who remained here with Madame Hayes. They do not seem to make any use of the other two rooms. They stay in the suite with her. I know this from the maids. And from our room service. They do not make use of our restaurant. These two take their meals in the suite with Madame Hayes. So far they have never left there."

Desiré turned from the window. "Do you know when the ones who went away with Hayes are expected to return?" His voice was quiet and steady. Nerves under easy control. He knew where Ilona was now and was setting himself to act on that knowledge.

"Not exactly," Salim told him. "They paid the kitchen staff to pack enough cooked food and water to last two days. But one of them said if they were lucky they would be back by tonight."

I asked him about the cars they'd driven off in. They'd gone in two: Hayes's white Volvo and the big blue Peugeot that Falicon had rented at the airport. They'd left behind an Audi sedan that the first four of Falicon's men had arrived in.

I said, "We need to know the layout of your hotel. And where the Hayes suite fits into it."

Salim gave us that, with some prompting from us about a few of the details.

Desiré looked at me and said, "Let's go."

31

WE GAVE SALIM A FEW MINUTES BACK IN THE HOTEL. THEN we strolled across: three natives with the hoods of our *djellabas* covering our heads. Hammou stationed himself in shadow against a palm tree at the rear of the parking area. On watch for Hayes's Volvo and Falicon's Peugeot. If either came back while we were inside, Hammou would hurry in to Salim so we could be warned by a ringing of the phone in the Hayes suite. This much Hammou enjoyed contributing. But if it came to fighting, he meant what he'd said about not taking part in it.

Desiré and I went in a side door from the parking area. It was always locked after sunset, but Salim had unlocked it for us. We'd promised him to go about our task as quietly as possible. He hadn't seemed overly worried. He was sure he could give harmless explanations to any hotel guests who heard noises they couldn't identify.

We went up a rear fire-escape stairway. From the top floor a steel ladder anchored to the wall led up to a trapdoor in the flat roof. It was latched inside but there was no lock. Desiré unlatched it and I followed him out onto the roof. We took off our native robes and left them there.

Hayes had taken a top floor suite at the rear, where the hotel had its best view. Out over a shallow, cultivated valley with a lot of fruit trees, watered by irrigation ditches fed from a thin stream. On the other side of the valley moonlight bathed a spectacular Kasbah growing out of a low cliff. We took care to be quiet about moving in the direction of that view, though small sounds were unlikely to be heard in the rooms under us. The roof was as solidly constructed as the hotel's walls.

When we reached the rear edge of the roof the suite's spacious balcony was directly below. No one was using it at the moment. There was only a round white table with a large vase of flowers on it and four white chairs around it.

Salim had said each of the suite's two rooms had a big window and a separate wooden door to the balcony. Squares of light from both windows lay flat on the balcony's tile flooring as sharply etched as if they'd been stenciled there. But there was no light from the doors. That meant both were shut.

I went down first, cautiously lowering myself from the roof edge until my feet rested on the top railing at one end of the balcony. From there I stepped down silently onto the balcony floor, against the wall between the side railing and one of the closed doors.

Desiré was poised on the roof, ready to lower himself with the same care when I signaled him to, or to jump if that proved necessary. He'd wanted to be the first one down, but I had held out against it. First I wanted to find out what we were dealing with. His daughter was in there with two of Falicon's men, and there was no way of knowing what was happening between them. If it was bad Desiré might barge in too hastily.

I took the Luger from my belt holster. Another item from my sack was attached to it: a silencer. Going to my knees crawled along the wall past the closed door. The suite's first window was closed too. I stopped short of it, then moved my head just enough to peek inside.

I was looking into the suite's bedroom. It was furnished like a modern room in any European luxury hotel, but with some colorful Moroccan touches. The central piece was a large four-poster bed, with a woven canopy and quilt in the same red and black design.

Ilona Szabo lay on the bed wearing a shirt and slacks, her feet bare. She had one forearm across her eyes. Her left ankle was attached to one of the bed's foot posts by a pair of hand-cuffs.

Zayid, Léon Falicon's pet torture expert, stood by the bed smoking a thin cigar and looking Ilona up and down with anticipatory greed. He took the cigar out of his mouth and spoke to her. She pulled her arm away from her eyes and glared up at him defiantly, and spat a few words at him.

Zayid laughed and took a drag at his cigar, letting the smoke curl from his nostrils as he continued to look her over.

I crawled on to the next window. This one was wide open. Inside was the suite's sitting room. The young marksman who considered himself Falicon's rising ace stood in front of a small bar opening a bottle of spring water. He wore jeans, motorcycle boots, and an open-necked sport shirt. His .22 was in a shoulder holster that had been trimmed down to make for a quicker draw. Billy the Kid.

I was set to signal for Desiré to climb down when the balcony door to the suite's bedroom opened. Zayid stepped out to finish his cigar in the open night air.

In the same instant that he saw me Desiré jumped off the roof, coming down with his feet lashing out at Zayid's head and back.

I was up on my feet aiming the Luger through the open window before Desiré reached his target. The double thud of their hitting the balcony tiles made the guy at the bar swivel toward my window, whipping his .22 from its trimmed-down holster even before he saw me there.

He was very fast. But anybody vain enough to try building a reputation with a .22 has certain problems to cope with. It's an efficient tool for a muzzle-in-the-ear execution. In a sudden gunfight it's not much good unless and until you can get it aimed perfectly at one of your opponent's few very vital spots.

I squeezed the Luger's trigger before he could get that aim. The gun made a small cough and jumped slightly in my fist.

The shot went where I'd aimed. It slammed into his right shoulder and spun him off his feet. The .22 flew out of his hand, bounced on the thick carpet, and skidded under a sofa. He fell to his knees with a thin squeal of pain.

I looked along the balcony. Desiré was going in through the opened door to the bedroom. Zayid lay sprawled behind him and it was obvious he wasn't going to get up. Not ever. Chalk up another failure in a gentle gardener's efforts to achieve a harmless way of life.

I climbed through the sitting room window. The guy I'd shot sat on the floor leaning his good shoulder against the bar and touching his bloody shoulder very carefully with shaking fingers. Bones in the shoulder were smashed to hell. It must have hurt him badly. Tears ran down his cheeks.

"What's your name?" I asked him.

He started to curse at me but a spasm of pain broke it in mid-run. I found his .22 and tucked it in my belt as I went to look into the bedroom. Desiré had gone back onto the balcony. Ilona was sitting up on the bed staring after him in shock, her ankle still shackled to the bed post.

She turned her head to stare at me. "You too . . ." she said, quietly and without emphasis, as though further wonders couldn't surprise her.

I jerked a thumb over my shoulder at the sitting room. "What's his name?"

"Lubrani," she told me as Desiré came back from his search of Zayid, carrying a handcuff key.

He sat on the bed to free her ankle from the post. Ilona studied her father's face in silence. When the cuffs were off she knelt up, wrapped her arms tightly around his neck, and began crying softly. Desiré put his arms around her back, awkwardly, and patted one of her shoulders. His back was to me so I couldn't see if he was crying with her.

I turned back into the sitting room, putting the Luger in its holster as I approached Lubrani. He took his hand away from his wrecked shoulder and cursed me again.

"You ought to thank me," I told him. "Unless you're too

stupid to understand what you just learned. If I can take you, you're in the wrong profession. You wouldn't have a prayer against somebody like Reju. Or anyone a rung lower, either.''

He looked like he wanted to curse me some more. But he suddenly passed out before getting to it.

Desiré came in from the bedroom. "We have to get out of here. I want Ilonka as far away as possible before Falicon and the others come back. On a plane to France would be perfect.''

"That may not be far enough," I said. "For you and me, either. Léon Falicon holds grudges. I saw what he did about one of them.''

"We can decide what to do about that after we're out of this country. That comes first—taking Ilonka away, out of immediate danger.''

Ilona had appeared in the doorway. "I'm not going away,'' she said, "not without Ray.''

I looked at her. "Ray—as in Raymond Hayes?''

She colored a little. "I'm sure Falicon intends to kill him. After he gets his hands on Ray's nephew—a man named Barney Kavanagh. I didn't realize before. I do now. And if Falicon kills Ray, it will be my fault.''

She had some of her father in her, after all.

"No it won't,'' Desiré told her. "It's his own fault. Nephew or not, Kavanagh is a giant thief. Hayes didn't have to have anything to do with him. He made that choice all by himself.''

"But he didn't know someone like Léon Falicon would be following his every move. Through *me*. Because I was with Ray. Because Ray loves me—and confided in me. And thought I cared for him, too.'' Ilona drew a breath and looked her father in the eyes. "And—I do. Very much.''

"What are you talking about, Ilonka?'' Desiré was close to shouting it. "The man's almost old enough to be your grandfather! He's ten years older than *me*!''

I'd seen him in a number of different roles by then. But the shocked, indignant father was a new one.

"That doesn't alter the way Ray and I feel about each other," she told him evenly. "I won't go anywhere until I know he is safe." And while he was struggling to digest that, she looked at me. "I need your help again. I know where they have taken Ray. I told you before that you can keep my ring. . . ."

"Anything I get for the diamonds in that ring," I said, "is already owed. I've been running on promises the last couple days."

"If it is diamonds you want," Ilona said, "there are many more. That is what Ray was taking to his nephew. A bag full of them. Worth about two million American dollars, he told me."

"Where?" I said.

"Where Ray and Falicon are," she told me—and having quietly dropped that tempting bit of lure in my lap she turned back to her father. "Dezsö," she said gently, "when you were afraid to have your new wife find out about me, I did what you asked of me, didn't I? What have I ever asked of *you*? Nothing—since I was a child of seven and you left me. Now I am asking you for something."

He stood rigid for a long moment and then I saw his heavy shoulders sag a little. He gave me a stumped look. "It is crazy, no?"

I didn't say that he was absolutely right. The possibility of coupling a critical imperative with an ulterior incentive was too intriguing. A chance to get the threat of Falicon off my back, and at the same time to maybe come out of this with a profit, after all.

◙ 32 ◙

IT HAD BEGUN ONE AFTERNOON IN PARIS WHEN RAYMOND
Hayes was having lunch at a brasserie near his apartment. A
man he didn't know sat down at his table. He told Hayes that
he had a message from his nephew Barney. He didn't seem
to know Kavanagh's last name. When Hayes mentioned it,
later in their short conversation, the stranger had become
briefly silent and thoughtful.

Ilona told me about it after we took her into Youssef's
house—where nobody would look for her if any of Falicon's
gang got back to the hotel while Desiré and I were gone. We
had brought Lubrani there too, still unconscious. One of the
women in Youssef's household had tended to Lubrani's
smashed shoulder, cleaning the wound and applying an oint-
ment that stopped the bleeding and was supposed to act
against infection as well. She had bandaged the shoulder as
neatly as any doctor. Lubrani was locked away in a window-
less cellar room now.

I had wired the ignition of the Audi that the gang had left
behind, and Desiré had driven off in it to dump Zayid's body
someplace where it would be unlikely to be found soon.
Hammou was on his way to another village in our rented
Thema. Looking for a man named Kateb who knew the place
we'd be going to much better than he did. Kateb was a young
smuggler who'd been Hammou's apprentice before he'd been
arrested—and he had grown up in this area.

Ilona and I were in the little room with the view across the road to the hotel. I had lit a wall-bracket candle that was close enough to be snuffed out in a hurry. Ilona sat on a large floor cushion with her back against the wall, smoking a Moroccan cigarette from one of the packs she'd bought at the hotel. I stood watch by the window.

Ilona flicked ash from her cigarette into a copper bowl on the floor beside her and said, "You don't have to keep looking out the window like that. I told you, if they haven't come back by now they won't until tomorrow, after daylight."

"You told me," I agreed. But I continued to stand by the window and give most of my attention to the road below while she gave me the rest of it:

The stranger who'd come to Hayes's brasserie table told him that his nephew needed some help and wanted to know if he could depend on his uncle for it. The man didn't know what kind of help. He'd only been told that it was a small thing, that wouldn't inconvenience Hayes much and for which he would be generously compensated.

Hayes's answer had been a flat no. He hadn't seen Barney Kavanagh in twenty years and was ashamed of what he'd done. He had no intention of getting himself into trouble by doing anything to help Kavanagh continue to evade the law. The only help he had to offer was advice that his nephew should give himself up to the American authorities.

His answer didn't disturb the stranger, who said he was merely an errand boy—paid to deliver the message and phone Hayes's answer to someone he'd once known briefly. But he'd also been told to say that Hayes's nephew begged him not to mention this attempted contact to anyone. Hayes promised he wouldn't, and the man went away.

My guess was that after the man discovered his errand job had something to do with the notorious Barney Kavanagh, he'd sold the information to the Falicons. Or had told someone else who'd done so. Because two days later Hayes met Léon Falicon at an art gallery *vernissage* to which he'd received an invitation. And that night, at a nightclub he went

to as Falicon's guest, he was introduced to several attractive
young women who were friends of Falicon. One of them was
Ilona Szabo—and Hayes had fallen for her, fast and hard.
Before long he was spending most of his days with her; and
all of his nights at her apartment. . . .

Ilona put out her cigarette and immediately lit another.
Her hands were steady, but it required an effort from her.
Like a drunk walking very carefully, trying to pretend he is
still sober. Her voice had the same kind of constricted steadi-
ness.

"Ray told me about Kavanagh trying to make contact with
him. Because he felt badly about how harsh his answer had
been. Kavanagh's mother was Ray's favorite sister and she
died young. At the end she asked Ray to look out for her
son, who was brilliant but unstable. Even as a teenager, Ray
says, Kavanagh was already showing an upsetting hunger for
money and contempt for the law. Ray promised his sister,
but after she died he lost track of his nephew. He worries
that he let her down. I told him not to think like that. Life
pulls people apart. He's not responsible for what Kavanagh
became."

She was silent for a while, her eyes narrowed, looking at
the opposite wall. "Ray is an easy man to get fond of," she
said softly. "He has been very good to me. . . . He is good
for me."

"But you kept reporting to Falicon," I said, to jar her out
of that.

"It didn't seem to be anything that would hurt Ray. Falicon told me he only wanted to locate Barney Kavanagh. So
he could meet him and work out a business arrangement with
him." Ilona crushed out her half-smoked cigarette in the
copper bowl and said savagely, "I didn't *care* what he did
with Kavanagh. Just another rich crook, stealing what belongs to other people . . ."

There hadn't actually been anything to report to Léon Falicon for a few weeks, she told me. Then, one evening when
Hayes was getting out of his car outside her apartment build-

ing, to pick her up for a dinner out, two men had grabbed him. They took him to another car. One of the men got in back with Hayes, holding a gun on him. The other drove them away.

The one in back with Hayes told him not to be frightened. They meant him no harm; and if he behaved himself they would let him go, after he had a talk with Barney Kavanagh. To prove they were from Kavanagh, he gave Hayes a gold ring. He looked at the inscription inside the band: it was the marriage ring of his dead sister. Kavanagh had taken to wearing it on his little finger after her death.

Hayes stated again that he didn't want anything to do with his fugitive billionaire nephew. But the man holding the gun on him motioned with it and told him to be sensible.

They drove to an isolated phone booth on the outskirts of Paris. And waited there until the phone rang. When it did, Hayes was ordered to answer it. The caller was Barney Kavanagh. Hayes didn't know where Kavanagh was calling from. Only that it was a bad connection that sounded very long-distance. What he did hear quite clearly was that his nephew sounded very frightened.

"I'm in deep shit, Uncle Ray," Kavanagh said. "I'm out of cash and there's no way that's safe for me to tap my number accounts in Switzerland. One of the men who've been hiding me tried it from his own bank. There was what they called a technical delay in the transfer operation. When he went back to collect, his bank was crawling with plainclothes cops waiting to arrest him."

What that meant, he told Hayes, was that U.S. lawmen must have discovered what and where each of his accounts was. They couldn't stop the Swiss banks from transferring funds from those accounts. But the American government had obviously persuaded the Swiss banks to inform its agents where the funds were going, and delay the transfer long enough for the agents to grab whoever it was going to.

"It's only a temporary problem, though," Kavanagh said. "There's a banana country in Latin America that's ready to take me in, make me a citizen right away, and not let the U.S. extradite me. I'll be able to open a legal account in a bank there, and have my funds transferred to it, bit by bit, and nobody'll arrest me. It'll cost, of course. I'll be giving half of everything I bring into the country to various of its highest ranking government officials. But what the hell, when there's a big pie everybody wants a slice. It's only natural, right?''

"You don't need any help from me then," Hayes told him.

"Yes I do, Uncle Ray. Because these men I'm with, they're a rough bunch. Very rough. They won't let go of me until they get *their* slice. A big one. And as I've explained, I can't get that out of Swiss accounts until I'm safe inside that banana country. That's the problem."

But Kavanagh had had the foresight to hedge against a possible temporary problem well before he had become a fugitive. Using an alias backed by false identify papers, he had made a long-term rental of a safe-deposit box in a small bank in another country. In it Kavanagh had stashed a bag of diamonds. Worth about two million dollars. Enough to buy his freedom from the men now hiding and holding him.

Kavanagh had also had the foresight to prepare for a future situation in which it might become unsafe for him to travel in person to the bank where the diamonds were. To the alias he'd used in renting the safe deposit box he had added the names of two men he knew he could trust not to steal from him. An old friend, and Raymond Hayes. If either showed up with proper identification papers, and a key to the box, he had the right to take out what was in it.

He had tried first to get in touch with the old friend, only to learn the man had recently died in a car accident. That left Hayes. "I'll contact you again and tell you where the bank is," Kavanagh told him. "All you have to do is go to Cannes for a while, the Hotel Majestic. And wait until you hear from me. I'll pay back whatever you spend, with a good chunk extra, as soon as I'm where I can safely make the bank transfers."

"No," Hayes told him. "I don't want anything to do with this, Barney."

"Uncle Ray," Kavanagh pleaded, "mother told me before she died that I could always turn to you if I needed help. And now there's no one else I can turn to. You've *got* to do this one thing for me. If you don't, these men I'm with are going to do terrible things to me. You can't imagine *how* terrible. . . ."

Their long-distance connection had been broken at that point. When he got back in the car with the two who'd brought him, the one sitting beside him gave Hayes a safe-deposit key. "I hope Kavanagh wasn't lying about being able to count on you," he said, and held up the wedding band again. "Because if he was, we won't just send you the finger he always wears this on. We'll saw off the whole hand and make you a present of it. For starters."

Hayes had arrived at Ilona's apartment very late for their appointment—and badly shaken. He had needed a couple stiff drinks before he was able to explain what had happened.

"He felt like he was caught in a nightmare," Ilona told me. "He didn't want to do what Kavanagh asked of him. But he couldn't stand the thought of being responsible for what those men would do to his nephew if he didn't. In the end Ray decided he *had to* do this one thing for his dead sister's son."

"And you passed the news to Léon Falicon," I said.

She pressed her hands together on her lap, hard, and bowed her head over them. "I didn't want it to go any further," she said in a low, constricted tone. "I was becoming frightened for Ray. I wanted to quit my arrangement with Falicon—and to stop Ray from doing what he'd been asked. But Falicon said he'd have me killed if I backed out. And kill Ray, too, if he stopped being useful because of me. I—was sure he meant that."

"Oh yes," I said. "He would mean it."

So they'd gone down to Cannes. Together, because Ilona

had insisted on going with Hayes—and because his need for her presence in his troubled state was too strong for him to refuse her. When Kavanagh had phoned Hayes there it was another long-distance call. No names were mentioned. He simply told Hayes to go to a specific public phone booth and wait. Kavanagh called him there and told him to drive across into Italy—alone—and register at a specific hotel in San Remo. This time Hayes refused to take Ilona along with him. During the time he was away, either Falicon or one of his thugs was with Ilona every minute. That included the boat cruise from which she'd swum to my place.

"Hayes was gone four days," I said. "Why so long?"

"He didn't get the next call from Kavanagh until the morning of the fourth day. Telling him which bank to go to—and that he should take the night plane from Nice to Marrakesh. Ray had the safe-deposit key and his passport and driver's license for identification. He had no problem getting the diamond bag from the box in the bank's vault. He drove back to Cannes and told me where he was going."

"And this time he didn't refuse to take you along."

"He was becoming very scared of what he was going to do," Ilona explained quietly. "He needed me—someone with him for emotional support. Someone who could make him feel the nightmare would be finished soon, and he would be free of it. I was the only one who could do that for him."

The call from Kavanagh to their hotel in Marrakesh had come soon after their arrival. Again, Hayes was told to go to a certain public phone booth. Kavanagh called him there and told him where to go next.

Hayes let Ilona accompany him—as far as the hotel here in El-Kelaa. He wouldn't take her the rest of the way, for both of their sakes. Kavanagh had warned him to meet him alone. If anyone else came with Hayes, Kavanagh said, it could turn deadly for all of them. So Ilona had to wait here.

"But he did tell you where he was going," I said.

Ilona had lit another cigarette. The smoke from it rose in a wobbly spiral pattern when she shook her head. "No. He told it, but not to me. Shortly after we were in the hotel here, four of Falicon's thugs came to our suite. With guns. They held us there until Falicon arrived with the rest of his men. It is Falicon that Ray told. Because Falicon said he would kill me—unless Ray explained all about the arrangements for the rendezvous with Kavanagh. Exactly where and how and when.''

I said, ''Tell me. Everything Hayes told Falicon.''

I gave close attention to every detail of it.

Barney Kavanagh had given Raymond Hayes precise instructions for reaching their rendezvous point. It was a place deeper into the desert; between Tinerhir and the Erfoud oasis. There an ancient village had once stood beside a stream from the far-off Ziz River. The stream had vanished long ago, leaving a dry wadi behind. The village had been deserted for a century, and by now it had almost finished dissolving back into the earth.

It's original name was forgotten. People of this region called it the ghost village.

It was there, in the dry wadi by the remnants of the village, that Hayes was supposed to meet Kavanagh and hand over his bag of diamonds.

Hayes had been told to get there at dawn this morning. Kavanagh was to arrive sometime today—or if not, he would come tomorrow. Whether it was this day or the next, the meeting would take place only when there was enough daylight to see that all the land around them was empty.

So if Kavanagh didn't meet him during this day, Hayes was to drive back to spend the night in El-Kelaa—and return to their meeting place at dawn tomorrow.

But Léon Falicon had decided on a different arrangement. He had gone out with his gunmen and Hayes last night. To reach the rendezvous while it was still full dark. And to carefully reconnoiter what was left of the village, finding the best places to hide and wait. If Kavanagh and the men with him didn't arrive during this day, Falicon planned to remain there throughout this night, too.

Because he was sure that Kavanagh and the others wouldn't come without sending a scout ahead of them, to warn of any danger there. Falicon intended to seize the man when he arrived, and force him to give the rest of his bunch an all-clear signal.

My estimation of Léon Falicon went up one small, grudging notch. He was vicious and had an overinflated faith in his own arrogant macho megalomania. But he wasn't totally stupid.

Ilona removed her cigarette from her lips and regarded me oddly. "Why are you smiling like that?"

"Falicon wants to get Kavanagh in his clutches," I said, "but first he has to get him out of the clutches of men just like him. That's why he took a little army along with him. They're going to fight each other for Kavanagh."

It was the only aspect of the situation I was heading into that I liked.

But I liked it very much.

⊠ 33 ⊠

THE DESERT IS AS COLD AT NIGHT AS IT IS HOT BY DAY. WE rode with the car windows closed, giving us a measure of body warmth inside. The track we were following had the same composition as the undulating, nearly barren land it crossed: a mix of gravel, sand, and clay. During the infrequent rains, Kateb said, it turned to deep mud and became unusable. But it was three months since the last brief rain. The track was like corrugated stone beneath our tires. We drove it with the car's lights off. The movement of artificial light can be spotted too far away in a desert night. Moon and stars provided all we needed to see our way.

Kateb was doing the driving. This was his land, and his profession had given him an intimate acquaintance with the ways through its emptier areas.

He was a younger, slightly shorter version of the Berber swordsman who had guarded our car in El-Kelaa. The same lean strength and dark hawk's face. Kateb had come to join us eagerly. Hammou had told him that the job would provide three of the four things he relished most. Action, profit and risk. The fourth, he said, was easier to come by. Pretty, adventure-seeking foreign women could always be found around the swimming pools of tourist hotels during his visits to Agadir and Marrakesh.

I rode in front next to Kateb, with Desiré and Hammou behind us. Hammou wouldn't be going all the way with us.

But we needed him to handle one essential noncombat function.

A long line of darkness materialized in the country ahead. When we got closer I saw it was jagged-flanked clusters of naked stone hills, joined together and stretching approximately four kilometers across our route. Moonlight showed sharp, low peaks rising from a staggered ridge line notched by ragged wind gaps.

The fused stumps of mountains thrown up by volcanic action, and then worn down by the abrasion of millions of years of sand storms.

"The ghost village is on the other side of that range," Kateb said. "This track swings around the north end of the hills and goes through the dry wadi past it."

"Be careful not to drive too much closer," Desiré told him, "or they'll hear the car."

"Not while we are on this side of the hills," Kateb said. "Not if they are on the other side. The hills act as a sound barrier." He laughed. "I have reason to be sure of this. Once I was waiting with some contraband over there, and an army patrol came along this track in three Jeeps. I didn't hear them until they were around the end and turning into the wadi. Luckily, I was well hidden. They went past without noticing me. *Inch'Allah.*"

The hill range rose higher as we approached, its long bulk blocking out much of the lower night sky ahead. The track diverted, beginning its swing to the north. Kateb left the track and continued straight on, slowing as we traversed ground that became progressively more uneven. The car jolted over a series of broken humps. Then high, outreaching cliffs loomed on both sides of us. Kateb steered between them, turning into a ravine that cut into the hills. The car crunched over loose stones and chunks of shale: detritus from slopes cracked by the alternating pressures of each day's brutal shifts of heat and cold.

Kateb brought the car to a stop in a narrow, deeply shadowed gap between a fissured cliff and a huge fallen boulder. "From here," he said, "we walk—and climb."

The four of us got out of the car and I opened its trunk. Most of it was filled by a very large, crammed-full nylon bag. That was Kateb's. He'd brought it from home after Hammou told him our destination—and after he'd done some thinking about our safest way in and out. When he adjusted its strap over his shoulder the bag hung down almost to his knees. The carbine that Kateb slung from his other shoulder was his, too. He'd fitted it with a telescope sight.

I offered him a spare revolver from my sack but he said no, he wasn't used to handguns. So I gave it to Hammou, just in case someone unfriendly happened to stumble on him and he needed to protect himself. He didn't refuse it.

Desiré and I had the Lugers holstered on our belts. We took some heavier firepower out of our sacks: MAC-11 submachine pistols. We tucked a couple extra ammo clips for them in our belts and slung the MAC-11s over our shoulders before starting away from the car.

I didn't intend to take part in a shooting war with that firepower. Just to start one—and get out while it was going on. With Raymond Hayes. Hopefully along with his bag of diamonds. That was the purpose of this expedition. And for that purpose there was something likely to be of more use than bullets, that Desiré had obtained in Marrakesh. A rare find. Three stun grenades. Kateb had one. Desiré and I had the other two.

We followed Kateb deeper into the ravine. After about ten steps he came to a sudden halt, raising a warning hand. We stopped and watched Kateb vanish into shadow under a cliff-side overhang. Seconds later he emerged and motioned us forward. Desiré and I reached him quickly, with Hammou a few steps behind. There was a large Peugeot sedan half-hidden in the shadow. The one Léon Falicon had rented.

"No one in or around it," Kateb said softly, and we moved on. We didn't find Hayes's white Volvo in the ravine, of course. Kavanagh had instructed him to drive to their rendezvous spot. The men with Kavanagh would expect to see Hayes there beside his car. It had probably taken two trips with the Volvo to carry Falicon, his gunmen and Hayes there via the track around the end of the hill range.

Kateb turned to his right. We followed him up a slope in the ravine. Other than having to be careful where we placed our feet it was an easy climb. After we reached the top the ground we crossed became fairly level. Until it ended at a sheer drop into a twisty, narrower ravine.

It wasn't a long drop. Not more than twenty feet. But there were rocks at the bottom with sharp edges and points that discouraged an attempt at jumping it.

Kateb sat down on the brink and opened his big bag. What he unrolled from it was a lightweight ladder: nylon with aluminum rungs. He attached one end securely around the base of a rock spur beside him and lowered the rest quietly down the sheer drop.

We climbed down one at a time. Kateb first. Then Desiré. Then me. Hammou didn't come down. After I stepped off the bottom rung he pulled the ladder up out of sight and huddled down with it. That was where we needed him: ready to lower the ladder to us quickly whenever we came scurrying back this way.

Before we'd left El-Kelaa, Kateb had sketched a detailed map for us of the ghost village, with the wadi in front of it and the fused chain of mountain stumps behind it. During the ride here he'd taken us over the details of that layout a couple more times. Including this approach to the rear of our objective.

There were several possible ways to get across these hills. Kateb had chosen this one for a specific reason. When we finished climbing down the ladder we were very near the rear of the ghost village. But we couldn't see it because of a sharp bend in the narrow ravine. The same bend had served to hide our descent from the enemy ahead.

We picked our way through the debris of shattered rocks with due caution. The ravine's bottom was in deep gloom, and this wasn't a good time or place for any of us to break an ankle.

It made for slow progress around the bend. But just beyond that the ravine reached an open end. We came out of the gloom, into the full light of the stars and moon. Kateb went to his hands and knees and crawled forward. We crawled with him, me on one side and Desiré on the other. When Kateb went flat and still, we did too.

We were at the top of a wide, gentle slope, behind the ghost village. It had been built on the slope, reaching down to the near bank of a wide, bone-dry wadi. What remained was a maze of low walls. They were almost formless, more like humps rising out of the earth. They filled the spaces they enclosed with dark night shadow. Kateb had said a few of the wall remnants were higher than a man's chest. From above most of them looked lower than that.

The wadi fronting the village was shallow, with crumbling banks. There was a scattering of trees growing down the length of it: wild palms and eucalyptus. That meant the ancient stream hadn't stopped flowing. It had just gone underground—something that happens now and then around the Sahara. The trees grew from roots that reached deep for moisture from that invisible stream.

The white Volvo was parked in the wadi, close to its near bank.

I couldn't see anyone in it or near it. Desiré was scanning the area below through his own binoculars. I raised mine, focusing on Hayes's car. Still nobody in it. I adjusted the focus as I inspected each section of the village remains. Half a dozen more trees grew out of what had once been rooms or small courtyards or passages between houses. But any people down there weren't moving around and were too shrouded by the darkness of the village maze for me to see them.

I lowered the binoculars. Desiré had already lowered his. He shook his head. Negative.

"The car," I whispered, "says they *are* there."

Kateb nodded.

Desiré moved one shoulder in a sort of shrug. "I still think this is incredibly foolish. But no one will listen to me. Including myself, it seems. So—let us get on with it."

We separated as we snaked our way down. Desiré moved toward the middle of the rear walls. Kateb diverged to his left. I angled off to the right.

I doubted that we would be able to locate Raymond Hayes in the darkness among the walls. But we could use the same dark to get into our positions. With the three of us spread out through the village ruins, one of us was bound to be near Hayes when daylight came.

We still had almost two hours left before dawn.

⊠ **34** ⊠

THERE WAS ENOUGH COVER ALL THE WAY IF YOU KEPT CLOSE
to the ground. Boulders and bulky slabs had detached from
the cliffs and found diverse resting places along the slope
behind the village. They cast long, dense shadows. Using the
shadows and the big rocks they belonged to I reached the
right flank of the eroded walls without drawing a shot or a
yell from inside them.

There'd been nothing to indicate that the approach of the
other two had been detected, either. Staying flat, I turned my
head and looked off to the left. After about twenty seconds
I thought I saw a momentary density shift inside a shadow
that reached from a boulder to a midpoint in the walls. Either
my imagination was overworking or Desiré was now inside.

Several boulders had rolled as far as the rear walls after
centuries of stops and starts. A couple more had crushed
through walls into the interior of the village. I could see one
of those directly in front of me, through the wall break it had
left behind. Its lower half was cloaked in blackness. The
upper part rose above the walls around it.

I crawled in through the break and didn't stop until I got
to where a jut of wall cornered against the boulder's base. I
turned and pressed my back into the protective corner as I
sat up. Making sure first that the top of my head wasn't
higher than the stumpy wall. Then I unslung the MAC-11

from my shoulder. The people who'd sold it to Desiré had modified it for full automatic fire.

A handgun is better in a close-quarters stalking duel—when you have enough light to see your target clearly. When it's too dark to take fast accurate aim, automatic fire is better. It spreads the damage around. You point in the right general direction and spray the bursts back and forth. It either hits your opponent or makes him scramble away and stop shooting at you.

I hoped nobody was going to start shooting at me and force me to that extremity. Because the ruckus would almost certainly prevent us from getting to Raymond Hayes and taking him out intact. But if the situation took a very bad turn I would be more inclined to lose Hayes—and that bag he'd brought—than to lose my own mortal self.

Some choices don't depend on conscious thought. The primitive part of the nervous system makes them for you. Some people you will sacrifice yourself for. Others, not.

So I sat there in my dark corner for a while, holding the MAC-11 ready for use while I listened intently and sniffed the air.

Nobody inside the low maze with me made any sounds close enough to reach my ears. There was no smell of drifting cigarette smoke. No one nearby cleared his throat or shuffled his feet or took a pee against a wall. I got my feet under me and left my corner with the MAC-11, hunching forward so what remained of the base of the buildings continued to shield all of me.

I crouched my way through a gap in an interior wall. It might have been the lower part of a lost doorway or simply a point where the last mud bricks had disintegrated entirely. Impossible to be sure. I tested each step of the way. The blackness at floor level was almost total. I went left through what could have been either a house corridor or an outside alley between buildings, and turned right through another gap. Halting regularly to let my senses of hearing and smell test for warning signals. Working my way downward.

The slope had been terraced for the construction of the village. The buildings went lower by stages until they reached the lowest line along the edge of the wadi.

Down there was the logical place for Falicon to have positioned his men. Strung out behind the last walls. Where they could overlook the wadi and fire into it at close range when the time came. I descended from each terrace to a lower one. With frequent detours left and right to find a hidden way through the complex of low walls, climbing over none of them.

My small group had one temporary advantage over Falicon's larger one. They would be relatively relaxed now. Not sleeping; but resting easy while they waited for dawn. Barney Kavanagh's rendezvous with his uncle was arranged to take place during daytime. That was when Falicon expected to have to deal with the gang holding Kavanagh captive. Falicon had no reason to expect that he might also have to deal with another variety of trouble, from an entirely different source, following him here and arriving in the night.

I was down to the next to last terrace when I heard a man speak to someone, off to my left and below.

The words were indistinct. The man's voice was quiet; though not as though he was keeping it down for fear of being overheard. It sounded familiar.

I moved slowly and silently to the left. When the voice sounded again it was very close, in one of the dark house ruins below me.

The man speaking was Léon Falicon.

". . . if you give the wrong signal," he was saying when I came near enough to hear him clearly. His tone had a malicious smoothness that made me remember his grandmother, The Old Spider.

"Remember," he went on, spacing out his phrases slowly and forcefully, "if they don't come after you've spoken to them . . . or if they come in some other way than what you've told me was arranged . . . For whatever reason . . . I will assume that it is your fault. . . . You will die so slowly . . .

with an agony that will make what you feel now seem like
bliss.''

Falicon had apparently guessed right about the men
with Kavanagh sending an advance scout—and had caught
him.

"I already told you I'll do what you ask," the man answered Falicon in a croaking voice. "I swear to God!" It
sounded as though something was painfully wrong with his
throat. He was speaking French, but with a bad accent. British, or maybe Australian.

"Not *asked*," Falicon told him. "I didn't *ask* you to do
what I want. I *told* you."

It sounded to me like his infatuation with his own power
and toughness was reaching new heights. No wonder—he
had a helpless man to torment and a small army about to
go into combat under his orders. Falicon was drunk with
it.

"Perhaps," he teased, "I should let Marcel play with you
again—to make absolutely certain you do remember."

"No—please!"

There was a guttural laugh from another man. Marcel,
presumably.

"Or," Falicon added softly, "I could tap that broken hand
some more with the blackjack."

The captured scout began to moan.

"The pain is good for you," Falicon told him. "It
will help you to remember to do exactly what I told you.
Now stop that disgusting noise; let us be quiet while we
wait."

The dark wall pocket below me became silent. I hadn't
heard anything to indicate that Raymond Hayes was down
there with Falicon. And I wasn't about to risk showing myself for a look over the walls into that pocket. Not now. It
would be too dark there to see who was who. Making the
risk worthless. But I was pretty certain that was where Hayes
was.

Falicon would want Hayes with him, under his personal

control. Like he had the opposition's scout under his personal control. That was part of his distorted character. What made me surer was the sight of the white Volvo's roof, showing above the wadi's near bank. It was almost directly in front of Falicon's hiding place.

I removed a pair of heavy clamp-on ear protectors from my belt.

Desiré had gotten three of them from his Marrakesh contacts, to go with the stun grenades. He and Kateb had the other two pairs with them now. They had also studied my photos of Raymond Hayes before setting out.

Our arrangement was basic. Details would have to be improvised quickly to cope with unpredictable developments. Whichever of us located Hayes would, when it came time to grab him, signal it with the explosion of his grenade. The other two were to trigger the war and then converge to aid whoever had Hayes. Sowing confusion along the way with their own grenades.

But a stun grenade thrown a short distance will temporarily immobilize the thrower as well as his enemy—unless precautions are taken before the throw.

I was hanging the ear protectors around my neck when a man stood up in the dark pocket below me to stretch himself. It wasn't Falicon and it couldn't be the slender, medium-sized Hayes. This man was much too big. Judging by his shadowy bulk, it could be one of the slabs of beef and bone I'd met with Falicon across from the closed hotel in Nice where Roland Mari had died. And now he had a name: Marcel.

I shrank deeper into the darkness between a low palm and a chunk of wall when he turned around in my direction. But he didn't look where I was. He gazed up at the sky; as though checking the positions of the stars and moon for how much longer it would be to countdown.

As soon as he sank back down, out of my line of sight, I shifted position. To the wall that separated me from Falicon and those with him. It was just high enough to shield me from them when I sat on the ground with my back against it.

By my reckoning it was less than three-quarters of an hour to first light.

I leaned my head back against the wall and waited.

🀫 **35** 🀫

Dawn arrived as it does in flat-horizoned deserts. Abruptly and completely. From my position against the base of the wall I couldn't see the sun lift above the distant horizon. Pale gold light spread swiftly over the land and flowed over what I could see: The raw, jagged flanks of the hills rising behind the village. The jumble of disintegrating walls above and around me. And all of the enclosure where I was waiting. The sunlight cast shadows, but none of them strong enough this early to hide anyone.

I hunched lower, pressing against the wall at my back, and held the MAC-11 ready with both hands. It was the only kind of protection available to me if any of the enemy came along now and looked inside my enclosure. But the odds were slightly in my favor that none of them would. All of them should be keeping down in their ambush stations, watching the wadi.

Léon Falicon spoke again, snappishly, on the other side of my wall: "Wake up, Piers—it's time to turn on your radio."

A groan of pain—then the croaking voice of the captured scout: "I wasn't asleep. Just—you didn't have to kick me like that. . . ."

So now I had a name for him, too: Piers.

"You'll get kicked harder than that," Falicon told him,

214

"if you don't sit up and get ready. This is when you said they will come."

Piers: "They should—if they stick to the plan."

Falicon: "Pray that they do." His voice was strung with tension now.

I heard the snap of a switch. Then a loud blast of static from a radio receiver. It was turned down quickly, until I could barely hear it. I held myself motionless, continuing to wait and listen. The rising sun was already heating the air. The sky was turning pale yellow, almost white, with streaks of lavender in it.

About sixteen minutes went by. Then there was another loud blast of static from Piers's radio. A transmitter, not far away, was tuning into its frequency.

A voice came through the static, badly distorted by it: "How is the weather, Piers?" A French voice, no foreign accent.

There was a click as Piers switched over to transmit. "Mild and snowing," he replied. The all-clear password, apparently. Then: "Hayes is already here. Alone, like he was told."

If his croaking voice was not his normal one it wouldn't be noticed through the distorting static.

Another click as he switched back to receive. The Frenchman's voice came through again: "With the diamonds?"

Piers switched to transmit and said: "Affirmative. He's got them right here with him."

Back to reception—and the French voice: "We're on our way. See you."

The static died suddenly. Piers had switched off his radio.

Falicon shouted to the men he had hidden elsewhere: "They are coming in! Get yourselves set for them!"

There was a wild exultation in his voice now. I didn't know if he stood up to do the shouting, because I didn't look to see. I was scrunched down as low as I could against my wall base.

"Remember, let them get close first!" he ordered. "Wait

until I give the signal! And you all know what Kavanagh looks like! Look for him and don't shoot anywhere near him! Anybody hits Kavanagh, I'll cut your abdomen open and feed a starving rat into it!''

General Falicon.

After a short silence, Piers spoke again, quietly and nervously: "I did what you said. Just like you told me to. You promised to let me go if . . ."

"Wait," Falicon cut in with a reasonable tone. "There'll be a little more for you to do. Nothing difficult. Do the rest of it right and I'll do better than let you go." His voice had acquired a seeming kindliness now. "First we'll get you a first class surgeon to repair that hand. Then you can join my employ. You'll find, I am sure, that it will be more rewarding and enjoyable than being with that bunch of ignorant hoodlums.''

He was playing in one of his private comedies again. But Piers didn't know that. He actually said, "Thank you." And meant it.

A different voice said, "I'm *very* thirsty."

Speaking excellent French. But the accent was definitely American.

I'd figured it right. Raymond Hayes was there with Falicon, separated from me by only a single low wall. His voice was taut with the effort to stem the fear coursing through him.

"Here," Falicon told him. "But just one swallow. Our water is running low."

After that none of them spoke again. I didn't budge from my position. The time to move would come soon enough.

Ten minutes . . . Twenty . . .

The sun was still not up where I could see it, but the sunlight had real fire in it now. Sweat trickled down my sides. I took one hand at a time away from the submachine pistol and dried my palms on the legs of my dungarees.

There was a distant sound of an approaching vehicle. I

turned toward my wall, keeping low as I quietly got my knees under me.

The wall's uneven top had a number of deep cracks where the mud bricks had pulled apart. I'd spent part of the dark before dawn using one finger carefully to remove some of the dust, sand, and crumbs of brick from one of the notches. When the sound of the vehicle grew louder I straightened enough to look through the notch with one eye. A calculated risk.

I'd calculated correctly. None of the four men below me was turned in my direction.

Falicon and the hulk named Marcel were on their knees behind the last wall section between them and the wadi. They were peering over the top at the nearing vehicle. It was a big Land-Rover. Extra-large wheels and wide tires and the bottom of its chassis high off the ground. The strong metal body, painted in an irregular brown and black pattern, looked battered and weathered. But the motor had an optimum-condition sound.

It was coming cross-country, using no visible track, approaching the other side of the wadi from the direction of the Erfoud oasis, over the horizon to the southeast.

Falicon held a Heckler & Koch submachine gun down by his thigh while he watched it come. An H-P Browning was holstered on his hip. Marcel, kneeling beside him, *was* one of the hulks I'd met in Nice. He had the same make pistol and was holding a long-range rifle with a scope sight.

Piers and Raymond Hayes sat on the ground behind them.

I could see enough of Hayes's profile to identify him. There were deep creases of strain and fatigue in it. He might still be young enough for Ilona Szabo's tender ministrations, but he was too old for what Falicon was putting him through.

Resting on his lap was a zippered bag, of some soft synthetic material that had a dark green shine. About big enough to hold a couple volumes of an encyclopedia; though I didn't think that was what it contained. Hayes had its long carrying strap hooked over his right shoulder.

The radio lay beside Piers: a compact two-way, short-range model. He was holding his left wrist up at chest level with his right hand. I couldn't see anything of his face, but I didn't need that to know he was suffering worse than Hayes. His left hand and fingers had been skillfully mangled: the bones broken without breaking the skin.

Their attention was fixed on Falicon, neither making any attempt to see what he and Marcel were watching.

The Land-Rover, with a long cloud of dust trailing behind it, reached the wadi across from the left end of the ghost village. It turned and came slowly along the top of the wadi's opposite bank. It was packed with men. There was too much dust to see if any of them were using binoculars, but it was likely. They were making a precautionary scan of the village ruins; still a bit wary though lulled by the all-clear message from Piers.

Falicon and Marcel crouched lower. But not too low to continue to see over the wall. The highest stretch of the wall was very lumpy. Even through binoculars, the top of a motionless head would appear to be just one of the lumps. I didn't move at all. Through the lightly shadowed notch in my wall, my eye would be invisible.

Without turning his head Falicon snapped, "On your feet, both of you. Stand up and wave. And *smile*."

Hayes and Piers got off the ground. When they were standing the wall between them and the wadi was no higher than their waists. The Land-Rover was almost directly across the wadi from them by then. Piers raised his right hand high and waved. Hayes used his left hand to do the same. I couldn't see if either of them managed a smile.

The Land-Rover continued on at the same slow speed, and then turned back in a wide circle. It came to a halt atop the opposite bank across from Hayes and Piers and the white Volvo. All of its five doors were thrown open at the same time. The driver and another man jumped out the front doors. Four more scrambled from the rear door.

All six had a similar look: sun-scorched, hard, and leathery. They were dressed alike, too: much-used khakis, desert boots, camouflage hats. Each carried an automatic assault rifle. They moved away from the Land-Rover swiftly, spreading apart as they descended the wadi's far bank. They were well strung out, with plenty of space between them, when they halted on reaching the bottom.

Then the remaining three emerged from the Land Rover's middle doors. Two were dressed and armed like the first six men. The other was Barney Kavanagh.

He was easy to recognize. Built like an elongated pear. Narrow shoulders and long torso and big pot belly. He had a round face and was almost completely bald. In his photograph the fringe of blond hair around that baldness had been barbered neat and short. Now it was long and scraggly. But he was Kavanagh.

I watched him climb down the far bank with the other two men. The one on his right held the end of a rope in one fist. The other end was tied around Kavanagh's chest, just above the pot. They, too, stopped when they reached the bottom of the wadi.

Not counting Kavanagh, there were eight men strung out over there. They outnumbered Léon Falicon's force by one. But they were out in the open, and Falicon's force was not.

The distance across the wadi was not too great for accurate shooting even with a carefully aimed handgun. For a rifle it would be easy. But Falicon held back the order to fire. He wanted them closer. Where he'd have his best chance to snatch Kavanagh—alive.

"Hayes," he rasped.

Hayes had obviously been rehearsed through his part in detail. He raised the dark green zipper bag above his head and called out: "Here it is, Barney!"

Kavanagh called back: "So bring it to me, Uncle Ray!"

Hayes lowered the bag and called: "First I want to be sure they'll let you go, in exchange!"

One of the armed men with Kavanagh shouted impatiently: "Piers—*bring* him out!"

Léon Falicon spoke quietly: "Only as far as . . ."

I didn't hear the rest of what he was saying. It was cut off, along with all other sound, when I pulled the protectors over my ears. I put the MAC-11 on the ground, unhooked the stun grenade from my belt, pulled the pin, and silently counted.

On the next to final count I flipped the grenade over my wall and threw myself flat with my palms pressed against my tightly closed eyes.

The blinding flash and ear-splitting howl of a stun grenade penetrates deep into a man's nervous system and knocks out its central controls—making it impossible for him to direct his own actions over the next five to thirty minutes. Only a little of the explosion's flash and noise reached my protected eyes and ears. But I *felt* it, through every pore in my body. When I ripped away the ear protectors and shoved myself off the ground my nerve endings were quivering wildly and my skull and brain were trying to part company.

But I was still in command of what I was doing. The four I'd dropped the grenade among were not. Hayes and Piers and the hulking Marcel were sprawled on the ground, eyes staring blindly out of faces paralyzed by the shock, their bodies and limbs and heads jerking uncontrollably. Falicon was huddled on his knees at the base of the other wall, head and hands pressing against it, trying to claw his way up.

He couldn't do it, of course. His hands kept jumping away from the wall each time his body went into another ungovernable spasm that sank him lower again. But that he could even try was incredible. There had to be a maniac frenzy driving the man. The kind that makes religious fanatics walk barefoot across burning coals.

The gang across the wadi didn't know what to make of the grenade explosion—except that it was unexpected. Some of them were sprinting toward the cover of trees growing along the middle of the wadi. Others were starting back up the far bank toward their Land-Rover; the one with the rope pulling Kavanagh after him.

From a midpoint inside the village ruins an automatic

weapon let go with a long burst. Desiré—and his MAC-11.
Sending a flail of bullets across the wadi, chopping fountains
of dust out of the opposite bank just above the men climbing
toward the Land Rover. Driving them back down.

A second after Desiré went into action Kateb fired his rifle
from inside the left end of the ruins—three times in rapid
succession. The first shot spanged off the Land-Rover's body.
The second tore its left front tire apart. The third barely
missed the gunman who had Kavanagh in tow. The man
dropped the rope as he leaped aside, tripped, and went rolling down into the wadi. He jumped up and ran crouched
after the others, toward the protective cover of the trees in
mid wadi, leaving Kavanagh behind.

Kavanagh walked slowly back down the opposite bank and
then stopped at the bottom, staring open-mouthed across the
wadi at the ruins and trying to understand what the hell was
going on.

Most of the gang that had brought him here had reached
the cover of the trees. Desiré and Kateb were firing at them,
but aiming to miss. Let Falicon's men do their own work—
and have their hands full of it.

The gang among the trees began firing back at the ruins.
Inside the ruins, Falicon's men must have been just as puzzled about what had happened. What they weren't puzzled
about was that the men in the wadi were shooting at them.
They began pouring their counterfire into the wadi.

The ball was rolling.

I went over my wall as low and fast as I could, and went
down on one knee beside Raymond Hayes. I picked up his
carrying bag and hung it over my shoulder. Falicon, his whole
body shuddering violently, was still trying to drag himself
off the ground and not making any progress. He was half-
turned in my direction but I was sure his blinded eyes didn't
see me. Piers and Marcel were as out of it as Hayes. I was
about to lift him when I heard a grenade explode, somewhere
off in the ruins. I hoped that meant Desiré and Kateb were
on their way.

I raised up a bit, cautiously, just enough for a fast look around. And just as the third stun grenade went off in the middle of the ruins. Even at that distance it dealt a painful shock to my eardrums and made my eyeballs hurt.

But it wasn't bad enough to put me out of commission, even briefly. I was reaching for Hayes again when I was stopped by the sight of Barney Kavanagh—and what he was doing.

He was running straight across the wadi toward the white Volvo on this side. Coming very fast in spite of his build. Making no effort to conceal himself from the gunfire of the two opposing forces.

You didn't steal a billion dollars unless you had more than your share of guts. Also, you didn't work your way into a position to steal that much unless you were very smart. Kavanagh was smart enough to know that no matter what was going on neither side would shoot at *him*. Nobody wanted him dead. They wanted him alive and coughing up all that ill-gotten wealth.

But another thing nobody wanted was Kavanagh driving away. He was almost to the Volvo when someone shot out a couple of its tires.

That took care of the problem for both gangs. Kavanagh couldn't get far on foot across this empty land. And he couldn't hide for long in terrain without water. Whichever side won the battle would track him, find him, and take him.

He stood staring at the car, trying to figure out what to do next.

I shouted at him in unmistakable American: "Come on Barney—shake your ass! Over here—with your uncle!"

He looked back and forth, trying to locate me. But he couldn't decide exactly where my voice was coming from. Finally he stumbled toward an outside wall off to my left. Too far away. But I didn't want to raise up any higher so he'd see me; and before I could yell at him again bullets began chopping pieces out of the wall ridges around me.

I dropped flat beside Hayes. And waited until the shots

stopped coming my way. There was still a hell of a lot of
shooting going on, but in other directions, when I straightened a little for another look.

Just in time to see Desiré rise up from behind the wall
Kavanagh had gone to. Reaching across it and seizing Kavanagh under the arms. Lifting him like a sack of potatoes
and pulling him in. Dropping out of sight with him as shots
thudded into the wall there.

I did a crouching turn back to Hayes. Raised him and
hauled him across the back of my shoulders. His spasms of
twitching and jerking didn't make it easy to hold him there.
Staying crouched, I got my feet under my weight and his. I
started to turn toward the nearest interior wall gap when I
saw what Léon Falicon was doing.

He had shoved himself to a half-standing position. A con-
vulsive shudder made him fall against the wall—but he didn't
go down. Using the wall for leverage, he steadied and
straightened himself.

No normal person could be doing that, this soon after
taking the full shock of a stun grenade. But Falicon was doing
it.

His hands clawed for his holstered Browning. A spasm
jumped his hand away from it. His face looked like it was
made of stone as he tried again.

Bowed under Hayes's awkward weight, I reached for the
Luger on my belt. I had it partway out of its holster when a
large part of Falicon's face below his left eye disappeared in
a spout of blood and splinters of bone.

He straightened a bit more, turning around very slowly,
and showed me the back of his head. Somebody's bullet had
made a much smaller hole going in than it had coming out.
He folded forward over the top of the wall, his toes turning
inward against the ground on my side and his arms and head
hanging down the outside.

He was draped over the wall like that, no longer shaken
by spasms, when I headed for my exit route to the rear of the
ghost village.

⊠ **36** ⊠

KATEB WAS WAITING FOR ME WHEN I EMERGED FROM THE rear of the village ruins carrying Hayes. I trudged past him with my twitching burden. Kateb backed up the slope behind me, holding his rifle ready to fend off pursuit. Desiré was on one knee beside the first boulder I passed, a fresh clip in his MAC-11, prepared to add its firepower to Kateb's. But there was no pursuit. What were left of the enemy forces in the ruins and the wadi were too engrossed in shooting at each other.

Barney Kavanagh sat behind the boulder, panting and perspiring from the surge of effort that had carried him all the way from the other side of the wadi. He looked at each of us warily, withholding any reactions to us until he got some information to base them on. When Desiré tapped his shoulder he rose without a word and joined us in climbing to the narrow ravine.

Hammou began lowering Kateb's ladder down the sheer cliff as we reached it. I eased Hayes off my back and tried to help him stand on his own. He couldn't, though the effect of the grenade was starting to wear off. He was no longer wracked by violent spasms. But he kept shivering and his expression was still stunned and his legs were rubber.

Desiré took his first real look at him. It was a hard angry look, but that was lost on Hayes. Finally, with a helpless grimace, Desiré took him away from me, slung his slim fig-

224

ure over one broad shoulder, and carried him up the ladder.
Faster and easier than I could have.

I went up last, hustling Kavanagh ahead of me. When we
were up on top, with Kateb rolling up his ladder, I began
working at relaxing. The danger was behind us, and no way
it could come up after us.

By the time we had crossed over the hill range and were
down into the bottom of the larger ravine, Hayes was able to
begin directing his own legs a little, with Desiré helping him
to walk and holding up most of his weight. And by then I
was relaxed enough to register the fact that the dark green
bag I'd hung from my shoulder didn't weigh as much as I
would have expected. I opened its zipper and looked at what
was inside it.

The bag contained some large crusts of dry bread. Nothing
else.

I turned back to Hayes and Desiré. "Where are the diamonds?" I demanded.

Hayes didn't seem to understand what I was saying. I repeated the question. Hayes worked at getting his voice
operative. When it came through for him it was a halting
stutter: "F-Falicon . . . his car . . . t-trunk . . ."

"Falicon's Peugeot?"

Hayes couldn't made his voice work again. He nodded.

When we reached the blue Peugeot I told Desiré to go on
to our car with Hayes and Kateb: "I'll follow in this one,
with Kavanagh and Hammou."

They went on, and I picked the lock of the Peugeot's trunk.
There was a chamois bag inside it. I opened its drawstring
and had a look. A lot of diamonds.

I dumped the dry bread on the ground, put the chamois
bag inside the dark green one, and closed its zipper. Barney
Kavanagh watched me do so, his expression still guarded. I
wired the Peugeot's ignition and told Hammou to get in front
and drive. I got into the spacious back seat, prodding Kavanagh in ahead of me. When we had the doors shut I put the

carrying bag down on the floor between my feet. Hammou drove the Peugeot carefully through the ravine's stony debris.

The other car was out on the dirt track, waiting. When we came out in the Peugeot, it headed back toward El-Kelaa. Hammou drove after it.

In the backseat beside me, Kavanagh spoke for the first time, in bad French: "Could you tell me who you people are?"

"Helpful gremlins," I said in English.

He regarded me thoughtfully. "You're the American that shouted at me back there."

"Uh-huh."

"Cop?"

"Nope."

Kavanagh took a slow breath. "Well that's a relief." But he didn't quit looking wary. "Do you mind explaining what just happened back there?" A reasonable man asking a reasonable question in a reasonable tone.

I gave it to him in brief outline.

"Christ," Kavanagh growled, "everybody's so damn grabby. The bunch trying to get their hooks into me sound as bad as the gang that had me."

"Worse," I told him.

"Talk about out of the frying pan and into the fire. . . ." He looked at me and smiled for the first time. "I owe you a lot for getting me out from between. I'm sorry if I failed to express my gratitude before this. But I thought you might be yet another bunch trying to grab and milk me. Or agents acting on behalf of the American government."

"You'll have plenty of those dumping on you soon enough," I said.

"Not necessarily," Kavanagh said, and he settled himself back comfortably and gave my knee a friendly pat. A pro player back on his own home field. "There is a Latin American nation that is prepared to give me citizenship and immunity from extradition. Once I'm there I will be able to draw funds from my various bank accounts. No way the U.S.A. can stop it.''

He patted me on the knee again. "What I propose is that you go to South America with me. You are obviously a man with a talent for coping with difficult problems. I can use a man like you. Come with me and I'll make you rich. Very rich. I am, as you know, extremely well off.''

"Right now," I said, "you're as well off as a turkey on the day before Thanksgiving. I'm turning you over to the authorities.''

"Why would you want to do that?" His tone was genial: nothing in it but friendly, skeptical curiosity. "When it will pay you so well not to?''

"For one thing," I said, "because there are a couple of specific law enforcement authorities that'll get very mad at me if I don't. I owe them and they're expecting me to pay off, somehow. You're the best kind of payment I've got to offer.''

"They won't be able to touch you once we're in South America together. I'll have them make you a citizen, too.''

"But we're not going there, Barney. Either of us." I said it as kindly as I could, and patted his knee. "Get used to the idea and start thinking positive.''

Kavanagh began to look worried. Just a little. "What is your notion of thinking positive?''

"I don't turn you over to the authorities. I introduce you to them. You give yourself up. Chock-full of penitence and cooperation. From what I hear, the U.S. government would be open to cutting a deal with you. In exchange for your giving evidence against your coconspirators. You'd probably come out of it with an easy sentence—maybe even get on the government's witness-protection program.''

Kavanagh grimaced. "But they'd make me give back the money. Every cent I stored away.''

"Easy come, easy go.''

But he hadn't quite given up on me. He pointed to the bag

between my feet: "That would have to include giving up those diamonds, you realize."

"Absolutely." I must have said it with the right tone and expression because Kavanagh appeared finally to believe me.

The belief did not make him happy.

In El-Kelaa I took a hotel room for Kavanagh and myself. For a short stay, so I could make some long-distance phone calls from there.

Desiré and Hayes took off with Ilona shortly after we arrived in El-Kelaa. Driving up to Marrakesh to take a plane back to France. Before leaving, Hayes told me not to sell Ilona's ring. He would buy it from me, and give it back to her.

I said that would be fine.

Desiré didn't have much to say when we parted. He was pensive. Gearing himself to introduce and explain Ilona to Mireille. And trying to adjust to the possibility that he might end up the father-in-law of a man a decade older than himself.

I took Kavanagh up to our hotel room and put through my first call. To Commissaire Juy in Nice. I told him just enough to get him on the next flight to Marrakesh.

My second call was also to the Côte d'Azur: to Dixon Chess. I didn't give him any details, but what I did reveal enabled him to scoop all other journalists with the story that Barney Kavanagh had surfaced and given himself up to law-enforcement officers.

One debt paid.

I waited until there was only an hour left before Commissaire Juy's plane was due to land at Marrakesh. Then I phoned Captain Hafidi and told him I had a present for him that would earn him worldwide acclaim—if he arrived in El-Kelaa together with Juy. Hafidi picked up Juy at the airport and came to El-Kelaa in a small military plane.

Captain Hafidi had a long phone talk with someone very high in the Moroccan government before he and Juy flew back to Marrakesh with me and Kavanagh. Three CIA agents from the American Embassy were waiting for us when we got there. So were some Moroccan reporters and a television crew.

Commissaire Juy and Captain Hafidi got their kudos, official and publicity-wise, for having cooperated internationally to learn where Kavanagh was and that he wanted to give himself up.

That paid off my obligations to Hafidi and Juy.

Though maybe Commissaire Juy now owed me one. He spoke to me, with harsh pleasure, of looking forward to being the first one to break the news to The Old Spider, in person, that her beloved grandson was dead.

Juy and Hafidi turned Barney Kavanagh over to the CIA agents—together with the bag of diamonds. The CIA men counted the diamonds carefully, and recorded their number, before taking them and Kavanagh to the American Embassy for later shipment to the States.

But since no one, including Kavanagh, knew exactly how many diamonds had been in the bag originally, nobody remarked the fact that some of the smaller ones were missing.

I had given one of them to Kateb before leaving El-Kelaa. I gave a second one to Hammou before taking the rest with me on my flight to France. After landing at the Nice airport I went to see a gem dealer I knew. One of the shady people referred to in that old crack about the sunny Riviera.

He didn't pay me top price for the diamonds, but he did pay me in cash. The equivalent of nine thousand dollars. Not a fortune, maybe, but I was never cut out to be a crook on the scale of a Barney Kavanagh. I guess I lack his brand of guts and brains.

I tore up Mireille's check and earmarked half the nine thousand for Fritz Donhoff, the next time I went to Paris. From my half I paid what was owed to Jean-Marie Reju. His full normal fee, not the cut rate we'd agreed on. That pleased Reju enormously. He was also pleased when I gave him the keys to my house and told him to regard it as his own for the week of vacation on the Riviera that I'd promised him.

Then I flew off to Dublin. Arlette Alfani had just succeeded in getting her client out of jail and out of Ireland. After his family had forked over a heavy fine and a generous settlement for the victim's hospital and recuperation expenses. When I arrived she was packing to return to France. Instead we drove to the west of Ireland and spent a holiday week at a fishing lodge on a secluded lake.

It rained almost the whole time we were there. And we were informed on arrival that the lake needed to be restocked. That suited us fine. We weren't much interested in fishing, anyway. Arlette and I spent part of our time taking long walks in the gentle rain, eating at a surprisingly good restaurant, and drinking and meeting new people in a couple of convivial local pubs. And more time enjoying our cozy room's soft, spacious bed and peat-burning fireplace.

One of the best weeks of my life.

About the Author

Ten of Marvin Albert's novels have been made into films. Several have been Literary Guild choices. He has been honored with a Special Award by the Mystery Writers of America.

In addition to being the author of books of fiction and nonfiction, he has been a Merchant Marine Officer, actor and theatrical road manager, newspaperman, magazine editor, and Hollywood script writer.

Born in Philadelphia, he has lived in New York, Los Angeles, London, and Paris. He currently lives on the Riviera with his wife, the French artist Xenia Klar. He has two children, Jan and David.

BIMBO HEAVEN is the seventh book in his *Stone Angel* series.